NEW YORK REVIEW BOOKS
CLASSICS

SUNFLOWER

GYULA KRÚDY (1878–1933) was born in Nyíregyháza in northeastern Hungary. His mother had been a maid for the aristocratic Krúdy family, and she and his father, a lawyer, did not marry until Gyula was seventeen. Krúdy began writing short stories and publishing brief newspaper pieces while still in his teens. Rebelling against his father's wish that he become a lawyer, he worked as a newspaper editor for several years before moving to Budapest. Disinherited, Krúdy supported himself, his wife (a writer known as Satanella), and their children by publishing work in newspapers and literary magazines. He became a figure in Budapest's literary bohemian café society and, after publishing two collections of short stories, found success with the publication of *Sindbad's Youth* in 1911. Sindbad, a ghostly lover who has only his name in common with the hero from the *Arabian Nights*, became a signature character and figured in stories written throughout Krúdy's life. Krúdy's novels about contemporary Budapest proved popular during the turbulent years of the First World War and the Hungarian Revolution, but his incessant drinking, gambling, and philandering left him broke and led to the dissolution of his first marriage. During the late 1920s and early 1930s, Krúdy suffered from declining health and a diminishing readership, even as he was awarded Hungary's most prestigious literary award, the Baumgarten Prize. Forgotten in the years after his death, Krúdy was rediscovered in 1940, when Sándor Márai published *Sindbad Comes Home*, a fictionalized account of Krúdy's last day. The success of the book led to a revival of Krúdy's works and to his recognition as one of the greatest Hungarian writers.

JOHN LUKACS was born in Budapest in 1924. He has written twenty-five works of history and criticism, including *Budapest 1900: A Historical Portrait of a City and Its Culture*; *Historical Consciousness: Or, The Remembered Past*; *The Duel: The Eighty-Day Struggle Between Churchill and Hitler*; and, most recently, *George Kennan: A Study of Character*.

SUNFLOWER

GYULA KRÚDY

Translated from the Hungarian by
JOHN BÁTKI

Introduction by
JOHN LUKACS

NEW YORK REVIEW BOOKS

New York

THIS IS A NEW YORK REVIEW BOOK
PUBLISHED BY THE NEW YORK REVIEW OF BOOKS
1755 Broadway, New York, NY 10019
www.nyrb.com

Originally published as *Napraforgó* in installments in the Budapest daily
Virradat during the first half of 1918, and in book form later that year. The
present translation is based on the complete, corrected version published by
Szépirodalmi Könyvkiadó, Budapest, 1978. It was first published in the English
language by Corvina Books, Budapest, 1997.

Translator's acknowledgments: This translation was made possible by a
Fellowship from Collegium Budapest Institute for Advanced Study, 1995–96. I
thank Rector Lajos Vékás for his friendship and support. I am deeply grateful
to Nick Woodin for his friendship, encouragement, and thorough criticism in
editing the manuscript.

Krúdy, Gyula.
 [Napraforgó. English]
 Sunflower / by Gyula Krúdy ; introduction by John Lukacs ; translated by
John Bátki.
    p. cm.—(New York Review Books classics)
 Originally published: Budapest : Corvina, 1997.
 ISBN-13: 978-1-59017-186-8 (alk. paper)
 ISBN-10: 1-59017-186-1 (alk. paper)
 I. Bátki, John. II. Title.
 PH3281.K89N3613 2007
 894'.511332—dc22

                                  2007006867

ISBN 978-1-59017-186-8

Printed in the United States of America on acid-free paper.
10 9 8 7 6 5 4 3 2 1

CONTENTS

Introduction · vii

1 The Touchable Eveline · 3

2 The Return of a Bygone Eveline · 17

3 The Lover Foretold by a Fortune-Teller's Cards · 43

4 An Unusual Young Lady and Her Unusual Beaux · 73

5 Our Lady's Fountain · 122

6 Toward Eveningtime · 141

7 Pistoli Goes on a Long Journey · 159

8 Life's Pleasures · 178

9 Pistoli's Twilight · 196

10 Pistoli's Funeral · 214

11 Autumn Arrives · 224

Notes · 231

INTRODUCTION

"The Sound of a Cello" was the title of the profile of—or, rather, an essay on—Gyula Krúdy that I wrote in 1986, published in The New Yorker *on December 1, 1986. Its entire text follows.*

"THIS CITY" wrote Gyula Krúdy, the magician of the Magyar language, about Budapest, "smells of violets in the spring, as do mesdames along the promenade above the river on the Pest side. In the fall, it is Buda that suggests the tone; the odd thud of chestnuts dropping on the Castle walk; fragments of the music of the military band from the kiosk on the other side wafting over in the forlorn silence. Autumn and Buda were born of the same mother." When he wrote this, he was thirty-seven, and well known. Yet few people in Budapest knew that Krúdy would be the greatest prose writer of Hungary in the twentieth century, and surely one of the great writers of Europe. Few people outside Hungary know his name even now. There are two reasons for this. One of them is the loneliness of the Hungarian language, which has no relationship to the great Latin and Germanic and Slavic families. The other is the character of Krúdy's writing, which, because of its lyrical and deeply Magyar qualities, is translatable only with the greatest of efforts, unlike the work of more superficial Hungarian writers.

He was not yet eighteen when he arrived in Budapest. His eyes must have been heavy with sleep; he had traveled through the night in the provincial train that came in before six in the morning. From the cool, smoke-laden darkness under the glass dome of the East Station he came into the sun. Now, he would remember many years later, his eyes were opened wide, as he marveled at the people gathering on the broad commercial boulevard that stretched from the station square tower toward the heart of the city. This was the wondrous metropolis, the fastest-growing city in Europe and the largest between Vienna and St. Petersburg—and this was the summer of 1896, the city half bedecked and stirring with a proud fever for the ceremonies of the thousandth anniversary of the founding of Hungary. This was the city that the gangling, inordinately tall boy set out to conquer with his pen. He was no mere Rastignac, the creation of a writer. He was his own creation. There was another difference. When Balzac's Rastignac arrived in Paris, he was still an innocent. Gyula Krúdy was not.

Already behind him were an angry father, a turbulent family, three different schools, occurrences of love, and at least three years of the life of a newspaper writer. He was born in the country town of Nyíregyháza, in the Krúdy family house: one story high, yellow-stuccoed, with a faded tile roof and large double-winged Empire windows overlooking the wide village street, where geese picked their way in the muddy rivulets between the pavement and the cobblestones. It was a town with the countryside not only around it but present at its very heart: the country of the Nyírség (The Birches)—flat, melancholy, foggy, mysterious, with silent copses, and rich marshes undrained and unchanneled, reaching to the bottom of the Krúdys' garden. This was the quiet, murmuring, backward Hungary of decades past, of peeling country houses in which an old-fashioned gentry lived, endlessly raveling the strands of their lives and quarrels and dreams. His grandfather was a hero of the Hungarian War of Independence of 1848–49, whose wife divorced him in his eighties, because of his innumerable escapades with all kinds of women. Krúdy's father was more sedate: a courthouse lawyer with an honest reputation—except that he lived with a common-law wife, a peasant maid who had fallen in love with him at sixteen and bore him ten children. He finally married her for the sake of his children, five years before he died. Grandfather, father, son—and, later, Krúdy's only son—were all christened Gyula. (Jules, Julius. The quick-footed Jules, the heavy-Germanic Julius: neither of these translations will do.)

He was an indifferent student, a quarrelsome boy. After a while, his father sent him away to the Piarist Fathers' cloistered *Gymnasium* in the small northern Hungarian town of Podolin. He spent his twelfth and thirteenth years there. What he remembered of that snowy, quiet little town, with its old burghers, its iron-hinged gates and iron-hasped doors, would eventually fill a dozen books and thousands of pages in his stories. "There are such towns in the north of Hungary," he would write.

> What somehow echo through the clanging of the town bells are memories of old kings and of ancient gentlemen who had come from afar. Men long dead, once loved or unloved by calm, indifferent women, since women customarily do not concern themselves much with history. During the embraces of her lover, no woman feels any happiness knowing that a chronicler would scribble about those arms and legs and beards after they had turned to dust. Beards, breastplates, hearts disappeared, the women went on knitting their stockings; they closed their doors early in the evening, and during the night no one came back from the bridge at whose stone railing he had once gazed long at his own countenance in the mirrory water.

The historic steps were gone, new steps were heard approaching; spring came, winter came, illnesses and loves came and went, the women ripened and then grew old, the men coughed, cursed, and lay down in their coffins. A small town was this, in northern Hungary, with foot-thick walls, convent windows, stoves from which smoke wafted off. Why should people look for the heroines of this story among the kneeling women at Sunday Mass or among the ladies waltzing at the fire company's annual picnic in May? One day the heroines will die, and the care of their graves will be the entertainment of those who are still alive.

He began to write when he was brought back to be enrolled in the Nyíregyháza *Gymnasium*. He began to be published at fourteen. He sent out fillers—short stories for provincial newspapers. In two years, there were a hundred of them. Then he fled from his family. He presented himself to the editors of newspapers in Nagyvárad and Debrecen. They were startled: they had thought that the Krúdy who had been plaguing them with his reminiscences was the grandfather, the noted veteran. He liked the coffeehouses of Nagyvárad, where the journalists and other writers argued and drank into the night. He went after soubrettes. His father and his favorite teacher hauled him home. They squeezed him through his baccalaureate. The father wanted him to become a lawyer. "I shall be a poet in Budapest," the son said.

In Budapest, he lived in the old Joseph district, among ancient smithies, dusty courtyards, cobblers' shops, taverns. Sometimes he returned home. His mother slipped him some money. There was a morning when his father called for his coach and pair; they were gone. The son was found drinking in a country tavern; he had mortgaged the horses and the carriage to the tavernkeeper. Except for a gold watch, his father disinherited him. He had little to live on, but he found himself in the cafés, literary conventicles, middle-class salons of the city. He met a pleasant, plump, literary Jewish schoolteacher, several years older than he, who had made a small name for herself writing stories under the pseudonym Satanella. He was not yet twenty-one. He married her.

This was the Budapest of the turn of the century. Summer was galloping in its skies and in its heart. Foreign visitors arriving in that unknown portion of Europe, east of Vienna, were astounded to find a modern city, with first-class hotels, plate-glass windows, electric tramcars, elegant men and women, the largest parliament building in the world about to be completed. Yet the city was not wholly cosmopolitan. In some ways, it was less cosmopolitan than the backward, unkempt town of a century before, whose population was a mixture of Magyars, Germans, Swabians, Greeks, Serbs. Now everyone, including the considerable number of Jews, spoke and sang, ate and drank, thought and dreamt in Hungarian. That ancient language, the vocabulary of which had been reconstructed and enriched with infinite care, sometimes haltingly, by the patriot writers and classicists of the early nineteenth century, had become rich, muscular, flexible and declarative, lyrical and telling. This was a class-conscious society: there was as great a difference between the National Casino of the feudal aristocracy and the Café New-York of the literary people as there was between the clubhouse and the grandstand at the racetrack. These worlds were separate physically, yet they were not entirely unbridgeable. A number of the aristocrats respected the writers and the painters; in turn, most of the writers and the painters admired the aristocrats, especially when these were to the manner born. They all read the same papers, sometimes the same books, saw the same plays, knew the same purveyors. They dined in different places, their tables were set differently; but their national dishes, their favorite Gypsy musicians, their physicians, and their actresses were often the same. In Budapest, there was no particular *vie de bohème* restricted to writers and artists; indeed, the city did not have an artists' quarter—no Bloomsbury or Soho, no Montmartre or Montparnasse, no Munich Schwabing. It was a grand place for literature. It was a grand place for the young Krúdy.

Yet he—at home in Budapest, at home among the famous and not so famous writers of the metropolis—did not write about Budapest at all. He wrote about melancholy provinces on the great Hungarian plains, about the little towns in the shadows of the Carpathian Mountains, feeding his pen with the memories of the few, very few, years of his brief adolescence. He traced the still visible path of sunken memories: the still living fragrances, colors, shapes, clouds of the past. He did not need the taste of the *madeleine*; his delicacies were always fresh and ready, stored in his mind. The way he wrote at the age of twenty-five reveals something astonishing to anyone who is interested not only in writing but in the mysterious alchemy of the human heart: he knew everything about old age during the physical splendor of his youth; he knew everything about autumn in the spring of his life. He knew something that the psychiatrists of this century do not yet know, which is that in our dreams we really do not think differently, we merely remember differently. He was not only a Hungarian Proust; he was a Homer, not of certain places but of certain times, a Magyar-writing Homer of the great subterranean development near the end of the Modern Age—that of historical consciousness. And, unlike Proust's, his prose was different from fine prose; it was thoroughly lyrical. "I shall be a poet in Budapest," he had said; but he never wrote a single poem there. Yet poet he was.

Much of his talent showed itself in his early books. His first volume of stories was published in 1899, when he was twenty. Now he wrote every day; his first long novel appeared in 1901.

His wife gave up her writing but not her teaching. They had four children, of whom one died young. She supported the family. Before thirty, Krúdy was already a legendary figure—as a presence, not yet as a writer. He had no money; he lived on credit. That was not unusual—so lived many of the writers and the journalists of his day, dependent on small cash advances and on the good will of certain headwaiters. But there was something extraordinary, even awesome, in the appearance of Krúdy, who at twenty-five was no longer a youth but a powerful, ageless gentleman. He was unusually tall, his handsome head leaning, with a kind of melancholy modesty, always to the right. He had large walnut-brown eyes. He spoke slowly. His voice sounded like a cello, as did his writing. He carried a cane. He was taciturn. He had few clothes, but they were always immaculate—clean white linen and a dark suit.

He was seldom at home. His home life was a shambles. He would disappear for days and nights, sitting up in wineshops and taverns. He would come home with empty pockets, a burning throat and stomach, yet few people had ever seen him drunk. He had many companions but few close friends. Women flocked to him. Eventually, he came to know Mme Róza, the owner and manager of the most famous house of assignation in Budapest, whose guests included the nobility of the Dual Monarchy, and the Prince of Wales. Mme Róza had literary ambitions; she, too, fell in love with Krúdy. Some of her letters to him survive, "I am ancient now," she wrote, "though, alas, not a venerable virgin. Were it so, I would offer that to no one but you." Another madam harbored Krúdy for days in her less elegant establishment, where he would sleep off the alcohol till noon, after which she took good care to serve him his favorite soup. (Once, she begged him to spend the night with her, instead of engaging in the usual fast hurly-burly on the chaise longue. If he wouldn't, she would jump out the window, she said. Krúdy told her that he had more serious business at night, with his companions. She did jump out the window—fortunately, not a high one—and broke her ankle.)

Around the age of thirty, Krúdy came into his own—or, rather, success came to him, with some money. The money did not last. As the great Hungarian critic Antal Szerb would write about Krúdy, he kept running after money but wrote masterpieces instead. Here and there, people began to savor his talent. He had found his genre at an early age, but now he found topics of a certain interest to the Budapest public. He had lived long enough in the city and knew its multifarious society well enough to write about it. Essentially, he remained the painter of the dream world of old Hungary, not of modern Budapest, but the peregrinations of his pen now included some of the latter, too. He invented an alter ego—Sindbad, the itinerant sailor of the Thousand and One Nights. Yet Krúdy was sailing not only from place to place but from one time to another. His most famous books were the Sindbad stories and *A vörös postakocsi* (*The Red Stagecoach*). Partly because some of their scenes took place in near-contemporary Budapest, partly because of their inimitable style, the reading public gobbled them up. Few people would now dismiss him as a journalist, an indefatigable scribbler, which, in practical terms, he was. A principal character in *The Red Stagecoach*, faintly disguised, was one of the few contemporaries whom Krúdy admired. This was the fantastic figure of M. Szemere, an aristocrat who had played (and won) in the Jockey Club of Vienna at such scandalously high stakes that the Emperor Franz Josef ordered his police chief to banish Szemere from the imperial capital for a while. Szemere was the lord of the Hungarian turf. On racing day, he would rise about noon in the old-fashioned hotel where he dwelt, descend among his respectful retinue, put twenty or more gold coins (his only instrument of exchange) in the pocket of his Prince Albert coat, and send a gold piece to the

Mother Superior of an Inner Town church, where the young novices were requested to pray for the success of his stable. Then he would order a carriage and trot off to the races, sometimes with Krúdy. It was around this time that Krúdy became addicted to his third and perhaps most destructive vice: after women and wine, gambling—horses and cards. When it came to horses, wine, women, it was his custom to choose outsiders.

He was a nocturnal animal. His head towered over the tables of the cafés, the nightclubs, the taverns, the gaming rooms of the writers' and artists' club, through the night; he sat up straight for hours, monumentally silent. He would fall asleep for several minutes, sometimes for half an hour, but people did not know whether he was asleep or awake. One of his loyal companions would carefully, awkwardly, pull away his own chips from their joint pile. Krúdy's hand would move and hold the defector's wrist: "Put it back." No one would dare to touch the carafe—always a carafe, never a vintage bottle—of the country wine that Krúdy drank (it was said that no one could lift a wineglass with comparable dignity). At late dawn, a tired colleague would attempt to leave, tiptoeing out of the cold smoky fug of the room. Krúdy's deep voice would break the silence: "Come back. Talk some more." One famous midnight, a hussar officer, a champion rider and fencer, sat down in full uniform at the crowded table where Krúdy sat. This officer pretended to ignore the writer. Krúdy got his anger up. "We had not been introduced," he said. The officer answered with an insult. Krúdy stood up, grabbed the hussar's sword, tore it off his waist, slapped his face, knocked him down, and threw him out on the pavement. Next day, he gave the sword to one of the afore-mentioned madams. The customary duel followed. The fencing champion was slightly wounded; Krúdy was not.

Sometimes he got restless. He would corral a companion, and they would drive to the station, board the Vienna express, sit down in the dining car. When their money or the wine ran out, they would get off. He would wire one of his editors for an advance and return to the city in a day or so. Once, in the pearly haze of a summer dawn, he climbed into a fiacre with another companion. "Where to, my lord?" the coachman asked. "Keep going," Krúdy said. "Drive slow." They came back four days later, having made a round trip of two hundred miles, with stops at the taverns and the garden restaurants around Lake Balaton. In the fresh breezes of the morning, he would order paper and ink, and in the empty restaurants he would write twelve or sixteen pages of magical, dream-haunted prose, sometimes about lonely travelers. In one of his finest short novels, *Az útitárs* (*The Traveling Companion*), he meets "an agreeable, quiet, sad-eyed, gray, and, above all, unpretentious gentleman."

We were traveling in the moonlight; through the shimmering fields ran those invisible foxes who by some magic always elude the hunters; wild ducks flew at a distance above a pond breathing silver; the shadows of trees moved like heartbeats...Like sadness, rain reached and overtook us, and from the darkening night it beat strings of tears against the indifferent window...and now only the words of my traveling companion echoed around me, as if Death were reading the Scriptures.

"I don't want to bore you with my circumstances," my traveling companion said. "That would be useless talk: like the usual, drowsy, uninspiring loquaciousness of fellow-travelers when they're waiting for the train in the musty room of a station and the signal bell is sullenly mute on the roof. I notice that most people travel for business. A bridegroom is the greatest rarity nowadays. And those fools out of certain romantic novels, with their bones shaken and hurting after ten, twelve hours on a train, in a stagecoach or a sleigh in winter—why? For the purpose of kissing a certain woman's hand, for being there to listen to her throaty mutterings, for the sake of getting a whiff of the scent of her petticoat or bodice; with their aim to say a few breathless words at the end of a path in a garden where the woman had stolen secretly from her bed—that kind of fool is now rare as a white raven. I was such a white raven once, exploding with love like dynamite in a quarry, the yellow smoke of which hangs for a while over the hillside until it disappears without a wisp of a trace."

Krúdy would return to the city, but seldom to his family. He now lived in hotels that he could afford—or, more exactly, whose owners were pleased to grant him credit. Yet his memories coursed in the opposite direction. They poured into scenes of a bygone patrician world of domesticity, peopled by spotless wives and honorable old men, and suffused with the quiet loveliness of country mornings:

To breakfast on a light-blue tablecloth, smelling of milk, like a child in the family home...freshly washed faces, hair combed wet, shirtfronts bright and white around the table. Everything smells different there, even rum. The plum brandy men swallow in one gulp on an empty stomach is harmless at the family table. The eggs are freshly laid, the butter wrapped in grape leaves smiles like a fat little girl, shoes are resplendent, the fresh morning airing wafts from the beds the stifling, sultry thoughts of the previous night, on quick feet the maid patters from room to room in a skirt starched only yesterday. Even the manure carts on the road steam differently on frosty mornings from the way they do in the afternoons; the rattle of gravely ill gentlemen quiets down in the neighboring houses; the bright greens in the markets, the red of the coxcombs, the pink-veined meats shining in the willow baskets, the towers of the town had been sponged and washed at dawn; and a piebald bird jumps around gaily on the frost-pinched mulberry tree, like life that begins anew and has forgiven and forgotten the past.

His words flew with longing for the provincial Magyar Biedermeier of the previous century. He would paint such scenes over and over, with a magic of which the addicts of his writing never grew tired. And this was part and parcel of his character: again, he was not so much like Proust, who loved high society and yet condemned it, as like Monet, who painted beautiful gardens because he loved them. At the tail end of his alcoholic nights, his clothes were still spotless. He despised loud carousers. He would, on occasion, send a message and a few banknotes to his wife: "Forgive me. Take the children on a Sunday picnic." "I'll be back soon." "Buy yourself some fine perfume." His wife had become corpulent and sad, tortured less by jealousy than by the continual lack of money. She did not forgive him. His children did. For decades after their father's death, they treasured their sad, loving memories, and even wrote short memoirs about him.

You do not understand, he told his wife and the other women trying to cling to him: I must be alone. I need solitude. We know, or at least we can surmise, that his incomparable scenes grew in his mind while he mused for hours, half awake. Yet they did not crystallize until he began writing. He let his pen saunter, amble, canter away, down endless roads and tree-lined paths laden with the honeyed golden mist of memories and the old Magyar names of innumerable flowers, trees, ferns, birds. I write "endless roads" because his novels and stories have only the thinnest of plots. They are four-dimensional paintings, whose magical beauty is manifested not only through shades and forms but through the fourth dimension of human reality—time itself—as the thin stream of the story all at once bursts into a magnificent fountain, the water splashing and coursing in rainbow colors. Like Balzac, Krúdy wrote every day, through his worst hangovers, because he needed money instantly and desperately. Unlike Balzac, he never corrected his manuscripts, and he cared little for the proofs. He possessed only a few books, and not many of his own. He wrote because he had to. He never cared for his reputation. Some of his companions and admirers were writers, but he would never—absolutely never—talk literature with them. The topics that interested him were the preparation of certain standard Magyar dishes, the odd habits of attractive men and women, stories of the turf, and the fascinating legerdemain of certain people able to lay their hands on money whenever they had to.

He would tuck his sixteen pages into his pockets, hail a carriage or walk to an editorial office, and request his honorarium. Then came a long midday dinner, well after the noon hour, in a half-empty restaurant, where he would be surrounded by the silent, respectful service of the owner and the waiters. Then the turf, the gaming table, and the night life. By midnight, he would have little or no money left. There was the memorable occasion when, having played and lost at baccarat for hours in his club, he stood up and said to an acquaintance, who was holding the bank, "Give me the *cagnotte*." That was incredible. The *cagnotte* was a box with a slot, sunk in the center of the green felt table, where winners would occasionally drop a few chips after a successful run. That club of writers and artists depended on the nightly *cagnotte* for some of its upkeep. "But, Gyula—" this gentleman said. "No 'Gyula'" Krúdy said. "The *cagnotte*." After a moment of deathly silence, the gentleman lifted out the box, opened it with a key, and poured out its contents before Krúdy. Krúdy ordered a waiter to cash them in; then he swept the money into his pocket, stood up, and left. The club did not expel him.

The best of his times—and the worst of his times—may have been the years of the First World War. The war came after the publication of the first Sindbad stories and *The Red Stage-coach*. Krúdy's writing had blossomed; for the first time, he had a considerable public. Perhaps because of the increasingly anxious and difficult years of the war, there was an appetite for his evocations of an older, better Hungary, an older, better Budapest, and older and better men and women—serious patricians, respectable virgins. Almost every Budapest newspaper carried a literary page. He wrote for most of these newspapers, indifferent to their political or social inclinations, interested in them only as the fount of honoraria. Yet his life was as disorganized as ever, perhaps even more so. He lived in the Hotel Royal, a large, modern commercial establishment on one of the noisy boulevards of the city, where it stands even now. The owner, a M. Várady, admired him. The owner's wife, a ripe woman in her thirties, loved him with a shameful, sensual devotion. At times, Krúdy had to resort to undignified stratagems to escape her desperate jealousies; once, at a summer resort where he was the Váradys' guest, he had a tall companion impersonate him in the evening shadows while he, bending his large frame, crawled silently among the bushes to the room of another woman, who had left a window open for him to climb in. Mme Várady had a daughter, seventeen years old, who adored Krúdy. Krúdy chose to love her. They eloped. It took two years for his first wife to consent, bitterly, to give him a divorce. Zsuzsi, his new love, was twenty-three years younger than he. She married him.

Much of this happened during the saddest years of the country. Hungary, in tandem with Austria, lost the war. A Hungarian republic was proclaimed—ominously, in retrospect —in late October of 1918, with disorderly shoutings, and rain splashing on the pavement under dark, soiled clouds, on a sodden day. There followed an ugly and unpopular short-lived Communist regime, a humiliating foreign occupation, and the reestablishment of a narrow kind of order, laced with the hatreds of a rent and diminished people. Meanwhile, most of the country had been amputated: two-thirds of the old Hungary was partitioned among the new states of Czechoslovakia and Yugoslavia and the swollen kingdom of Rumania. Krúdy, who never wrote a false word when describing a flower, a tree, a woman's garter, or the odor of the midnight air but who was an instinctive opportunist when it came to money, had written a few things—paragraphs, sentences—here and there in accord with the ideas of the now despised revolutionaries and leftists. This was but one of his difficulties under the new regime. There was now no atmosphere for his music; even the acoustics of nostalgia were out of date. The dust bath of abject poverty covered a truncated, misery-laden nation. After a while things improved. Hungary and Hungarians tend to be unsuccessful after their most astonishing triumphs, but they have an instinctive genius for recovery and rebuilding after their worst disasters. During the most miserable of those years—1919, 1920, 1921—Krúdy wrote several more masterpieces. Perhaps his new marriage and the birth of his adored youngest child sustained his spirits. He had not much changed his habits: the night before his young bride gave birth, he was at the gaming table in his club again. He sent her a tender note, saying that it was lucky that he had lost that night, since she would now have an easy delivery. A little girl, Zsuzsika, was born. She weighed "four quarts and three pints," the elderly father would say proudly to his companions.

For he had become an elderly gentleman. He was not much over forty, still handsome, but his head had turned silver, as had his mustache. His vices were changing, too: fewer women, more wine; fewer turf days, longer tavern afternoons. But he wrote like a fiend. His feuilletons filled the pages of newspapers of every persuasion or denomination. Eventually, these writings would be gathered together and published in modest, thin, paper-covered editions. They brought him little money. His public had diminished. His reputation was running down. He had written often about autumn, about country autumns that "stretched out long, like a single shining strand of red hair." In Budapest, too, the autumn mists were coming closer, there were "weeping young clouds, a damp wind whistling through the keyholes... when the Danube boats sound their horns like forlorn ghosts who cannot find their way in the night." He himself was in the autumn of his life now—*dans les faubourgs de la vieillesse*, as the lovely French phrase has it. Yet there were moments of happiness ("Happiness," he had written once, "is a moment's interval between desire and sorrow")—or, rather, of contentment. An ancient apartment was found for him and his family, in surroundings that could hardly have been more suitable for Gyula Krúdy, though comfortable they were not. It was in a century-old house in the shadow of giant plane trees, on Margaret's Island, in the middle of the Danube, between Buda and Pest. Decades before, the greatest of Magyar poets, János Arany, had sat under the island's noble oaks, in a grove beyond the ruins of a thirteenth-century monastery. In the early nineteen-twenties, the island had few telephones; it was traversed every hour by an open horse-drawn trolley. It had an old hotel, frequented by writers, among them some of Krúdy's companions. He and his family had to take their baths there; their apartment had no bathroom. At times, they led a country existence in the midst of the heaving city, which was gradually filling with buses and cars.

He had less and less money, while he gambled and drank more and more. "There are mornings," he wrote about another writer, in another age, "when literature resembles a kind, sad wife, weeping without a word, alone; she is always in one's mind but one does not talk about her." He spent a few unhappy months near Vienna, in a former imperial château rented by Baron Lajos Hatvany, who, besides being a baron, was a noted left-wing litterateur and dilettante, in temporary exile from Hungary for political reasons. During those months in the elegant house in the Vienna woods, Krúdy was morose and solitary. Once, he roused his host at four in the morning in order to break open an ancient armoire that, according to Krúdy, must have belonged to Franz Josef himself. Eventually, he came back to the island without a farthing, having urged Hatvany in vain to provide a substantial loan for a child-care establishment that his wife was trying to launch. The valves of his heart were leaking badly. He was lucky to have among his admirers a fine doctor, Dr. Lajos Lévy, who was one of those saintly giants of medicine from a past age who took it as their sacred duty to care for and attempt to cure men such as Krúdy without asking anything, material or spiritual, in exchange. He took Krúdy into his hospital, to cure and rest and feed him. Of course Krúdy had to be bereft of wine. But one early evening the nurses found him in his whitewashed room with a beaker of wine and a lone Gypsy playing softly, very softly. The young doctors of Lévy's entourage were shocked. Lévy only shook his head. His patient was on the road to a limited recovery, and a little wine might be good for him, he said.

There was no money in the Krúdy house. There were sad, tremendous quarrels. He passed the age of fifty. He was an old man now. He failed to pay the minimal rent on the apartment. From the island, he had often looked across to the western side of the river, the old quarter of Óbuda—Old Buda—with its one-story houses inhabited by thrifty working-class people, its rough cobblestone streets, and its peasant-baroque church towers under the high Buda hills. Now he was forced to move there, taking three rooms in an old yellow house, in some ways reminiscent of the house of his childhood. There exists a photograph of Krúdy leaning out of his window and contemplating the street with his large brown eyes. Yet his headquarters were not in that house, Templom-utca 15 (No. 15 Church Street), which is marked with a plaque now. They were in Kéhli's ancient tavern, in the next street, whose yellow flat-country wine he liked.

He wrote and wrote in the mornings, at a plain table covered with wrapping paper that was held down at the corners with big No. 2 steel thumbtacks, always with an old-fashioned steel pen, always using a bottle of violet ink. He had written more than seventy books. His wife and daughter took temporary lodgings elsewhere, returning to him from time to time. His writings were no longer popular. His advances from publishers were exhausted. Most of his former publishers would have nothing to do with him, because they could not; the Depression of the early nineteen-thirties made the publishing situation even worse. Krúdy could still place short pieces in some of the newspapers, but this income was far from enough. His most faithful readers now were a small group of people, among them some of the best writers of Hungary. They understood what his prose meant for their Magyar language, that lonely orphan among the languages of Europe. One of these writers, the novelist and poet Dezső Kosztolányi, arranged things so that in 1931 and 1932 Krúdy would receive literary prizes amounting to considerable sums. Krúdy asked that the awards be given him not during a ceremony but privately; he wanted to avoid his creditors. By the spring of 1933, he had not paid his rent or his bills for many months. The city authority that owned the house informed him that he would have to vacate his rooms. His electric current was cut off. On the last day of his life, he coursed through the city unhappily, stopping in governmental and editorial offices with indifferent results. He sat for a few hours in Kéhli's, with his long white hand around the small wineglass. He borrowed a candle and ambled home.

Alone in his apartment, he stuck that cheap brown candle in an empty bottle and lay down to sleep. A cleaning woman found him dead, at ten o'clock on a bright morning.

That was the end of the writer Gyula Krúdy. The sun was shining in the incredibly blue skies over Óbuda when they laid him out, in his last spotless piece of clothing—his full-dress suit. A companion recalled that, a year or so earlier, Krúdy had told him that he had tried to pawn this suit but that the pawnshop could not use it—it was too big, he was too tall, they said. To his funeral came writers, journalists, editors, waiters, headwaiters, porters, street girls, an official delegation from the city of his birth, and a small Gypsy band, which played his favorite air as the coffin was let down. His first wife cried out, "You had it coming, Gyula!" There was a hush. His friend the newspaper editor Miklós Lázár spoke at the grave. M. Lázár gave me the tear sheet of that beautiful speech, in New York, in 1963—a yellowed, brittle page from an old newspaper.

For almost a decade, Krúdy was forgotten. His grave, only faintly marked, was sinking into the ground. Then came a marvelous event—not only in Krúdy's posthumous annals but in those of modern Hungarian literature. A book appeared entitled *Szindbád hazamegy* (*Sindbad Comes Home*), by the great haut-bourgeois writer Sándor Márai. What Márai (who was twenty-two years Krúdy's junior and knew him in the last years of his life) had composed was a Krúdy symphony, in the form of a reconstruction of Krúdy's last day, in Krúdy's style. It begins with his solitary rising and dressing in his rooms in Óbuda; it ends with his last night, enveloped in the comforter of his unforgettable dreams—dreams that carry Sindbad the sailor to another world. I read this book when I was seventeen. Afterward, I read as much Krúdy (and Márai) as I could lay my hands on, buying Krúdy volumes often in antiquarian book-shops. And I was not alone. All this happened during the Second World War, in the middle of a German-occupied, bru-tal, and often very vulgar world, when people found happiness and inspiration in the presence of nobler and better things of the past. I left Hungary in 1946, even before its regime had be-come wholly Communized, because I thought that there was no place for me in the "new" Hungary—or, rather, not a place I would want. So did Sándor Márai.

I left my family and, among other things, perhaps two dozen Krúdy and Márai books. I was convinced that Hungary was lost; besides, I knew English rather well. I wanted to be-come an English-writing and therefore English-thinking histo-rian, not an émigré intellectual who writes about Central European history in English. Twelve or thirteen years later I be-gan to notice something extraordinary. Krúdy's books were be-ing reprinted in Hungary, one after another. There was—there still is—a Krúdy revival, to an extent that he (or I) could not have dreamed of. People who had left Hungary after the 1956 Rising began importing his books from Budapest. I got some of them, and as I turned their pages on quiet winter evenings in my house in the Pennsylvania countryside my eyes sometimes filled with tears. Another exile, the scholar and critic László Cs. Szabó, has written what Hungarians, exiled or not, know: "How can a foreign reader understand Krúdy without ever hav-ing seen the Óbuda towers from Margaret's Island under gath-ering snowclouds; or the flirtatious scratching of the blushing leaves of birch trees in the sand, down the Nyír; or the inward smiles of the fallen apples lying on the bottom of the Lower Szamos? How could he, when he had never heard the sound of a cello through the open window of a one-story house: the sound of the bow pulled by an unseen gentleman, playing for himself alone, just before the evening church bells begin to peal from the Danube side?"

So there is the problem of Krúdy's Magyar language. There is the question of his place in the history of Hungarian literature. And the question of his place in European, and world, literature. Allow me to turn to what I think are the essentials of these questions before I return to the language problem.

More than sixty years after his death two considerations are indubitable. The first is that Krúdy was one of the greatest writers, if not *the* greatest writer of Magyar prose. The second —not unconnected with the first—is his unclassifiability.

The recognition of Krúdy's importance within the ranks of the greatest Hungarian prose writers developed slowly, and perhaps erratically, but this recognition is no longer questionable. During his lifetime the extraordinary significance of his style and the quality of his talents were asserted only by a few of his greatest contemporary authors. Then during the last half-century as more and more of his books were reprinted, many scholarly and critical essays and monographs about Krúdy appeared. One main result of this is that we have now a rather clear view of the successive phases of his oeuvre. (Note that because of the staggering quantity of his writings there can never be a complete Collected Works of Krúdy; and that despite the most assiduous work of researchers a complete and precise bibliography of Krúdy's published pieces will not be possible either.)

During his first phase, from approximately 1894 to 1911 (recall that his first published writings appeared when he was fourteen!) we can already detect without difficulty most of the elements of his extraordinary style and vision. At this time he may be still somewhat classifiable, because of the similarity of many of his themes (though with hardly any similarity in style) to those of the great Hungarian novelist Kálmán Mikszáth, of the previous generation. The second period began with the

Sindbad books, in 1911–12. It may be said (though imprecisely) that it was then that Krúdy reached his full powers. What is more certain is that it was then, and then only, that he became a well-known writer among the considerable reading public in Budapest. This had something to do with the fact that most of his work now dealt with scenes and people in Budapest—but the significance of this must not be exaggerated. He wrote much more of old (nineteenth-century) Buda and Pest than of the modern Budapest of the 1910s; while the symbolic and impressionist qualities of his prose developed further and further.

The third "period," 1918 to 1923, corresponded with the greatest tragedies of his country and nation as well as with lamentable upheavals in his personal life. Perhaps his greatest masterpieces—including the present *Sunflower*—were composed in these years. He now turned back from the present to the past, from Budapest to the provinces, to an older dreamlike country—which, however, must not be attributed to an escape into nostalgia. These books are suffused with what, perhaps surprisingly, Maupassant once wrote: that the aim of the "realistic novelist" (and Krúdy was anything but a "realistic novelist") "is not to tell a story, to amuse us or to appeal to our feelings, but to compel us to reflect, and to understand the darker and deeper meaning of events"—in Krúdy's case, particularly of people. Krúdy writes of imaginary people, of imaginary events, in dreamlike settings; but the spiritual essence of his persons and of their places is stunningly real, it reverberates in our minds and strikes at our hearts. This Introduction is not the place to explain or illustrate this further; but perhaps readers of this book will recognize what this meant and still means.

The last eight years of his short life were his saddest years, interrupted twice by serious illnesses and leading directly to his premature death. There was no deterioration in his style; but there was less of a concordance of his themes and of his interests. Much of this was due to his personal constraints and difficulties. We may, however, detect yet another emerging element in the evolution of this extraordinary writer: his increasing interest in the past history of Hungary, perhaps propelled by his sense that the eye of a great novelist may see things that professional historians may have missed. In these often sketchlike reconstructions it is again and again evident that Krúdy is *sui generis*, and unique.

Indeed, one of the marks of Krúdy's extraordinary position in the history of Hungarian literature (and if I may say so, in the history of Hungarian mentality) is the character of his unclassifiability. During the twentieth century there has come a break, a veritable chasm, in Hungarian literature, as well as in ideology and politics, between "populists" and "urbanists" (or between "nationalists" and "internationalists," though none of these terms are quite accurate). Again this is not the place to analyze or even to describe this—often regrettable—phenomenon further, save to suggest that similar scissions exist in other nations too (e.g. between "Redskins" and "Palefaces" in America, or between "Westerners" and "Slavophiles" in Russia, etc.) Now it is not only that Krúdy does not belong into either of these categories. Nor is he a "hybrid," writing about Budapest one day and about the old provinces on another morning. He is—not at all consciously, but characteristically and naturally—above them, without even thinking, for a moment, about their differences. That alone is a mark of his greatness. The unclassifiable character of his style, of his vision, of his very Hungarianness is more than the mark of an eccentric talent: the talent exists not because it is eccentric, and the eccentricity is remarkable not because it is talented. Like a Shakespeare or a Dante or a Goethe in their very different ways, Krúdy is a genius.

But then even a genius cannot be separated entirely from his place and time. Krúdy belongs to Hungary; and he belongs to the twentieth century. He is a modern writer—though there may be plenty of problems with that overused adjective. (The time may come when we, completely contrary to the still accepted idea, will recognize the works of French Impressionists not as breaking away from representational art but as its culmination.) The words "impressionism" or "symbolism" would have meant nothing to Gyula Krúdy. Nor was he a "subjectivist" writer. But within his capacity to see and to describe people (and places) beyond the constraints of mechanical time, to understand the confluences of dreaming and wakefulness, of consciousness and unconsciousness (*not* sub-consciousness!), of the ideal with the real (and *not* with the material!) we may detect elements of those recognitions that appear in the works of such different artists and thinkers and composers as Bergson, or Mallarmé, or Debussy and Ravel, or Proust (with whom he has been often compared, though the French prose writers closer to his style are Alain-Fournier and Valéry Larbaud), or even—perhaps—of Virginia Woolf (with whom otherwise he had nothing in common). Krúdy, in sum, is one of the greats of European literature of the twentieth century.

This brings me, in conclusion, to the last problem, which is that of the Magyar language—and, consequently, to the enormous difficulties of Krúdy's translatability. "Everything suffers from a translation, except a bishop," wrote Trollope in dear old Victorian England. Yes, and this is especially true of works from the Hungarian—but not only because of the already-mentioned uniqueness of the Magyar language, and the unrelatedness of the small Hungarian nation to the great linguistic families of Europe. Nor is the main problem—though problem it is—inherent in Krúdy's prosody and vocabulary which are earthy and ethereal at the same time, sometimes within the same sentence. Krúdy is a *deeply* Hungarian writer. That quality has nothing to do with nationalism (the mistaken belief of many a populist), though it has much to do with the older, more traditional virtues of patriotism. His prose is poetic, and profoundly national, soaked with history, with images, associations, including not only words but rhythms recognizable only to Hungarians, and among them only to those whose imaginative antennae naturally vibrate not only with such words and their sounds but with what those descriptions historically—yes, historically—represent.

That is why his translations require unusual talents. *"How can a foreign reader understand...?"* From that passage by Cs. Szabó with which I ended "The Sound of a Cello" I left out his last two sentences:

> Hopeless. Hopeless.
> Still...go ahead and try, my friends.

Well, Mr. John Bátki has tried. And largely succeeded.

JOHN LUKACS

SUNFLOWER

1. THE TOUCHABLE EVELINE

THE YOUNG miss lay abed reading a novel by the light of the candelabra. She heard faint creaks from another part of the townhouse: was someone walking in a remote room? She lowered her book and listened. The hands of the clock were creeping up on midnight like some soul climbing a rock face.

Miss Eveline at age twenty had already more or less got over mourning for her first love, except for the occasional recollection, whooshing by like a gull on the north wind, of a young man who had threatened suicide. Otherwise she was the very image of health and serenity: she favored a serious aspect; in summer she wore white, in winter black; she made her autumn devotions in the Franciscans' Church, with the same fervor with which she hoed the spring garden at her country estate; she believed a great happiness awaited her somewhere, and for this reason she remained calm as the days flew by.

However, the midnight noise alarmed her.

At first she could not recall whether she had locked her bedroom door. But she was sure the small door to her bathroom was unlocked. And so her eyes fixed on that door. Softly, she slipped out from under her comforter and tiptoed toward the bathroom. With trepidation she saw that she had left the key in the lock on the other side of the door. She watched mesmerized as the copper doorknob started to turn with the softness of a coffin being lowered into the grave. Such mastery of locks could only mean a practiced hand on the other side of the door.

Eveline took one last look around—her window faced the December garden. It was a mezzanine window protected by a cast iron grill in the style of old town houses in the Josephstadt district of Pest.

Next she looked about for a weapon, to defend herself. Her eyes passed over a Turkish-style paper cutter, to rest on a hat pin.

The doorknob, by now, had almost completely rotated. The moment arrived for the stranger to try the door.

Now the rose-colored door, indeed, began to open.

Eveline's shout was so loud she didn't recognize her own voice:

"Get up, Kálmán! There's a robber in the house!"

In her terror she flung her sewing kit at the window with such force that the pane broke with a loud crash.

The doorknob, released, clicked back into place.

Then a door slammed in the distance like a loud oath.

The footfalls she next heard from the street could have come from anyone out for a melancholy meditative midnight stroll.

Heart thumping, Eveline ran to the window. The white garden resembled a graveyard. Old trees stood motionless, wearing their overcoats of snow. The distant wall at the end of the garden loomed white. The house grew quiet again, like a discarded diary whose heroes and heroines have departed from this world.

The young woman hurriedly donned a fur coat: it felt against her nightgown like a fawning tomcat. Her perky little slippers appeared as if on command from under the bed. A glance in the mirror showed a dark female with small lively eyes and chalk-white face. She stood motionless, heart pounding murderously, and broke out in a cold sweat. With the immediate danger gone, she did not know what to do. She could only stand there frightened, oblivious to everything.

"Could it have been him?" she wondered.

Her former fiancé, Kálmán. Certainly familiar enough with

her house to find his way in the dark labyrinth of zigzag corridors with doors opening left and right. He knew about the spiral staircase leading from her mezzanine quarters down to the garden, built in the days when Jacobins lurked in old Pest and the owner of the house had been part of the conspiracy. The aristocratic palaces lined her street as stately as illustrations in a travel guide. Among them, the mansard roof of her narrow single-story house stood like a little old lady guarding the family silver. An ordinary robber would have gotten lost inside this antique house. The midnight intruder had to be Kálmán.

But what did he want? He was free to drop by any time, in broad daylight, and ask for whatever he needed, as he had so many times before, for instance when bankrupted by cards or the horses; in such cases like some benevolent relative she had always helped him out generously. Crisp, faintly perfumed banknotes rustled in her rosewood money box at whatever odd hour Kálmán appeared in the boudoir overlooking the garden. Her delicate, white fingers handed over the largest of these banknotes as casually as if it had been a handkerchief. Out of superstition, she had always asked for a penny in return so that good fortune would not leave the house. But Kálmán appeared on other occasions, as well: whenever he had been wounded, abandoned or betrayed by some woman. At such times the rosewood box in the corner contemplated Kálmán's downcast head with compassion. The girl's snow-white fingers were kept busy chasing away the clouds from the young man's brow.

But Kálmán had not visited here in two years.

What did he want now?

Did he have money troubles again? Before their final breakup Eveline had paid all of the young man's debts. So he could start a wholesome new life with a clean slate. So he could forget Eveline, who in turn would do her best to forgive him.

Eveline sat by her window until dawn. She watched the trees soak up the light. Dawn poured over the city like farm-fresh milk. The dwarf shrubs emerged from the gloaming like schoolchildren with snow on their hats after the long walk to the schoolhouse A solemn cypress in its black and white robe loomed like a melancholy gambler returning home at dawn.

Eveline opened the window.

She saw footprints in the snow-covered garden.

Light snow still falling turned the footprints into paling memories. And just as hunters distinguish a wolf's tracks from other beasts', so did Eveline, hands pressed against her heart, recognize the tracks left by her nighttime visitor. In a flash, she was on her feet, through the bathroom, down the spiral stairway, and out in the garden. Never mind that the doors were left open behind her.

She tiptoed toward the first footprint as if it were a butterfly in noonday sun. And knelt, as in front of an altar. Then bent down and kissed the snow where her midnight guest's foot had landed.

She kissed the mark left by the heel. Because that's where the body's weight rests, its strength, courage and resolve. Her lips touched the imprint of the arched sole, the part that rests on the invisible stirrup that ever supports the rider, keeps him from being unhorsed. These perpetual stirrups steer the wanderer's footsteps this way and that. Sometimes they lead to surprises in uncharted and wondrous lands where never-to-be-imagined women await their man, all practiced smiles, shameless knees, and breasts as unclean as the pavement in the street. These same stirrups will guide the wearying footfall in other directions. From the wild booming of the contrabass to the faintest murmurs of the heart; from the antic swirl of the masked ball to the gentle flames of the hearth; toward the barely audible gravelly crinkling of freshly sprinkled garden paths under plantains that exhale deeply like sleeping virgins. O these stirrups one day will completely overpower the poor, hesitant feet. Who knows where they will then speed the lost traveler?

The Josephstadt church bells were ringing for the Advent mass. From beyond the garden wall came the coughing of kerchiefed old women bent into salt pretzel shapes.

The afternoon mail brought a letter.

Eveline at once recognized Kálmán's handwriting. The envelope contained a single frozen stem of rosemary.

"Please forgive my robbing your garden. I repent my transgression and herewith return your flower, for I have no right to keep it."

The wilted flower revived in the warm room, raising its head like a frostbitten bird. A wonderful fresh icy scent pervaded Eveline's chamber, like a token of reviving life.

At Hideaway, the estate in Bujdos, even the snow fell in a different way.

A few days after the midnight visitation Miss Eveline packed up her whole household and traveled to her estate by the upper reaches of the River Tisza, as was her wont whenever the smoky ghostriders of depression descended on her house in the capital. By stealing away to her village residence she fled the grim faces of these unfriendly shades, nor did she dare open her eyes before reaching the signal box of the Bujdos station.

It was honest to goodness wintertime here. Snow every day, just like in the Alps. The marshy groves, the reeds and snaking rills were all snowed under, disappearing for the duration of the season like enraptured women lying sequestered with pagan lovers. The landscape lay bewitched, as in a dream. This was old Hungary, silent with the sleep of the blessed, the humble, the poor. At this time of year the tracks of the North-East railroad line lay under snow; telegraph poles now served only as signposts for vagabonds; the rime-frosted windows of the midnight train hid strange travelers, who could have been madmen, or the damned, heading for unknown destinations.

At Bujdos-Hideaway life stood stock-still like a snowman stuck in a corner of the yard.

But under the archways of the old manor house it was snug and toasty. The iron-barred windows, serene and secure, regarded the landscape. The clock's musical chimes invoked the tones of some ancient kinsman's resonant chant. The serving folk had served here all their long lives. They knew by name each flower and tree, each trail, each horse and dog—they were all members of the family at Bujdos-Hideaway. Even the crows were old acquaintances. The stone saint by the roadside was ready to speak out in response to the greetings of the village folk. Ghosts returned from the graveyard sure to find their old pipes still waiting on their customary rack.

This is where Eveline was born; this is where she felt herself truly content. Across the cast iron grill at the entrance of the family crypt she could see her parents' sandstone monuments. She greeted them and they spoke back to her. All creatures here —dogs, horses, humans—saluted her as their queen. And to pay his respects, Andor Álmos-Dreamer of Lower and Upper Álmos came on horseback from Álmos Isle across the frozen Tisza. Leaning from the saddle, he knocked on the dining room window, rapping on the exact same pane as his father and grandfather, dropping by to inquire what was cooking for dinner.

This particular Álmos-Dreamer was a village savant, around forty years of age, a wiry, hard-headed bachelor with gentle eyes. He lived in solitude on his island in the meandering river, where a stone wall sheltered his retreat from people and the spring floods. He spoke softly, and had not been heard to laugh aloud in years. His aspect was as calm as twilight in the country. He loved the winter silence. In the spring he liked to smoke a cigar and listen to passing raftsmen's songs. He was neither extravagant nor a maniac. He remained on his island with the utter tenacity of an otter—a scientist whose name had never seen the light of print. He was one of those bygone Hungarian gentlemen who, just to amuse themselves during long winter nights, learned French or English by perusing the tomes in their libraries. As septuagenarians they would take up the study of astronomy. They knew their Horace and Berzsenyi by heart. But they would not speak out at the county assembly because of their disdain of electioneering and politicians. Calfskin-bound, yellowing classics carried their ex libris. Surely book-marks still remain at the pages they were reading on their deathbeds. And their beloved women were like potted plants. Back in those days the lady of the house was a fair, fragrant and calm being, who went about her days at a leisurely pace, with little noise; her voluptuous curves provided eveningtime pleasures. These were leisurely, Rubenesque, tender romancings, slow and endless like the village hours. They brought peaceful, wholesome dreams—and children who were precious fulfillments of a promise, like feast days vouchsafed by the calendar. Within the walls of these fortunate old-time manors, Don Quixote's amorous follies, Manon Lescaut's tortured miseries and even the poet Kisfaludy's melancholy lines set heads a-wagging in quiet amazement, as if they were tall tales told by a far-flung traveler.

Andor Álmos-Dreamer never declared his love for Miss Eveline. Their affinity had always been taken for granted like a childhood friendship that survives throughout a lifetime, serene, questioned by no one. It was as natural as the mating of birds, the springtime rut of domestic animals and the white blossoms of an orchard, as easy as the East wind that heralds spring and sets the reeds in motion, dries up the floods and caresses the grass with a benevolent hand.

"Are you feeling miserable again?" asked the horseman, having dismounted, brushed the snow from his shoulder, and kissed the girl's cool forehead.

Teardrops showed in Eveline's eyes as she fixed her placid gaze on Andor, as on a trustworthy elder brother.

"I've been thinking of him again...that creep."

Andor's handwave was gruff:

"You should winter here. Stay the whole year even. Hideaway will cure you. Poor girl, you seem so miserable. This is the only place where you can find your former self. I won't even ask what happened. I'm sure something must weigh heavily on your mind if you left the city in the middle of the season. Please understand...I'm not interested in hearing about young Master Kálmán or any other man about town. I just won't let you leave before you are fully healed."

Eveline's smile was hopeful, evoking childhood Christmas bells and carolers. It was wintertime. They would go sledding...and skating in the bright high noon sun on the frozen Tisza flats...and there would be a pig-sticking...The mailman would deliver books still smelling of snow, frozen magazines and Christmas supplements somewhat the worse for the wear after the long journey, and together they would browse through these...They could look over the scrawled accounts kept by her bailiff...Talk about their dead parents, and old friends who had passed on, women who had danced away their lives, and the mysteries of the City. The watchdogs would bark nonstop—perhaps it is the Grim Reaper himself flying above the landscape, passing over the blizzard-wrapped old manor house where pillows exude the faint scent of floral cachets and the dream book offers the right solution to one's dreams. Check the calendar, what day is it? The fragrance of Yuletide and New Year's season creates those reveries of an ever-hopeful childhood, when faded schoolbooks that we had practically absorbed by heart, and stern old schoolmasters who seem menacing even when viewed through the spectacles of dream still provided us with a gossamer film of happy expectation...that had absolutely nothing to do with the life to come.

Eveline grasped her friend's bony hand:

"Too often you've let me go like a child sent off to a distant land. Will you please not do that again? Who knows if I'd ever come back..."

Andor Álmos-Dreamer caressed the girl's hair.

"You are a dear creature, and I know you haven't a mean bone in your body. I've always felt easy about you even when I didn't see you for a long time. Your heart is noble because you never had to deal with demeaning, low things. Your soul is pristine because you were never troubled by woeful need, dream-depriving cares, or sinful thoughts whispered by poverty in your ear. You are gracious and peaceable, like a young woman who at eveningtime kneels in front of the fireplace and sinks into reverie lulled by the swirl of snowflakes. But those dream chevaliers, lovers mounted on steeds, soaring over rooftops on swallows' wings, they all vanish without a trace when the lamps are lit. The morning and daylight are sober, serene and delightful like fresh water. The winter sky hereabouts is mostly gray, just like our lives. But it also happens to be as warm as rabbit fur. I'm not worried about you, my sweet angel. You'll always come back here because this is where you find everything worth living for. Your home, your grave, your sky and the land that nurtures you. Eveline, you are a village miss at heart, homegrown rosemary, even if you like to think of yourself as a cosmopolitan lady. Your world is really made of falling snow, autumn leaves in the wind blowing free and springtime greens on the river bank. In the depressing city you are only a hotel guest, rather bored by the hustle and bustle of humanity, and spend your time yawning in the monotony of your room although even its musty air seemed exciting on first arrival. What would you want from those total strangers?"

"I don't really like them and yet they fascinate me like travel descriptions of distant continents. For me to be alive means coming across ever new acquaintances, new voices, new names, new faces. Even each handshake can be so different. And people's lies make the most beautiful fairy tales. Everybody tells such lies." Meanwhile the bachelor made himself at home in her dining room. He opened the cupboard, found the bottle of plum brandy, cut himself a slice of ham, sniffed the aroma of the bread loaf, and proceeded to have himself a leisurely and self-indulgent snack.

"Men aren't worth a pipeful of tobacco, mark my words. You are twenty-two now. You love travel and travelers, fairgrounds and market women, stylish overcoats and flashy lights. You'll go back a few more times for a taste of that sorry masked ball. You'll need life's disappointments and storms to find the path to happiness. Yes, go on and step out, have a good time and laugh a lot, dazzle and dance on. Sooner or later you'll have your fill of the masquerade. I'll be here waiting for you, I won't go anywhere. But bear in mind that if you decided not to come back one year...I'd be very sad ever after." So spoke Andor Álmos-Dreamer.

He said his good-byes and set out. The horseman's snow-laden figure soon disappeared into the white night.

Three days later on his island he received a letter from Eveline, requesting Mr. Álmos-Dreamer's presence at once, for she had important things to tell him. And so the recluse again abandoned his tame otters to find Eveline sitting by her stove, as pale as one afflicted with an ailment of the heart.

"I seem to have become quite a coward. At night I keep hearing footsteps around the house. I wake up and stare at the door as if somebody were here, who won't let me sleep. I fear the bell-jar silence of the winter night, the noiseless dying of the embers, the shadows of antique furniture, this treacherous provincial house with its lazy hounds and indolent servants. I could be murdered in my sleep, for all they care."

Andor Álmos-Dreamer growled in response.

"You'll get used to the quiet. Soon you won't mind the moaning of the wind. Part of you is still in the big city."

"Mademoiselle Montmorency, my paid companion, sleeps

as soundly as an aged nun, while my aunt enjoys happy dreams about the gallants of her youth. My maids scribble love letters to Budapest. The bailiff gets drunk every night. I am all alone here, and I am afraid. Someone is lurking around my house. Maybe a vagabond or a highwayman, or else a . . ."

Mr. Álmos-Dreamer smiled. "A lover . . . Just leave it to me, I'll take care of it. I'll come back at night and patrol the neighborhood on horseback."

That night the moon shone as radiant as a carnival clown. The snow-covered landscape sparkled with built-in stars. The groves stood immobile in their shrouds. It was a blessed winter night, the crowing of the rooster still a long way off. Time to die a hundred deaths until then. A mounted figure resembling a highwayman passed in front of the house and surveyed the moonlit landscape. His horse snorted smoky clouds into the bitter cold air. There came the windowpane-shattering report of a firearm.

Eveline, trembling from head to foot, opened her shutters and called out.

"Is that you, Mr. Álmos-Dreamer?"

"Yes, it's me," his hoarse voice replied. "You can sleep without fear, my angel. The ghost is laid to rest."

"Give me your hand, my good sir."

Andor reached in through the cast-iron bars of the window.

Eveline slowly pulled off the fur glove and bestowed a lingering fervent kiss on his hand.

"I thank you," she whispered.

The warmth emanating from her nightgown, the gentle nestling caress of her kiss, the fervid grasp of her hand, the fragrance of the night befuddled the middle-aged knight errant. Leaning from his saddle, he regarded the young woman with shining eyes.

"My angel," he mumbled, blushing, and caressed the girl's exposed neck.

Uttering a quick oath, he snatched back his hand and spurred his long-maned little horse. Enormous wolfhounds mutely sped through the swirling snow in his wake like the hounds of night.

Eveline's insomnia proved to be of long duration.

If you are sleepless in the big city you may gain some consolation from street noises that tell you there are others who find no relief in the night. But in the village the midnight hours can drive you to distraction, their slow passage as sluggish as the creaking of the deathwatch beetle. You may well imagine yourself a portrait of an antique ancestor hanging on the wall, whose wide-open eyes must contemplate one generation after another. The years whiz by with the wind and the rain, the rumbling storms, the migrating birds, the unctuous words of the priest and the mourners' bent heads by the open grave, stallions collapsing in a heap and fine old watchdogs laid low to rest, serving maids who were once young and fair, and tumbledown fences, desolate wishing wells and overgrown gardens... One after another, the years whoosh by. Only the insomniac looks on with open eyes, like a cadaver who forgot to die. A fine dust descends from the moldering ceiling to cover everything: bright faces and haymaking hips, merry neighbors, springtime smiles, flashing white teeth. Transience squats by the foot of the bed like a moribund, faithful old servitor. And the hand reaches less often for the thirst-quenching goblet.

At last the roosters began to crow.

And night shatters like a worn-out curse. At the call of that crazy bird, the sluggish, motionless curtain of darkness begins to stir. Other sounds filter from the far distances. Perhaps it is the wild geese passing high overhead, following their obscure paths, obeying a mysterious command to cross night's vast gulf like wandering souls conversing in otherworldly tongues.

But cock's crow signals the arrival of those never-glimpsed vagabonds who stand stock still under your window in the dead of night, with murder in their hearts, guilt and terror in their eyes. Come morning, they regain their original shapes and turn into solitary trees at crossroads or hat-waving, curly-haired young travelers with small knapsacks and large staffs, humming a merry tune and marching bright-eyed toward distant lands to bring glad tidings, fun and games, new songs and youthful flaring passions to small houses that somnolently await them. There they sit down at the kitchen table, earn their dinner by telling glorious tall tales, help pour the wine, chop the wood, nab the fattened pig by the ear; they also repair the grandfather clock that had not chimed in forty years and leave in the middle of the night, taking along the young miss's heart as well as her innocence. How enviably cheerful the lives of these vagabonds who pass your house at cock's crow after a night of sleeplessness...As if their knee-deep pockets contained some seed they drop in front of the window, to sprout into a yellow-crowned sunflower; no sooner are they gone than it is already tall enough to peek through the window pane. While, inside, the young lady of the house is already fast asleep, like Aladdin in the enchanted cave.

In the daytime Eveline dared not think of the night. Like a good child or an old-fashioned bride, she preferred to listen to tales told by Mr. Álmos-Dreamer who, being the village beau that he was, in order to keep the thread of conversation going, surely must have conned a page or two in some antique tome before leaving his island.

Mr. Álmos-Dreamer brought into the house a fresh winter scent that smacked of plain everyday life and prompted one to quickly confess everything—sins, diseases, meanness, weakness, desperation and bitterness—and rapidly reel off one thing after the other, to be absolved as quickly as possible, so that refreshed, reformed and bathed clean, one might turn a new leaf, and launch upon a carefree, openly selfish, relaxed and ordinary life. It meant leaving behind forever the curses of civilized life, its soulless pleasures, exotic agonies and neurotic dances. It meant pulling on a pair of peasant boots, biting into a garlic sausage, and joining the washerwomen on the frozen river by the hole cut into the ice; it meant lugging grimy little kids in a knapsack on one's back. It meant eating plenty and squatting on the snow like the nomadic Gypsy women who can run like gazelles, and give birth and die in birch groves, where crows congregate.

Eveline was petite, with black hair. She loved the color red. To amuse herself at home she dressed as a Gypsy girl, and told Mademoiselle Montmorency's fortune: she predicted the wilting old maid would have ten children.

2. THE RETURN OF A
BYGONE EVELINE

ONE FINE day Mr. Álmos-Dreamer up and died.

He did this every year after spending some time in Miss Eveline's company, at times when love, the torments of lone wolves and the howling winds assailed him. At times like these, he started to play the violin in the house on this island frequented by the wind and storm-tossed birds. At such times his servant boy, with his brass buttons, shabby white gloves and antique spats, would retreat into a cubbyhole. Mr. Álmos-Dreamer played the violin from dusk to dawn in front of his lectern like an officer in Queen Maria Theresa's bodyguard preparing for a duel to the death. He played old melodies from a score on which the writer's hand had doodled roses and ladies' faces. French chansons: grandmothers' reveries. German student songs: souvenirs of Hungarian gentlemen traveling abroad. Viennese waltzes: the light-hearted, floppy perukes of forefathers. Compositions by Lavotta and Czerny: fantasies of musicians returned to their homeland to muse over the aimlessness of life.

While making music, Álmos-Dreamer neither ate nor drank. He sat wearing a black tailcoat, white vest and lacquered pumps. His face as serene as an autumn landscape, his eyes brooding over dry fallen leaves, his lips proudly pressed together—all this was no mere histrionics. He was in truth a specimen of the dreamy, retiring and scornful Hungarian country gentleman who asks nothing more of the world than a nook from where all obnoxious climbers are banished. A place where life's business may be conducted with the occasional small gesture or barely audible word. Such behavior would be called depressed by some people, yet it is in fact a splendid human trait, this regal disdain.

He liked to call these hours "withdrawing from life."

He did not have to go far, in his solitude, to arrive at his goal. The house, built on this remote island wilderness by an eccentric ancestor to escape the "yellow peril" that would one day overrun Hungary and all of Europe, was a natural home to death and extinction. Around this household there could be no lust for life, for life was a succession of monotonous, idle days, its sole purpose, a preparation for extinction. The gutter hung from the roof, slowly dying like a superannuated watchdog. There were chairs that limped like grandfather himself. The cupboard had a vertiginous stance, prone to fainting spells like a fat old lady. The lamps gave a tired light, the walls were crumbling, windowpanes cracked without being touched, the carpets shed knots like hair falling from a head and the chimney emitted laborious puffs of smoke, as if tired of life. Everyone and everything was getting ready to leave the place like rovers at a tavern when the wine gets tiresome after the dreams of ecstasy wear thin. The portraits on the wall, once viewed with such youthful pride, had yellowed to the point of unrecognizability. The ideals carried in the heart, the colorful chords, solitary caterwaulings and songs hummed by one's lonesome self had all turned into a meditation unrolled like some rare, treasured rug in the quiet hours around midnight. The wisdom of books, the dust of sunsets, the puppylike energy of the morning hours, had all faded away like the used-up toys of childhood.

Such reclusiveness, if intruded upon, comes charging out of its cave brandishing a club, like a hermit aroused from his dreams. One's mood reaches the freezing point, and becomes bearish, like a black cloud over the woods. At night the wind howls like some terrible hellhound immune to ordinary bullets. The furniture, as a rule so obedient, now turns obtrusive so that the room's inhabitant bumps knees and elbows against fiendishly protruding edges. The mirror's reflection grows faint, or perhaps the face itself does, taking on an acrid, fastidious look like that of a cobwebbed old daguerreotype set by senti-mental hands on a headstone. In the pupil of the eye tiny, swimming dots appear: they are rowboats steered by melancholy boatmen conveying luggage and traveler—departing life—from the shore to the vast old bark awaiting.

At times like these the quiet man opted to die.

By way of the violin's melodies he took his leave of all that was pleasing and dear to him. Friendly faces cropped up in the hedgerows of miniscule black musical notes. Green mansions, porches wreathed in wild grape, stretching greyhounds, loud, friendly greetings, merry eyes and fancy bow ties. Men, companions who raised their glasses in a toast to homeland or womanhood. White table linen, cool arbors, fine, lingering autumns, frost-nipped leaves, orchard scents and places where he had been happy without being aware of his happiness. Years that yawned leisurely, poplar-bordered walking paths, rippling waterways, playfully curling chimney smoke, distant creaking of the well windlass, brown gateways and bedsteads that promised wonderful, untroubled dreams. The odor of fur on a winter's journey, a tavern room redolent with marjoram, a lady's name traced on a frosty windowpane, and a lingering pause over a small footprint in the freshly fallen snow. Women, glowing white under Christmas trees, indolent women whose soft flesh was made for embraces, romantic girls who tied their garters with fancy ribbons, reddish streaks in blonde hair and rings on slender fingers whose touch meant happiness once upon a time. Prayerbooks full of devotions, crucifixes at cross-roads, high masses complete with kettledrum celebrated in childhood, playful strolls on the castle hill, girls with firm calves, and tiny earlobes that he could no longer place. Illnesses that were so good to recover from, convalescence like a breath of spring air, the buzz of the alarm clock signaling frozen dawns that smelled of the crypt, the coachmen's ample capes exuding the scents of the road, and the mysterious bearing of the lady who happens to be your fellow passenger. Memorable hounds and majestic trees in the corner of a courtyard, strange old men, red autumnal twilights, birds' cries and storytelling old women ... All of life swept by during the violin's play. Now Mr. Álmos-Dreamer was ready to die. He sat in the armchair, wrapped a rosary around his hand, closed his eyes and expired, for that was what he wanted.

His servant boy rode off posthaste to relay the news to Miss Eveline.

She put on her fur-trimmed skirt and boots, called for her sled and drove off across the frozen Tisza taking along only two large hounds.

The Álmos-Dreamers died for women. These dreamers, loiterers on bridges, strollers under shaggy-browed weeping willows, musers on solitary dark benches surrounded by the burgundy red tones of autumn: by now all of them painted in oil and vermilion, and hanging on the walls of this ramshackle old island domicile, the mansard roof so thickly layered by moss that storks landed there as in a meadow. All of the portraits showed Andor Álmos-Dreamer's thin face as if every member of the family had been born into this world half-heartedly, tentatively, and always one-fourth obscured by shadow. Their true and majestic form had remained over there, in that netherworld, the solemn appendages of a headless, taciturn knight. Only their feminine aspect arrived in this world, like a white flower handed through an open window. Here they were, all of them, holding the wake over their dead impassively, without batting an eyelash. Over the past century every male in the

family had ended his life with his own hand. Serene and resolved, having said their benisons and devised complicated last
wills, they died premeditated, ritualistic deaths, for the same
cause: the love of a woman.

They were called the crazy Álmos-Dreamers.

Once upon a time the family had possessed extensive holdings in the Uplands of Northern Hungary; these were probably
not acquired in notably delicate ways. For centuries the Álmos-
Dreamers had stalked wealthy widows, moneyed elderly
women and females with prized dowries, pretty much the way
they hunted the rarer kinds of egret in the marshy reeds of the
Tisza.

That was back in the family's heyday.

As a result, they acquired historical ruins; forts, forests and
castles. Women's curses, the shrieks of imprisoned spouses, the
sad and vengeful shades of wives dispatched to the other shore
haunted the Álmos-Dreamers. Back in those days women were
given short shrift. Wild orgies, spilled ecstasies, virgins' red
blood, the mad rage of frenzied hunting parties drugged and
lulled the pangs of conscience. Most of the ghosts in today's
castles had originated in those times. What else was left for
these poor women? They would return from the other world,
shrouded in white, to put the fear of God in their grandchil-
dren. Ghosts are no mere figments of the popular imagination,
cropping up like sempervivum on a stone wall. Curses turned
into an owl's hoot, echoing crypts and mysterious moonlit
forests loom in the remote history of many a Hungarian family.
It was not unusual for one of these brutally powerful men to
wear out three or four women in one lifetime. Men in their old
age married as lightheartedly as the young. They would abduct
their women if necessary. Their rivals' blood dripped from the
steps of the wedding altar, and terrorized, violated brides covered their eyes in shame. The daggers were always close at hand,
ready to be dipped into someone's heart. Old family histories

all resemble each other. When the men were off on a crusade, the women were happiest, rocking the cradle by themselves. They could choose their own lovers.

After all this violence there came a turn in the history of the Álmos-Dreamer family.

One day they abducted a blonde witch whose blue eyes flashed with all the colors of a mountain stream. She was as supple as a silvery birch in springtime. And like tumbleweed, she clung to men. She spoke the language of grasses, old trees and crossroads. She could make herself understood to beasts. The windmill's blades stopped when she blew at them.

The name of this witch was Eveline.

Eveline managed to keep in line the men in a family where women had as a rule been locked away into caskets like old silver. Ákos Álmos-Dreamer, father of the newly-dead Andor, had unsuspectingly married her in the 1840s. He became the third husband of a woman widowed first by a colonel then by a high-ranking government official.

Eveline's former husbands met identical fates on the dueling ground; in those days this was a legitimate exit for men. The Colonel's heart was pierced by an épée, after an excruciating fit of jealousy inspired him to challenge an itinerant Frenchman whose only known occupation was kibitzing at the faro table and fleecing tipsy swine dealers playing billiards at the Turkish Sultan. This dubious foreigner had eyes for a Parisian dancer who happened to be a guest artist at the National Theatre. In the evenings he would leave the gambling casino to stand like a statue with arms crossed during performances, as it happens, just below the box reserved, on alternate days, by Colonel Sükray. The dancer appeared as an entr'acte between the second and third acts when she hovered, fairylike, over the stage, performing a dance of her own choreography, with superhuman grace.

"Madame, I adore you," sighed the statue beneath the railing of Colonel Sükray's box, and, doing so, he happened to fix on the Colonel's wife the blazing torch of his eyes—eyes that were actually bestowed upon him by the Creator for the express purpose of keeping tabs on the legerdemain of one Buzinkai (a notorious local cardsharp) so that in the case of a successful deception he should imperceptibly yet significantly tap the gambler's shoulder.

The Colonel had heard the Frenchman's words only too clearly. One look at his wife's beaming face was enough to turn his suspicions into the darkest despair, even though at home, in the privacy of their canopied bed, they had frequently made fun of the eccentric Frenchman so hopelessly in love with the untouchable star of the stage.

Sükray was a nobleman and an officer. Speaking in an undertone he requested his wife to leave quietly with him before the hall lit up again in all its splendor at the end of the show. During the fairy's dance the entire house was plunged into total darkness, to the great delight of the local heartbreakers who made use of this interval to pass love notes or whisper sweet nothings in their chosen ones' ears without being observed.

Eveline, shaken, grasped her husband's arm as he led her to the back of the loge. As soon as she was outside the door, the Colonel turned around and with a light gesture tossed his white glove, crumpled into a ball, into the face of the French chevalier who stood with his customary stillness below the box. At the touch of the glove the chevalier staggered as if hit by a poleax. The blood left his face; he lowered his eyelashes in pain. Being the most ill-fated lover in town, he was desperate. His face resumed its everyday devil-may-care expression only when the door closed behind Eveline and the Colonel, making any further histrionics unnecessary.

A decade earlier or later the Colonel would have handed over the fly-by-night Frenchman to the military or the municipal authorities for incarceration until the next transport of vagrants.

But this happened at the height of a Romantic era when the salons were seething with daily tales about the generosity and self-sacrifice of men in love. Women fell for heroic characters of the stage and many a lady in the capital felt an urge to elope with the first dance instructor or musician she encountered.

Therefore the next afternoon the Colonel acknowledged without comment when the Frenchman's two cronies, birds of a feather, asserted that the impudent dandy he had insulted the previous night at the theater happened to be a French nobleman, a descendant of Saint Louis, dispossessed of his rank and estates by the French Revolution...A routine claim of the French gamblers and impostors who roamed the continent of Europe and usually ended their lives in some German prison, for the Teutons had no sense of humor in such matters.

The Colonel requested Captain Asszonyfái and Count Leiningen to assist in the speedy settlement of this affair. The officers were forced to respect the Frenchman's claim to competence only in the épée, whereas the Colonel would have preferred to fight with the curved Hungarian sabre.

However, the dueling regulations of the day were clearly in favor of the offended party. The officers did not keep a detailed record, noting the events only in their private diaries. Pages cut out from the diaries later exonerated these officers in front of the military command.

The duelists met on an early spring morning in a remote corner of the city park. They chose the secluded woods on purpose. At this time it happened more than once that women, for whose sake the men faced each other with drawn swords or at pistol point, had penetrated the ball room of the Seven Electors or the riding school at the barracks. Dressed in mourning, they threw themselves screaming between the duelers, and produced theatrics that left a bitter taste. Colonel Sükray had conducted his affairs in utter secrecy but he could not vouch for his opponent's discretion. Especially since he noticed that the last two nights Eveline had only pretended to be asleep in the canopied bed. Her heart was palpitating and every once in a while she let out a loud and uncontrollable sigh. The Colonel, wrapped in melancholy thought, lay motionless next to his wife, nor did a single twitch of his face betray his awareness of her sleeplessness.

On that fatal, foggy morning he had intended to tiptoe out of his room, since there was not a sound from where his wife lay asleep. As he was about to silently open the door, Eveline popped up pantherlike from among her frilly, lacy pillows.

"O, you miserable wretch . . . You'd leave me without one last kiss?" she shouted, beside herself, and showed him her leaden, haggard, sleepless face.

For the last time the Colonel commanded his aching heart be still. With cool courtesy he brushed his lips first against Eveline's hand, then her forehead.

Wildly, uncontrollably sobbing, she threw herself back among the pillows. The noble Kamilló Sükray, Colonel of the Hunyady regiment, quietly closed the bedroom door for the last time. With an aching heart he directed his steps toward the woods at the edge of the city.

No matter what the Romantic novels claim about desperate, angry husbands who kill their unfaithful wives without a second thought, let it be known that a woman's treachery first of all causes pain; sentimental, cowardly and sad pain . . . Shame comes later, then vanity arises like a raging bear, followed inevitably by angry remorse.

On the way to the duel, Sükray decided to kill the Frenchman, who, to all appearances, had been carrying on a secret affair with his wife.

Who can fathom women's mysterious feelings, their secret errands, their never-acknowledged adventures? Why, the dear lady who could pass for Saint Cecilia, misted in dewy scents at the soirée, might have spent that very afternoon in the woods with a mysterious stranger, and her knees might still bear the traces of ant bites...Her sweetly fragrant mouth pronounces carefully chosen phrases, picked from the works of unhappy poetasters or frazzled novelists, to dazzle everyone with her witty repartee—whereas an hour before, in her uncontrollable passion for her secret lover she might have moaned words used by a kitchen wench at a sailors' bar...An English governess or a boarding school may teach a girl impeccable manners, sweet-scented modesty and the chastest dances, all of which will be most useful in society, but to love madly, in joy and misery, to love with gnashing teeth, this a lady can learn only from depraved men, the trashy men kept by streetwalkers. Is there a bored society lady who, deep down in her heart of hearts, does not crave to be acquainted with the mysteries of love?

On the way to the duel these were the thoughts of Colonel Sükray who, as a young lieutenant had nowhere near the sacred regard for the tenth commandment he professed now, when unclean hands threatened the fragrant rosebud in his possession.

Each dueler wore a black silk shirt over his bare chest and on the second passage of arms the Colonel's fiery lunge left him impaled on the Frenchman's épée, like a magpie on a hedge-thorn. The wound penetrated the heart and proved fatal within seconds.

The two captains solemnly adjured the roving chevalier to leave town before they took steps to expel him. The Frenchman announced that he could only do so after he apologized to the Colonel's widow...He asked the gentlemen to remain with the corpse until his return, whereupon he would immediately depart from town.

The stunned officers looked askance at each other. The astonishing brazenness of the Frenchman rendered them speechless. A resurgent spout of blood from the corpse's chest signaled the dead man's awareness of his impending dishonor.

"How much time do you need?" asked Captain Asszonyfái.

"Half an hour."

"Hurry up."

The Frenchman grabbed his overcoat, put on his stovepipe hat, and left the scene of the duel with rapid strides. We have no way of knowing whether he in fact looked up the blonde lady to notify her of the sad news, in lieu of the reluctant officers. Eveline, the only one who knew the circumstances, preferred to keep silent. Many are the meetings about which women maintain a wise silence.

Asszonyfái and Leiningen stood guard by their Colonel's corpse until nightfall, as if it were the Saviour's body on Good Friday. Then they placed the cadaver on a cart and had it taken to the cemetery. Eveline wore mourning for the first time. Her blonde hair, white neck, and rustling skirts soon landed a second husband. He was Mr. Paul Burman, a high government official at Buda.

Mr. Burman had remained a bachelor until the age of forty-five, just like the late Colonel, for whom Eveline had the Requiem sung at every church in the capital. Paul Burman was a dashing, witty, and ceremonious gentleman, a welcome guest in the townhouses of the upper-crust bourgeois and wealthier merchant families. Gentlemen in those days still knew how to keep secrets, and Mr. Burman never allowed a single look to betray the women who had favored him with their graces once upon a time. The only telltale fact allowing some insight into his former lifestyle was that Mr. Burman was as familiar as a seamstress with the trade secrets of feminine wear. He had more than a passing acquaintance with those white stockings that grandmothers tirelessly knitted so that their daughters could always wear spotless white hosiery on their outings to the Buda hills. Mr. Burman had intimate knowledge of those butterfly knots tied above the knee, on garter ribbons that coyly showed themselves only in moonlight. Flannel knickers with those long, zigzag stitches persisted as faithful friends in his memory. He was able to remove, with a single twist of his hand, sensible shoes of the "Eberlasting" brand from petite female feet. He knew all about the monograms embroidered on shirtfronts over the heart, the loving labors of poor girls who ruined their eyes. After all, the ladies of Pest had always taken great pains over their wardrobes. Their petticoats had sparkling clean edges, with adorable frills. Surely these women must have been constantly washing and ironing when they were alone.

Mr. Burman never, not once, let on what an awful lot he knew about the clandestine amulets on necklaces concealed under women's garments. For his afternoon naps at home his head reposed on a silken cushion stuffed with female hair, curls that women bestow only on especially favored lovers; he had also collected in his apartment and held in the most sentimental regard various feminine mementos, such as ladies' shoes, forgotten petticoats, unforgettable hosiery, shifts, handkerchiefs, and hat feathers; moreover, on winter afternoons standing behind the yellow silk curtains he was wont to dream of those women who had once upon a time pulled his doorbell, to swear solemn oaths on entering that they could never set foot in this apartment again, they would die of fear, of the risks they had had to take... Meanwhile, from Mr. Burman's closet the lady's nightgown would materialize, having been brought home by him on an earlier occasion... His guests used to run about the house in slippers and kept tabs on his linen closet... They would settle in an armchair or on the sofa with such happy abandon as if they had meant to stay the rest of their lives... Totally forgetting proper decorum as well as their convent-taught manners, they hummed naughty songs, romped about like children, and studied with misty eyes Mr. Burman's collection of small hand-colored photos, scenes of a medieval mass... And these Budapest ladies never let on that they had glimpsed each other's souvenirs at the apartment on Lövész Street.

This Mr. Burman had fallen so in love with Eveline that he was as impatient for the year of mourning to end as a child waiting for Christmas. At Eveline's request he destroyed all of his trophies, every last souvenir of his past affairs. The old tile stove had plenty to feed on, as it merrily incinerated all those loves of yore, loves that had once upon a time arrived with a promise of life-giving springtime, of Easter resurrections. Only a single key was left as a last remnant of Mr. Burman's once mighty manhood. This was the key of the Russian Orthodox chapel at Üröm, where in bygone days Mr. Burman had enticed those women who had been too timid to set foot in his apartment on Lövész Street. But Eveline had taken possession of this key after a jealous tantrum and already in the sixth month of their marriage made use of it, for an assignation at the chapel where a solemn crypt held the mortal remains of a Muscovite princess, the wife of a former viceroy.

(In Pest there were few women of the Orthodox faith to make use of the holy chapel for their devotions. Therefore ladies of the Catholic, Protestant and Jewish persuasions, who, in their respective houses of worship, would not have dared to lift their eyes in the Almighty's majestic presence, felt free to frolic without guilt in the Russian chapel with Mr. Paul Burman, high official of the viceregal government. The Buda hills had seen many a Pest lady making this excursion to Üröm, having departed early in the morn by coach, accompanied by a faithful confidante, and eagerly awaited by Mr. Burman, who, in his impatience for the moment of consummation, passed the time by examining the icons and devotional objects of the Muscovite *popa*.)

Before long Mr. Burman had occasion to note that Eveline was a pious creature. That fine spring hardly a week passed without her making an excursion to the chapel at Üröm.

"It's the only place where I can truly pray," was what she said, and, amazing to behold, her husband did not doubt her veracity. Husbands tend to credit their own wives with superhuman powers of abstention. They refuse to believe that their wife in any way resembles those married women with whom they had innumerable liaisons in their bachelor days. In fact, Mr. Burman experienced heartfelt satisfaction whenever his wife expressed an urge to repair to Üröm for her devotions.

Until one fine day an anonymous letter, written in a hand that Mr. Burman recognized as belonging to one of his former lady loves, opened up the eyes of this gullible husband. "Eveline, not content with her civilian husband, has renewed her penchant for the white uniform of military officers," went the letter, which the cocksure Mr. Burman threw away without a moment's hesitation.

"Of course, many women must be jealous of my wife," he mused. "But I've had enough of love bites, and those tormenting, clandestine, fearsome couplings, cuckolded husbands, anxieties... Enough of those blundering little women on whose account I had so often felt the noose tighten around my neck."

The second anonymous letter reached Mr. Burman at his office chambers. The writer of the letter warned him that, for those women of Pest who still thought of him fondly, their former chevalier was now an object of pity. In the salons they now referred to him simply as "that poor man."

Mr. Burman's temples flushed red.

When the third warning arrived, Paul Burman stood tall as a poplar, clenched his fists and vowed that he would no longer suffer being made a fool of. He stealthily followed his spouse the next time she set out on a jaunt to the Üröm chapel. There he managed to catch Eveline in flagrante with a tomcat-whiskered officer of the cuirassiers who knelt as worshipfully in front of her as if she had been a holy icon untouched by human hands.

"You poor jackass," shouted Mr. Burman and spat in Eveline's face.

"I hope you'll avenge this," screamed Eveline, her eyes flashing, and indeed the honest cuirassier had no alternative but to challenge Mr. Burman to a duel.

The combat that ensued resulted in Mr. Burman's unnecessary death. In a wooded corner of the city park, perhaps the very same place where the Colonel's blood had spilled on the fallen leaves, Mr. Paul Burman dropped face first, the cuirassier's bullet in the middle of his forehead. It must be noted that this austere civil servant behaved most calmly before the duel, and stated in front of his seconds more than once that were he to die in the duel, he would consider his death as absolution, for his sad end would serve as a memorial to all husbands who, in spite of being deceived by their wives, still leave an exemplary last will and testament.

He left everything to Eveline, who had asked his forgiveness on the final night, confessing that she herself had written the anonymous notes because she had started to doubt her husband's love for her. She announced that she had always loved him, and him alone, just like a plant loves the soil it grows in. Thus she consoled and prepared him for death, giving much pleasure and gratification in the process.

And so, at the age of thirty, Eveline became Ákos Álmos-Dreamer's fourth wife.

All we know about Ákos Álmos-Dreamer, the father of our Andor, is that he was an even-tempered, phlegmatic village gentleman who enjoyed sound sleep and digestion, a man who had buried his three former wives without undue emotional distress. From each woman's trousseau and belongings he selected the useable items—clothes, shoes, furs, shirts—and carefully saved them for the next. For his fourth wife he did not bother to remake the marriage bed in which the previous one had expired in particularly agonizing circumstances. The ill-fated woman had swallowed poison, and the assembled midwives and medicine women did everything in their power to remove the ingested substance from her stomach. Repulsive traces of the sickness were still evident in the bedroom when Ákos Álmos-Dreamer brought the pampered Eveline from the capital down to his rustic mansion. Eveline immediately fainted upon arrival.

"My poor ex-wife," murmured Ákos, "her passing was definitely not for the weak of heart. Well, it's up to you now to put the place in order."

As it turned out, Eveline would even put up with the occasional beating, as long as she could amply console herself with vagabonds, peasants, and itinerant musicians. She routinely told her husband about all her affairs. Ákos Álmos-Dreamer roared like a lion, and with each passing day his love for his wife grew stronger. It was an aging man's desperate, sleepless passion.

Ákos Álmos-Dreamer suffered the torments of a woodcock winged by a poacher. He was the unhappiest man in the entire windy Nyírség—The Birches—a region wrapped in dreamy veils of mist. Men laughed at him and women scorned him; no one pitied him except his court jester, a failed student who in all likelihood had assisted at the former wives' burials. Older folk still recalled one subprefect of the county, a certain Krucsay, who had his faithless wife beheaded. They called Álmos-Dreamer spineless; in his defense, his well-wishers cited the old saw, "hoary-headed groom, fiery young bride." Others opined that the old milquetoast ought to be horsewhipped out of the county. And so he took his shame into hiding, out on the remote Tisza island where Álmos-Dreamers have lived ever since, as if ashamed of a mother's misbehaving. But Ákos kissed his wife's hand for following him into exile and solitude.

What happened now to this robust, strapping man who used to laugh at women who shed tears for him? What changed this aloof man, so miserly with his words, kisses and caresses, who only once in a blue moon condescended to acknowledge a woman's loving stratagem or her artful attempt to please? His giant frame became broken and bent as a gatepost that has out-lived its use. His bloodshot eyes watched over his wife's healthy, deep slumber; he savored each tender little moan, murmur and sigh that escaped during her sleep, and absorbed them into his heart. He would have loved to hear her call out lovers' names in her dream, so that he could have those men instantly assassi-nated, or at least beaten up, tarred and feathered, banished for-ever. But this woman playacted in her sleep like a born actress. She cooed and giggled, mumbling Ákos's name in a faint voice. She hugged a pillow as if it were her lover's muscular neck, her promise-laden mouth shaped into a kiss, as if she were wooing a swaddled infant or a gingerbread hussar. Her breathing was sheer music, like the delicate notes from a small wooden box lightening up one of those grim old Magyar dining rooms with silvery Viennese waltzes. Ineffable delights emanated from her neck, her shoulders, her full calves and thighs. Precious, savory love, sweet as ripe pears, love that has no need to conjure with closed eyes shapes of other women in place of this one, no need for furtive thoughts recalling memories of dear distant loves, like a retired guardsman licking his chops on recollections of the beauteous queen he had served in the days of his youth. Even Eveline's little toes radiated a love that is full recompense for all earthly woes. There was pleasure in her hair, in those fresh honey-blonde curls on the nape of her neck. For one of those locks in days of yore noble knights would have gladly re-turned from the most distant crusades in the Holy Land. Her shoulder alone was worth a kingdom. For one of her kisses, one of her embraces, a man would have willingly placed his neck on the chopping block, for possession of this exquisite woman meant knowing all of life's secrets and mysteries.

And so Ákos Álmos-Dreamer, contemplating Eveline's sleep-ing snow-white and tawny body, began to understand the Colonel and Mr. Burman, who had died for her sake. Ah yes, he, too, would gladly give his life if only Eveline forgave him the coarse, rude and unfeeling welcome he had contrived on her arrival at his house. But Eveline did not forget, did not relent, merely laughed at his threats, calmly faced the barrel of the shotgun he pointed at her, and simply shrugged off threats of deadly violence. She was not moved by Ákos Álmos-Dreamer on his knees, nor by his bitter sobs. Instead, she kicked like a mare attacked by wolves.

Ákos Álmos-Dreamer therefore ended up spending his nights alone, flanked by two candles in that great, grim hall that has ever since accommodated the occupant's gloomier moods. The torments caused by this remarkable woman were easier to suffer when she was not in sight. He read the French Encyclopaedists, the history of England, and *Fanny's Posthumous Papers*. These tomes still remain as he left them, the pages folded where the suffering man stopped reading. He fondled the loaded pistol and spent hours staring at the barrel. Later—during the second winter—he started to drink. At first, it was humble local wines that produced a light-headedness resembling early autumn's feathery clouds, with undercurrents of melancholy like mist floating above a thinning stand of gorse. Later came the gold inlay of Tokay vintages that buried life's unbearable torments within the triple coffins of Attila's funeral—and this made him see ghosts. He turned into a well-known Hungarian type: the village squire who is drunk day and night.

And so Ákos Álmos-Dreamer lived a life as melancholy as the jack of spades. He could never forget his wife's past. The many men who had figured in her life now stood like waxworks figures in the corners of the dour hall where Mr. Ákos doused with wine the fires of his body, the headless dragon thrashing in his soul.

He was stumped; he could not find the secret of winning his wife's love, even though in his time, in the salad days of his dashing, nonchalant, resilient youth, when rain and snow and frost had been no obstacle, he had made a whole slew of women cry. Yes, he had kicked about their hearts, trampled upon their fragile innocence. Enjoying women's gracious favors, he cavorted like a deaf hog in a field of corn, as the saying goes. He got tired of their embraces, their natural desires, their sonnet voices, their miseries. He would give his mustache a twirl, and one glance from him was enough to penetrate to the core of many a female's fancy, although these white-stockinged village women lived in daily fear of damnation and hellfire. When he spoke, his voice went straight to the heart. His caresses were like rare silk. Those passionate kisses of his, impossible to forget. And now every night he strode, bent, aimless and totally disillusioned, back and forth past the portrait of Eveline he had had an itinerant artist paint on the sly—for the woman was so determined not to serve him she refused to pose for her portrait in oils. And he moaned and groaned like an epileptic:

"Why can't you love me, my wife, my sweet angel?"

He paced under that framed face like a moon-sick child until one night it spoke up—the portrait did, or else its original had slithered into the room full of wine fumes:

"I'll love you when you're ready to die for me," the voice cooed in answer to Ákos Álmos-Dreamer's laments.

Subsequent nights advised Álmos-Dreamer about how to execute his suicide.

The island that sheltered from men's eyes his beloved wife (like stolen treasure) was surrounded by the Tisza floodlands. In the distance lay The Birches, monotonous sandy hills barren of all thought, darkling furze thickets asleep on the horizon like so many trembling widows, the wild geese departing from this region under night's dark tapestry like fleeing spirits honking their farewells in weird voices from the sad heights, as if summoning every unhappy person below.

"Ghee-gaw!" cry these enigmatic birds of other worlds and other shores.

That's what these voices sound like to the marshdwelling fisherman in his lair, but one who loves life's wonders will find all sorts of meaning in the voices emanating from the dark. Ákos Álmos-Dreamer awaited the wild geese to summon him into the blue yonder. He would depart from here like a drenched, dark, frost-winged wild goose and go far, far away... And once the gander is gone from the nest the female, too, would follow on the mysterious highways of the heavens. At sunrise, when it is still too dark, in high altitudes' golden oceans the bird would swim after her mate, just like a sad, worry-worn swan.

"Ghee-gaw!" comes from the other world Lord Álmos-Dreamer's cry, and Eveline, humbling herself, would obediently follow in his wake to the land of dreams.

Spring was on the way, the Tisza region full of witching vapors and miasmic exhalations. Sir Álmos-Dreamer spent a moonlit night in the boggy fen, with a clear view of the ladder stretching up on which souls like tiny dust motes climbed toward milky heaven. The spring night sparkled miraculously above the toady clods of earth. Fogs, mists, and plumes of fume floated up toward the heights like bygone beauties' curves on dallying display for the moonbeam's benefit. Now the water snake sheds its old skin, fish and lizards borrow their brightness from the moon and ancient, mute waterfowl vow eternal silence. The earth below splits open like a bivalve, and mysterious night betroths the seedling never yet seen by human eyes.

The time was here for Sir Ákos Álmos-Dreamer's tragic demise.

Swamp fever, on the Tisza island, stole snakelike into his indestructible system, slithered down his throat and through his eyes like poison fumes, terminally deranging an already unbalanced psyche. His case baffled doctors: the so-called malaria, like most other Indian diseases, usually treated with quinine, took the form of delirium in Mr. Ákos Álmos-Dreamer. His actions, at least, indicate that the tragic gentleman went mad in his insular solitude.

One May night, after prolonged staring at a rufous moon that appeared to squat on the marsh's edge, coming down on the furze thickets like visiting royalty among rustic wenches, the thought ripened: he must end his tortured existence. But first...

With the stealth of the insane he approached Eveline's bedroom. That merciless lady always bolted the oaken door for the night, although her husband had quoted the Bible to her to prove she had no right to do so. Eveline looked away and shrugged. Who cares about the Bible?

But on this night, as if she had had a premonition (the way her little finger could sense changes in the weather), this extraordinary woman left the door ajar, and woke from a deep slumber to a heavy hand on the nape of her neck, a trembling, joyously quivering palm cleaving to the mound, not unlike the mons veneris, found in buxom women below their neck vertebrae and from where miraculous cables and telegraph wires signal the nuptial moment. An ancient minstrel song already calls the nape the most desirable and most vulnerable bastion of that splendid castle known as the female physique. Eveline had a neck equally suited to the necklace and the noose. Beauteous feminine necks, as self-possessed as if they led their own swan-like existence, and seemingly without the brain's overlordship, execute their fairylike motions; they see and hear, speak, rise and humbly, submissively bend—such necks have been known to send the brains of many a man into his bootlegs.

Eveline suffered the caresses only until her dream had flown out the window. When the bird was gone, she hissed a question:

"Why did you wake me?"

"Why indeed..." mused Mr. Álmos-Dreamer. "Because I want to say good-bye to you, my dear wife, my darling."

"Is that why you woke me?"

Mr. Álmos-Dreamer sadly nodded like a wanderer stranded in the night:

"That's right, my child. I shall be leaving life in an hour. Like a runaway cat, the movements of my hands and feet are abandoning me as I descend on slippery steps down to the ice-house and the door slams behind. I want this last hour of my life to be happy. Not to think, not to dread, not to quake, not to recoil from invisible blows... For one hour, eyes open or closed: to sense and see only you, oh ecstasy, whose chalice I never drank from."

Eveline angrily knit her brows—then cast a sly glance from under those eyebrows as if weighing whether to believe the promise. Would he deceive her like a wandering organ-grinder, who plays sad songs under the window, making your heart ache and cry, waking the sad ghosts of the house, while laughing to himself as he licks the last drop of wine from his mustache?

Eveline was a bold and businesslike lady. She had never done anything that she later regretted. She was concerned that all this might be a trick.

"Word of honor?" she asked, mostly to stall for time, to better appraise the situation.

Mr. Álmos-Dreamer nodded without emotion, a most peculiar nod, like a one-legged man confronting his lost limb preserved in spirits.

"Swear on the cross," murmured Eveline, having noted nothing suspicious in Mr. Álmos-Dreamer's behavior.

Ákos Álmos-Dreamer dropped to one knee. Eveline's hand reached for the heavy silver crucifix that had for centuries served to pacify and silence the dying curses of forebears. The crucifix could have passed for a weapon, at a pinch. Rightly swung, the hefty silver object indeed could have promoted one's passage to the other world.

Álmos-Dreamer took the crucifix in hand and softly swore a clearly audible oath in the vaulted room:

"I, Ákos Álmos-Dreamer, swear by the Almighty and by the seven wounds of our Lord Jesus Christ that after an hour's passage I shall no longer be among the living but will lie stretched out dead, never to return from the nether world."

Eveline nodded her assent.

She took one glance at the glass-encased clockworks where at the stroke of midnight the twelve apostles would pass in single file.

It was a clock face worn out by all the expectant, desperate, fatal glances cast by eyes that had long ago turned into varicolored pebbles along the Upper Tisza. The Roman numerals had faded, the hands were bent like a drooping mustache, the circumambulant pilgrims' robes tattered. But the tireless mechanism labored on, it still had so much left to accomplish here on earth: such as marking the hour of someone's death.

"When the apostles appear, your time's up," she murmured and blew out the candle.

And what happened to Eveline after she had taught the first Álmos-Dreamer how to die of joy and grief, for love of a woman? For, ever since then, curious little females have been asking Álmos-Dreamers, and with good cause: "Could you do something grand for me? Would you die for me?"

Nine months later Eveline gave birth to a wistful, moody little boychild, whom she would take many a time to his father's green sepulchral mound, located, in deference to the deceased's wishes, like Lensky's grave, in a small copse of white birches. On the bookshelf, to this day you may find *Onegin* (in French), with the page folded at the appropriate place.

At his christening the child was given the names Andor Zoltán, the latter fashionable at the time in Hungary, favored by widowed mothers who followed the example of the poet Petőfi's young widow, née Countess Szendrey. Widows who do not stay faithful to their husband's memory sense their kinship from afar, like nomadic Gypsies who leave behind intertwined straws or some other sign of their passage across the country-side; women, by donning a certain ball gown or particular chapot, let each other know that they don't mind bestowing their favors upon newcomers. This is a strange fact, but true. In bygone days village dames read through lists of guests at soirées, participants at masked balls, and were able to tell at a long distance whom their lady acquaintance meant to please with her carnival outfit. Via the pages of *Conversation Pieces* and *Ladies' Courier*, Eveline kept in close touch with events at the capital. Even from her rustic hermitage she could partici-pate in the eventful life of Pest. The mail coach delivered lengthy epistles. From fashion magazines she could determine which ladies were the latest trendsetters, what hat and hair styles were the current vogue. For the same reason she wore her hair short like Petőfi's widow, mused about love by her es-critoire, kept a romantic diary in which she lamented her un-happiness and never bothered to recall any of her former suitors, while she more than once invited to her country estate Kálmán Lisznyai, the fashionable poet of the day, and often looked out of the window to check whether the poet who af-fected the *szűr* (an ornamentally embroidered shepherd's cloak) had at last arrived. When she died at fifty of consumption, the *Capital Herald* carried an obituary citing her patriotism and her artistic, noble soul, ever true to the black veil and to her tragi-cally deceased husband.

This was the parentage of the most recently expired Álmos-Dreamer, whom the living, touchable Eveline now visited on his island in the Tisza.

The bygone Eveline's life-size portrait hung on the wall, and next to it the living Eveline now appeared, the very image of the painting come to life and stepped out of its frame. The re-semblance was striking. As if that extraordinary woman—who had wreaked such havoc in the lives of gullible men, setting frozen hearts ablaze like a bonfire built by woodcutters shivering at the edge of a forest—it was as if this woman had come back to life. Being exceptional, she had been given a second life to live, for one life was not enough to accomplish all that was waiting for her to do here on earth. As if she had turned back at the gates of eternal repose, having noticed that her limbs were still youthful, her eyes still fiery, and the candle flame still unextinguished in her cold heart. She had returned for another round, to meet new men, to drain love's goblet anew... Only her rich, honey-blonde mane had been left behind, underground. At the time of her emergence from the soil, along with the cowslips and dragonflies, the fields bore a thick crop of rye. For a crown of hair she plaited herself a wreath of ripe rye, spiky russet and yellow grasses. Now her hair had red-brown streaks, like tiger spots. The first moonlit night taught her the arts of witchcraft and sorcery, when among the trees' sleeping boughs the souls of the dead glide like so many bats. Young birch trees ooze a sap that the pale-skinned women of the region lick up so that their legs stay forever limber, and even in old age they can ride the broomstick with bright gleaming knees. In The Birches there is no need to take lessons in giving men the evil eye. The women's voices are woven of the strange melodies of springtime birds; their hips radiate the comforting warmth of a brooding duck; their glances emulate the sun-worship in the eye of the lanky sunflower straining after the sun. Their hair, like the tender young crop in the fields, is raked by the capricious fingers of the wayward winds.

The touchable Eveline stood lingering under the portrait of the bygone Eveline and exchanged a look of sympathy with her predecessor. Her heartache was gone like a child's hurt blown away by a mother's kiss; she immediately felt her strange power in this house where all things owed her allegiance. She felt she had come home to claim the heritage of the former mistress of the house whose swaying skirts were almost still visible just around the doorposts. All she had to do was follow her trail.

On the painter's primitive oil the elongate, white hand was pointing ahead, a magical sign, as it were, for women who enter this abode. Eveline followed the pointing finger. Andor Álmos-Dreamer, as his ancestors had done, had in life provided for his fragrant walnut coffin, and now lay in it with hands clasped in prayer, wearing a full evening outfit, with courtly black dancing shoes, a token of his esteem for the post-mortem visitor.

"Álmos-Dreamer, how could you leave me?" said Eveline. "How can I live in peace from now on, calling for you in vain?"

The deceased did not stir, even though Eveline crooned like a mourning dove.

"I know you're truly dead, you've taken your leave solemnly and ceremoniously, closed your eyes forever without any theatrics or falsehood, and you wouldn't protest if we laid you under ten tons of sod. Still I beg you, won't you come back, for I simply cannot go on without you..."

This is how Eveline addressed the deceased, who quietly sat up.

He looked at Eveline in wonder yet without surprise, as if the girl were simply the continuation of a pleasant dream.

"I think I've been through a grave illness," he murmured and slowly emerged from his coffin.

3. THE LOVER FORETOLD BY THE FORTUNE-TELLER'S CARDS

THERE lived in the Inner City of Pest a strange young man whose white spats, carefully ironed trousers and curled hair were visible mostly in the evening hours.

The outward appearance of this young man resembled one of those figures on antique amulets worn around the necks of pious elderly princesses or seduced daughters of the bourgeoisie. His auburn locks, combed in an old-fashioned style, his weary smile, his rather melancholy aspect and his way of dressing in imitation of fashion plates from the Romantic era of fifty years before, were all calculated to make women's hearts open up, to accept and forever remember this young man. His appearance was as refined and fragile as that of a morganatic prince. His cream-colored gloves and freshly shaven face implied he was heading toward the National Casino, although his usual attitude toward that neighborhood was to eye the young aristocrats with a distant and disdainful smile, which dismissed them as idiots.

At the time of our story Kálmán happened to be homeless.

The aging dame who, in part out of charity, in part out of undying love à la Ninon de Lenclos, had adopted the youth, on this day discovered that someone had tampered with her cache of gold coins. These were not ordinary shekels. Ninon, in her youth, had received them as presents from reigning sovereigns and cardinals, English peers, and pretenders to diverse thrones, all of whom had paid court to this amusing and charming woman. Heads of kings and queens from all parts of the globe adorned the ducats brought by her chevaliers in their vest pockets. Ninon, when alone in her diminutive palace in Képíró Street, liked to claim that she could never be bored as long as she spent her days in such illustrious company. Amidst her guldens, she could turn from the Prince of Monaco to Queen Victoria. It was these notables that had of late been preyed upon by Kálmán who, by the third month of his sojourn at her house, had contrived to pick the lock on her strongbox.

Kálmán did not think the expulsion tragic. Ninon would forgive him any time he felt like it, once she had installed new locks on her safe. In all likelihood she was already on her way, scouring the city for him, possibly disguised as a market vendor à la Mrs. Baradlay in Jókai's novel.

As was his wont, he turned his steps toward the Josephstadt, toward a dreamy townhouse complete with donjon, whose gray-curtained windows had witnessed his daily strolling past, to confirm that the bird had not yet returned to her cage.

Around the Museum lounged palazzos as changeless as the Papacy. Here life is never rushed, for it never ends. The families' bloodlines run in endless streams: it seems the same individuals who die return rejuvenated to carry on the line. The selfsame figures inhabit the selfsame palaces, daughters get married the same as ever, countesses' hair turns gray just as their ancestresses' did. In the portals, the same old bearded, bald, gloved grooms loom, handling well-trained, highly bred steeds, while the same guests as ever take their places in the same carriages. The days pass without desires of an unattainable nature. Perhaps the medicinal-smelling doctor on a house call prescribes an occasional remedy. The books contain the same old romances. The christenings are unlikely to produce a name that has not yet occurred in the family.

Kálmán thought fondly of this genteel world. He would have given anything for a peek at a countess's boudoir or bedroom! How did these heavenly angels spend their earthly days? Is it true they paid their feet the same painstaking attention as dancers? Did they ever harbor loving thoughts toward an etching or a sprightly verse? Their aloof, nonchalant and splendid faces, the distinctive style of their curls, their swan necks and little earlobes burnished vivid memories into Kálmán's brain after a scrutinizing stare through a carriage window... He would have gratefully welcomed even one of their chambermaids, who in all likelihood wore stockings and shoes handed down by her mistress. But he had to make do with their serving men, whose conversations he overheard at Ivkov's little tavern on the ground floor of the Üchtritz House.

As the bird had not yet returned to her cage, Kálmán sank into a reverie, forehead pressed against the bars of the cast-iron gate, then with hesitant steps waded through the dry leaves that littered the small round garden—it resembled a filigreed reliquary that contains the cheerful dreams of youth. This diminutive French garden with its white belvedere, green-skirted pines, and walls overrun by wild grape vines served to remind Eveline at spring and autumntime of the calendar's turning leaves. Kálmán at times thought he was totally, maybe fatally, in love with Eveline, and could die for her, as a knight would. On this basis he considered the small French garden his natural kin and ally—a piece of the city's most precious real estate that dedicated its flora solely to amuse a lovely girl.

Here he stood each night, facing the iron grillwork of the gate, like a penitent whose thoughts forever rehearse the same scenes of the past. Joy's fleeting clouds, the trembling play of sunlight on a carpet, visions waving farewell. This was his moment of piety. Had religion been on Kálmán's mind, the twilight hour would have found him entering the Franciscans' Church in the wake of mallow-scented Inner City girls, along with the stately, distinguished gentlemen who came to pray there daily. If only once he could have won at dice in the gambling den where he spent his nights, at dawn he would have stopped in at St. Roch's Chapel where the poor nuns, like white seagulls by the ocean's dark shore, sat in the pews, row after row, saying prayers as adventitious as birdsong. But Kálmán was an unlucky son of a gun and—although not yet twenty-five—had lost all faith in both man and God. This deserted garden, strewn with dead leaves, had come to mean both redemption and purification for him. It reminded him that he had been young and innocent once, when spring mornings had impelled him to kiss the sumac blossoms, and when he had absorbed those distant, profound, serene autumn afternoons, as one does the teachings of a gentle sage who preaches only charity. Like fading sepia tints in photographs he had lost long ago, his mother's and father's faces floated above the path he trod in the sentimental worship of Eveline. The distant, innocent past loomed up before his eyes, sad and unaccusing. Oh, if only once he could hear a chiding voice from the past! But the past was silent, like a beloved mindlessly and irrevocably killed in a fit of passion.

Sunk in this emotional reverie, Kálmán sauntered from the Josephstadt district back to the Inner City, where in small taverns smelling of beer and braised pork *pörkölt* he ate his meals and was slowly going to seed, spending his time with devil-may-care, constantly harassed yet eternally hopeful cronies who knew nothing of his heart's deep wound. Paprika-laced dishes flushed his face, foaming brews cooled his gullet, the grease-stained newsrag apprised him of the day's events, while his associates retailed bawdy and hilarious yarns. Thus he passed tolerable, jolly, carefree evenings. At times some streetwalker would arouse his interest, but these trysts left him feeling as if he had embraced death. He was amazed that the other wanderers in the gutter, all those women swathed in veils and cheap perfume, had not been collared by the lanky escort with his death's-head grinning above a smartly-knotted white silk scarf.

Midnight would regularly find him at a gambling den, among same set of pallid faces. The waiter, bright and merry, was quick to bring a cup of steaming black coffee, high hopes reflected in his sly eyes. The air of the halls was still fresh, the carpets unsoiled by cigar ash. Gentlemen with gleaming shirt fronts beamed, amiable and jolly, as befitting well-bred men about town. They shook hands ceremoniously, and traded pleasantries with the croupier, even though everyone knew he cheated. The hostess, freshly coiffed, diamonds in her earrings, extended her plump, soft hands to be kissed; her neck emanated a fresh, sweet scent. The footman continually opened the secret door upon the proper signal to let in more and more players who brought the latest news from coffee houses, theaters, restaurants and clubs in various parts of town. A lively and enviable hubbub animated the salons of this establishment. Lapels still sported the flower pinned there by a woman's hand earlier in the evening. Everyone felt like being witty and pleasant—until the bell rang at the gaming table.

A dyed mustache, meticulous shave, pomaded strands of hair pasted across his bald skull like dark twigs on winter trees: this was the croupier. He wore a green hunting jacket and tight pants, like landed gentry on a city outing. He let the nail grow long on his little finger, and wore an oversize signet ring bought at a pawn shop. He was on familiar terms with everyone present, for that was the style of the house. His bulging frog's eyes took in his guests from top to toe, the rock in his tiepin was the size of a pea, and he wore his watch chain short, in the manner of army officers. His platinum-capped false teeth smiled enigmatically behind blue lips. This man was never bothered by the thought that outdoors it might be springtime . . . He wore great big American shoes, was equipped with ear- and toothpicks in a silver case, a gilt-backed mustache brush, a silver cigar-cutter, a pocketknife with a handle fashioned from an antler, and matching morocco leather notebook, mirror, wallet and change purse; his back pocket hid a Browning automatic, his lapel sported an ivory edelweiss, the kind they sell in Austria; in his vest pocket reposed a hundred-crown gold coin and a case holding an amber mouthpiece for cigarillos and cigarettes. He puffed clouds of smoke from an A'Há brand Turkish cigarette with the relish of one who had just dined. Yes, he savored life to the fullest. Only his temples betrayed telltale signs: those ominously bulging veins that hinted he would not be around until the extreme limits of human longevity to quaff French champagne with his little finger sticking up next to his dyed mustache.

(Kálmán, in his mind still back in the neighborhood of the Museum Boulevard, imagined his nose detected, in the aroma of steaming black coffee, the ineffably sweet scent of a young lady's lingerie. He paid less heed to this dubiously genteel crowd than he would to a street urchin lounging by a lamppost on the corner. Eveline kept reverberating in his head, an incantation, a mantra protecting him from all danger.)

Before the mustached croupier set to work, he dug up a monocle from a vest pocket, the kind set in the eye socket by a gold spring. For he was a gentleman now. Why should he strain his facial musculature to balance a monocle? The glass lens rested effortlessly over his right eye, lending an air of prestige.

He had a penchant for French words in directing the game, much as a dance master conducting a quadrille. Had he chosen a political career, he would have achieved great success by pompously parroting the sententious slogans and pronouncements loved by the press. In fact he had been a small-town revenue officer in the Alföld lowlands before marrying the hostess, the infamous owner of several "champagne parlors" in Pest. Although the lady was somewhat over the hill, her connections were unimpeachable: she knew just about every spendthrift in town through the salons she had kept. The decision to run a gambling casino meant that Mr. Zöld would never again have to don a bureaucrat's frock coat.

Nothing earthshaking was brought about by Mr. Zöld's turning up in the capital. There was simply one more scoundrel in town, another chiseler who assumed the airs of a Hungarian country gentleman. Without batting an eyelid he would have forged a promissory note, without a twinge of conscience committed highway robbery, or done away with one or two customers, afterwards sleeping the untroubled sleep of the just, snoring ever so heartily. Pseudo-gentry of his kind, lording it in the capital, was becoming the vilest ingredient in the body of the Hungarian nation. Putting on aristocratic airs, they cheated and stole while complaining that you cannot prosper in Hungary because of the Jews. Mr. Zöld was a typical example of the con man who is forever blowing his own trumpet, sends out a pair of witless dueling seconds whenever he feels insulted, whose arrogant, aggressive glances darken the local horizon until he finally meets the person who cracks his skull.

In the midst of the assembled tailcoats and tuxedos there would turn up an overweight and prematurely old Jew who had once upon a time received illicit commissions from Guszti, tonight's hostess, in the days when she still dealt in champagne and love for sale. Back then Diamant held another outlook on the world, when the stock market, cards and women had abundantly provided for life's necessities. At nightclubs and gambling dens he had been the number one big spender, the kind who would send lavish bouquets to celebrated danseuses and who knew cab drivers and music hall doormen by their first names. He had been the very soul of conviviality, sparing no expense for a friendly get-together. However, his luck had turned. He grew gray-bristled, fat and bald. Asthmatic, he drank excessively, got into fights, owed the headwaiter, lost his seat on the stock exchange, his credit at the tailor, and finally, his friends; cards and horses stopped favoring him. Yet he accepted all this with equanimity, for he was a wise man. His Achilles' heel was hearing about the good luck of men he judged his inferiors. Face flushed dark in scorn and anger, he would stop talking, puff on his cigar, and express his contempt with a dismissive gesture.

Diamant detested Mr. Zöld for having been a revenue officer, for having married Guszti, for running the roulette game and diverting a pittance for Diamant from the house's winnings only at the wife's intercession.

On these occasions Diamant had to lounge about in the salon until after the patrons departed at daybreak, when he would clearly overhear the conversation between man and wife in the next room:

"Listen, Zöld, we should give Diamant something," she began.

"Let'im go jump in a lake," the sporting man retorted.

"I think he owes rent money."

"He can rob a bank," suggested Mr. Zöld.

"But listen . . ." she persisted, and whispered the rest, inaudibly for Diamant's vigilant ears. But the croupier's shout rang out loud and clear:

"Why should I pay for your old boyfriend?"

Diamant, by his lonesome self, flicked his wrist in a resigned gesture but did not budge, assured that Mr. Zöld would soon emerge, yellow with bile, and wearily drop a few banknotes in the dawn intruder's palm.

Diamant liked to converse with younger men who presumably respected his illustrious past. Therefore he joined Kálmán in the salon where the old manservant, a billiard marker back in Guszti's younger days, now served ample libations of complimentary champagne.

"See, my young friend, your two basic types in Hungary are the count and the Jew. The rest don't count. They're a bunch of big zeros. And so is our landlord." So opined the prematurely old, fat man, who had consumed the greatest number of oysters in Budapest. "Now the historical nobility behaved like simpletons. Always paid up before the loans were due, as if they needed to shore up their credit. Back in '48, or whenever, they gave up their last holdings, the nobility's privileges. They voluntarily degraded themselves into commoners, although if there'd been a single Jew in the company, he would have surely spoken up: 'I'd rather die than let myself be persecuted...' The Hungarian nobility settled the debts of the past without litigation, dispute or insisting on the highest bid—and what can a tribe expect, when it has voluntarily divested its privileges?"

In the neighboring room the ivory ball was already spinning in the wheel.

For the time being Mr. Zöld manned the roulette wheel, with the expertise of a veteran Monte Carlo croupier. (Should the wheel perform poorly, the Madame was ready to spell him; her ring-studded plump hands turned up numbers that made the players curse.)

Neither Diamant nor Kálmán had the wherewithal for a stake—not even a five-crown piece—to try their luck. Therefore they had a leisurely, heartfelt chat in the salon, while the players' chaotic hubbub and the jingle of gold and silver filtered toward them like sounds from a distant, exotic province.

"I'd love to be a tenant leaseholder on some village estate..." continued Diamant, signaling the footman for another bottle of complimentary bubbly. "I'd keep young maidservants who'd give me a hand adulterating the wine. Ah, my wife would have money to stuff her straw mattresses with. As for the outlaws, I'd either be pals with them, or else take potshots at them from behind barred windows. I'd have my horses, cattle, children and freedom. Wear a blue housecoat and marry a young girl when I'm a hundred. Yes, I'd grow a beard like my father's and be lord and master of my house like an Oriental potentate. Now I am just a bum in the big city. A village cur lost in the metropolis, because he ate the folks out of house and home. And who do you think you are, my young friend, Kálmán Ossuary?"

Kálmán calmly waved his hand.

"I won't challenge you to a duel, Mr. Diamant, no matter what you toss in my face."

"I know: you'll give that satisfaction only to gentlemen! But do you know who are the ones lording it in Hungary these days?"

Before Diamant could continue, a dreadful howl of rage rang out in the gaming room. A man roared as if he had caught his wife in flagrante. A drowning, raucous howl of murderous intent.

Kálmán jumped to his feet.

His stout friend tranquilly restrained his arm.

"Let'em be. Only scoundrels and idiots get into fights."

In the roulette room Kálmán witnessed the following edifying scene:

A gentleman in tails, his eyes reduced to red circles by alcohol and rage, clutched an empty champagne bottle, and threatened at the top of his voice to crack the croupier's bald skull. The dramatic intermezzo caused only a brief interruption in the progress of the play. The croupier's cronies, who hovered like executioner's assistants behind Mr. Zöld, and cheered the house's winnings with spasmodic gesticulations and inarticulate shouts and turned cadaverous, livid faces upon less profitable runs of the ball, now saw the time ripe to demonstrate their usefulness and servility. In a trice they surrounded the fuming player. One set about convincing the man of the impropriety of his conduct, another protested in a rapid patter that Zöld's play was unimpeachable, while a third shook his knobby butcher-boy knuckles at the tipsy gentleman's nose.

"You're disturbing the game!" squawked others who sat hunched over the green baize tabletop clutching pocket notebooks or slips of paper, dead serious about recording the run of numbers.

Shouts of "Throw him out!" echoed, like some cabbalistic formula, incanted by a potbellied, hedgehog-eyed, swine-dealer sort who had just collected sizeable winnings by staking on zero.

"Take it easy, Colonel," bleated others, trying to appease him, while, wrinkling their brows, they took advantage of the fortuitous pause to appraise winnings and losses.

"I was under the impression I'm among gentlemen," bellowed the personage addressed as Colonel, whereupon one or two of the players started to tug at their shirtcuffs, and one sneering, bald fop with a face just begging to be slapped screwed in his monocle.

"How amusing," he lisped. "The Colonel was under the impression . . . Most amusing."

But his comment proved ill-timed. The enraged Colonel, unable to reach the croupier, vented his pent-up fury by slamming his fist into the monocled face, and sent the man sprawling under the table.

That fine gentleman emerged deathly pale (sans monocle) from below and produced a revolver as big as a hambone from a back pocket.

"That's all we needed!" exclaimed Guszti, the cheerful hostess, almost gladly. And without so much as straining her biceps she hustled the gun-toting dandy into the adjoining room.

Mr. Zöld seized the ensuing pause to remove his monocle, and assuming a rather innocent and even pained expression (perhaps regretting the fop's *malheur*) he rose, radiating empathy.

"Gentlemen, we're not playing for beans here. I believe it's in everyone's interest that we continue playing fair and square."

"The police ought to be told about what's going on here," the Colonel persisted, grinding his teeth.

Mr. Zöld gestured unctuously:

"These gentlemen are my daily guests," quoth he, deferentially looking around as if the company assembled around the roulette wheel were the very cream of the nation's paladins and standard-bearing knighthood. "They will testify that the play in these rooms is strictly above the board. And anyway, in roulette the croupier is a mere intermediary handling the players' bets," he added, as an edifying afterthought.

"The person who brought me here assured me zero wouldn't count," the Colonel bellowed.

Mr. Zöld raised a palm to his ear, as if unsure he had heard the Colonel's words right—although for the past fifteen minutes the debate had been over this very point. Mr. Zöld merely shook his incredulous head, and asked in tones of deepest injury:

"What could the Colonel mean by that? And anyway, who was the idiot who duped him into believing such nonsense?"

"It was Jalopy!" the Colonel sullenly replied.

"Jalopy," Mr. Zöld echoed, and emitted a gentle peal of laughter. "What a rascal."

"Jalopy!" shouted the other players, amidst ironic and derisive guffaws, upon hearing such an absurdity.

Mr. Zöld, pleased as Punch, resumed his seat, and the Colonel, muttering, sucked on his cigar, with only an occasional glance of his bloodshot eyes around the table. Meanwhile in the next room the much-derided Jalopy was the recipient of a cold compress applied by Madame Guszti's ringladen fingers. Ah, the glitter of those rubies, emeralds and turquoises on this woman's marvelously white hands! What a manicured, soft and delightful female hand—Jalopy could have spent all day admiring it. He resolved that, were he to marry, his wife's fingers would be lavish with rings—even if he'd have to beg, borrow or steal.

Diamant, having crept unnoticed into the card room, now stood, hands in pocket, behind Kálmán. The older man thoroughly despised these whiny, jittery, loud and insolent card-players who were incapable of concealing their jubilation or disappointment. Why, back in his days as a celebrated player, he and his confrères would wager entire fortunes without batting an eyelid, and lose without complaint! Yes, back in those days the women left at home started to pray the instant their men stepped out of the house . . .

Diamant watched the game's progress in silence, with a disdainful smile, the unlucky gambler's bitter, scornful expression, observing the sizeable stakes swept away by the croupier. Some of the gentlemen's faces had already developed a deathly pallor; trembling hands fingered coins after repeated losses; others clutched charms, lucky pennies, as if already fondling the barrel of a revolver, shoulders hunched, like hills crushed by ice, faces stiff in craven prayer to Fortuna, like fire victims before a burnt-out hovel; frenzied groans emerged from throats as players whimpered at unfavorable turns of the ball; one lip-biting, twitching gentleman uttered shouts of "But my dear Géza!" as if that was all he could remember; eyes practically rolled out of their sockets following the thalers and guilders like the rear wheels of a cart, or else they cast hopeful glances toward the croupier's pile of winnings, as if expecting the soiled banknotes to turn into a white dove that would ascend with a flutter of wings.

The Colonel had by now lost all he had and stood in grim thought, his evening coat dangling crumpled like a circus attendant's. The henchmen behind the croupier stood shoulder to shoulder, beaming with delight, nudging each other and casting malicious glances at the Colonel, as if they could think of nothing more amusing than a player who had been cleaned out. The spirit of camaraderie egged them on to cruel and inane jests. An old gentleman, absorbed in his calculations, received a playful tap on his bald pate. When he turned around, the culprit was already hiding under the table. But with all their clowning they maintained a deeply respectful and submissive attention to Mr. Zöld's back.

"Fifty forints on the zero," the Colonel yelled out, a drowning man's call for help.

Mr. Zöld snatched back the ball as it spun out. Treacherous and evil was the look he directed at the ashen-faced Colonel.

"Let's see the dough," he said softly.

But the Colonel had no "dough." He fumbled futilely through his wallet. He had not a penny, much less fifty forints.

"Let's see the dough," repeated Mr. Zöld. "You can't play without it."

"But I'm a Colonel," roared the officer, straining his voice.

Mr. Zöld's hand wave was pitying; the other players cast grumpy glances at their fleeced companion who was obstructing the progress of the game. ("It's already the second time tonight.")

Diamant took Kálmán by the elbow.

"Let's go. We'll only get in trouble here. I bet the Colonel will sign an I.O.U. and keep on playing. I've seen it happen plenty of times," growled the fat, prematurely old Jew. "Look, it's almost dawn; why don't we go have some breakfast...I know a small tavern open all night right here on Franciscans' Place. You're my guest."

With a reassuring wink, Mr. Diamant revealed a ten-forint banknote peeking from his vest pocket.

Where did he get the money? Possibly the landlady had pressed it furtively into the palm held out behind his back as she crossed the room, all violet-scented party-going briskness. Or perhaps the banknote had been found on the floor, under the chair of some frenzied gambler, by the eagle-eyed Mr. Diamant, who never loitered in vain around the card tables.

Ten forints was a lot of money. Enough to make the heart-sick Kálmán cheer up, and nearly shake hands, as Mr. Diamant did, with the cagey old doorman who let them out through the secret passageway. (Only later did it occur to him that he had been received in this house like a lord while his money and credit had lasted, in the days when he would lightheartedly fling Eveline's perfumed banknotes on a number on the green baize, confident that the kind maiden's rosewood moneybox would be forever at his disposal. But Eveline had gone far away since then...At the gambling salon they soon noted his penury, no matter how Mr. Kálmán tried to hide it. The fiacre, naturally on credit, would still wait for him all night on Posta Street; he still bestowed the usual two-forint tip on the doorman, and with a blasé expression chewed on a thick Havana cigar, while observing the progress of the play. In the adjoining room, where he felt sure he was out of sight, he would ask winning players for a small, gentlemanly loan, in strictest confidence. However, Mr. Zöld's hawkeye saw everything, and no longer was seat number ten reserved for him at the table.)

On the predawn street a tiny woman and a lanky gentleman were walking arm in arm, apparently taking their daily constitutional.

Diamant, who knew everyone in town, purred with satisfaction.

"This is what happens when you sell yourself to a woman. Mr. X gets married, but he can only take his dwarf wife out for fresh air in the dead of night...I remained a bachelor, although I had my chances...To marry like Zöld, that would have been easy."

The morning light reflected from windows of the Inner City's antiquated houses like lantern rays shining from the Rákos cemeteries. Former burghers of the Inner City, now turned to water and dust, were sneaking back into their old apartments. The light gilded the faded shop signs. Diamant pointed at the lit-up windows on high:

"That's where they sleep, the good, the pure, the decent ones, the happy families, the untouched daughters. Ah, if I could have had the love of an honest woman just once! If only my fate had brought me an innocent, lily-white, heavenly creature, I'd now be going to the Jesuits' red-brick church to give my thanks, instead of this..."

Diamant grabbed Kálmán's arm, and spoke as emotionally as a romantic hero. (Kálmán eyed him incredulously: maybe his friend had had too much champagne—although Diamant for decades had been quaffing champagne like water.) His eyes were as doleful as a ghost's, his voice dolorous as a cello sounding behind a curtain.

"My life's been spent among women of ill repute. I was no lady-killer, no, I wasn't even handsome, and what's more, I never spent much on women. I just sat and smoked quietly and kept their company night and day. I'd give offhand answers, you'd never see me bend down to pick up their dropped jewelry or flowers; a glass of beer from me made them more delighted than a bottle of champagne bought by a count; some mornings I'd take them to the carnival peep show on a one-horse buggy, order hotdogs, have their fortunes told, things like that made them unforgettably grateful. At night I stood in the back at the nightclub, along with the applauding waiters, but the girls would still notice me. Every now and then I gave them a flower, and they'd dance all night wearing it in their hair and saved it in a glass of water in the morning. I offered them cheap Sport cigarettes, because I knew they didn't really care what they smoked. I'd drop in at their rooms in the afternoon, like some relative paying a family visit. Then they'd tell me about family matters, unlucky love affairs, and show me the fiancé's photo or love letters received from some simpleton. On rare occasions I'd let drop a word of advice, a mere suggestion. But mostly I smoked in silence, and solemnly listened to their Tarot readings. I pretended to believe all their superstitions, nodded sympathetically when they reviled a treacherous friend or expressed their disgust with the monotony of life. I'd put on my glasses—

black horn-rims—when they consulted me about their contracts, and I coached them about making a statement when they were in trouble with the police. I never told them they were pretty, or that I loved them, I simply sat and sat, smoking, taking it all in, quietly, acting serene and wise. That's how I possessed the diva and the flower girl. Neither my body nor my soul really craved them, for I'd always dreamed of something else, something unreachable."

Thus spoke Diamant, and he pointed his cherrywood walking stick at the windows in the gray dawn light:

"There...up there...where the whole family sits at the fully laid table, cups of fresh coffee steaming on the red placemats, and where even before their ablutions the girls of the house smell of hyacinth, from the kiss exchanged with the potted plant on their windowsill, first thing in the morning. Their hands are white and translucent, just right for the little green can they use for watering their flowers. At times I felt a drop of water fall on my face...That was the entire extent of my acquaintance with pure, innocent maidenhood. Their polka-dot kerchiefs, the hair brushed straight back, those earlobes, those corals paling and blushing in turns, the down on the nape of the neck, cheeks cool as springwater, forehead full of godfearing faith, melancholy temples, dreamy curls, aloof noses and those resigned lips always shut tight, as if they would speak only once, and for the first time, on the wedding night—all this I never saw from up close, and could only imagine the flowery scent of their breath. Innocent, gentle, churchgoing, white-footed were the women whose acquaintance I'd always craved, and instead I got actresses and somersaulting jezebels. If only once a pure maiden's palm had caressed my forehead, I would have been a different man. If only once, just once I'd have noticed that in the world outside it was Easter morning, and my heart full of love for a springtime woman—I would have walked a different path. Not once did a chaste woman smile at me, or take my hand, and inquire about the salvation of my soul . . . I merely stood on tiptoe behind dancing girls' sagging petticoats. That's why I never got anywhere in life. Soon I'll be fifty and ready to die like a dog."

Kálmán felt a voice humming in his throat, a psalm that would have to be sung as soon as the organist gave the signal:

"Eveline, Eveline . . . Pure virgin, sweet Eveline."

But he held his peace, for she was the sole treasure of his life.

Lovers, every last one of them, these strange participants in the card game of life, tend to see all other men as inferior knaves.

While Mr. Diamant mused over his wasted life like a melancholy jack of diamonds, Kálmán, in his jaunty heart and cocky complacence, reflected that he happened to possess the very woman whose praises the wise fat man just sang.

An upsurge of woes and sorrows, to a lover's ears, sounds like mere lyrical plashing of white-capped waves.

What a fool, the Hungary of his day deemed the poet Kisfaludy, when he sounded his plaintive lover's lyre! The blue hill of Badacsony, the dreamy, fleecy cumulus clouds evoked sadness only in a few similarly afflicted hearts. Few folks had cared to remember that, wandering through the greengage woods on the vineyard-studded mountain, was an unhappy swain for whom all of life, the entire universe depended on the whim of a young girl's eyes.

Even the man in love is always ready to laugh at another one—apart from his own emotions, are there still other varieties of that fancy ivy that entangles the heart? Love can be a most ridiculous and childish thing, as long as it amuses or torments others.

It is the clown's pancake makeup daubed on our fellow men's faces.

Or a flamboyantly long pheasant feather stuck in a dunce's cap.

Or worthless filberts used by children and old men in games of chance.

Everyone appears ridiculous when in love.

Only the daring ones admit the extent of their torments over a woman. Therefore the lyric poet is actually surrounded by a hostile audience when he sings of his folly. And as for an overweight, barrel-toned, beer-bellied and prickly-chinned man, already suffering from all kinds of bodily ills, to talk about love, why, the weary corners of his mouth are more suited for obscene or scornful phrases than plaintive verses...

That dawn Kálmán made a silent vow that he would never again hold forth about love. Henceforth he would only hum to himself, "Eveline, I love you so," like some solitary autumnal fly droning among reeds and rushes.—Kálmán was a red-blooded young man, who would have died rather than be heard singing those songs crooned daily by tenors the world over (songs that women never tire of hearing).

"Damn!" exclaimed Mr. Diamant who in his thoughts had been making wedding arrangements with Inner City misses at the Franciscans' Church and would have gladly approved the young maiden's wearing long, laced knickers, such as her grandmother had worn to the fair on St. Gellért's Hill. Possibly deep down in his heart he had desired a wife who would knit her stockings herself—just as the same men who profess to set things right in the world end up guzzling booze from dancing girls' shoes.

"Damn, something spilled on me..."

His feathered green hunting hat indeed showed traces of a suspect fluid, flung from above into the early morning Inner City street; at the same time a white-curtained window was quietly closed on the second floor.

(It would have been easy to go into flights of fancy about the white hand and the lace-frilled nightgown, the sleepy little face, the snowy shoulders, and the long eyelashes stuck in a thousand-and-one-nights' narcosis by sleep, heavy sighs exhaled into the pillows, thoughts aflutter like moths in the night while the stockings were being pulled off, the fairy dust of sweet reveries sprinkled on the brow, the orphaned little hand of the sleeping woman, her heel peeping out from the silk quilt in telltale exposure of the dreaming virgin in the dawn light—but Mr. Diamant was past his serenading mood. Interjecting brief curses, he explained to Kálmán that certain irate old bachelors in the Inner City poured water from upper stories on the heads of the early dawn passersby whose footfalls, resounding in the deathly silence of the neighborhood, disturbed the citizens' sleep.)

These were the circumstances preceding their arrival at The Veteran, a rare all-night tavern in the Inner City of old Pest, permitted by the police to stay open all night. And so the nightlife was lively here, even though the tavern sign showed a Hat Street janitor decked out in the uniform, complete with feather, sword and other insignia, of a Mexican campaign volunteer from Emperor Maximilian's time.

The vaulted rooms belonged to a building on Franciscans' Place; printers, newspapermen, women of easy virtue and other such nocturnal refugees camped out here, so many tumbleweeds, transients blown by the whistling autumn winds and left stuck on the cemetery steps. Misplaced lives found a nook here, much as wanderers' wet cloaks are spread out to dry on a roadside kiln. The pilgrims left the crosses they had toted this far, resting them against the wall outside, before stepping from the night into the alcoholic fumes of this musty tavern. They dropped in here for one last hour of merrymaking, shouting, table-thumping, arguing, maybe a song or two—before laying themselves down to a sleep from which there might be no awakening. All around in the big city, the Budapest of myriad lives, people were asleep. Groaning in their dreams of lottery numbers, white-legged girls, nightmarish hags, tomorrow's cares, money turned to ash—as if they had all fled the city for night's distant province. Sleepers don't pay taxes, don't litigate, they lie tranquil, stretched out, wonderfully silent. Of the city's legions of voices, feelings, longings, only The Veteran's patrons remained awake. If the sleepers were never to wake again, The Veteran's patrons would remain as Budapest's sole survivors, having stayed up carefree, gay, open-eyed, keeping the watch during the night when archangels came to lay waste apartment houses whose gateposts were marked with the blood of the lamb.

Here they sat, tippled their wine, downed their beer, and consumed freshly boiled meats and palate-tingling seafood, the folks who would have nothing to do with the city's daytime, who had exiled themselves into the night, having found no daytime faces worth facing. Those who, without this tavern, would have been forced to become magic hunters, galloping ghosts astride dry twigs, wanderers gliding over the highway, blurry patches of moonlight on the roof ridge, stuck-in-the-doghouse, doorway-lurking shadows, stray smoke rings wreathed around the moon, starbeams' loosely flung motes, persuaders lurking at the foot of the suicide's bed, pied pipers wearing the trickster's tall hat, disembodied bawdy thoughts sneaking in to tempt sleepless virgins. They sat dipping their beards into tankards, as befits liberated, formerly bewitched spirits who have nothing else left to do at night in the city. Executioners and victims, trembling sinners and meek fishermen flocked together under night's shelter. Those whom a faithful wife's chaste kiss and undefiled limbs awaited in a warm bed had already left the premises, the way a dragonfly soars away, apparently aimless, toward the sun's rays.

These desperate, sad pub crawlers respected Mr. Diamant, whose form emanated at least as much bitter experience as the pyramids of Egypt. A separate table was secured for the melancholy man who proceeded to salute by first name a few individuals who looked like coachmen, after being greeted by them.

"Boiled beef...and, if you happen to have one, a marrow

bone," said Diamant to the spindle-shanked tavernkeeper, all the while emanating an air of official ceremoniousness, as if the job of food inspection had been what made him stay up nights.

The teeth had hardly begun masticating the meat, Diamant had barely downed a single stein of barley-brew (his eyes fixed vacantly on a far-off point), when the front door's glass, veiled by steam like the women's compartment in Purgatory, flew open.

She was smartly dressed, fresh and perfumed, as if all night she had preened in front of her mirror, instantly replenishing evaporated essences. She shimmered and hovered like a beauteous woman in a ruined gambler's imagination, the one he could have bought had his luck taken a different turn. Her vanished youth, expired like a swallow on African shores, now returned for this one night. She was woman, a jealous tigress maddened by pains surpassing those of childbirth. She was the ruddy disk of the sun dying behind the hills, mirroring the wrestling twins: the moon's leggy, breezy, flute-playing daughter and the sun's hammersmith son.

One of her eyes had a cast, as if there, behind iron-barred windows, cried out the prisoners condemned to death row: love, youth, song and recklessness.

Her other eye stared fixed at Kálmán Ossuary like a gold-tipped arrow seeking the bulls-eye.

Kálmán, paralyzed, could merely look on at this fiery sallying forth of bustle, ostrich-feathered hat, sweet perfume: la dolce vita itself, on parade like some superannuated circus steed that, come tomorrow, might be harnessed to a hearse.

But Diamant had his wits about him.

He flew toward the onrushing lady and addressed her in the unctuous, churchwarden-like tones of a village uncle:

"Madam, this place is most unsuitable..."

"I want to be near my betrothed," replied Ninon, who had had plenty of time on this sleepless night to rehearse her say.

"But this is a cabdrivers' club," Diamant insisted, expending considerable energy to achieve a kind of asthmatic emphasis. "Men may go anywhere, even to a morgue if they feel like being diverted by the sight of a woman beaten to death. But you are a refined lady, men kiss your hand wherever you go."

"That used to be the case, but this man proved to be my undoing," she faltered.

"Let's go, my lady," Diamant replied relentlessly, and at once took the hysterical woman by the arm.

In two strides he led her out of The Veteran, and seated her in a cab waiting by the curb.

"Please go home now..." he said.

("And feel free to read your old love letters, my unhappy child," he added, in his mind.)

When he returned, he addressed Kálmán in a more familiar manner.

"Son, you must get away from here. Only misery and the sufferings of hell lie in store for you here. And lest you forget, the prisons are empty nowadays, just waiting to be filled... Get away from here, go someplace where there's fresh air and a breeze. Where you can hear whoops from a long way off, and the heartbeat's steady like a bull's low-key, casual bellowing. You're still young, you're master of your own fate. Find some innocent, saintly woman who will pray away your sins and will gladly suffer anything for your sake, be it a toothache or martyrdom. Times are getting tough around here."

Ossuary hung his head.

A slew of melancholy images came to his mind with cruel alacrity. A narrow Inner City street, the flickering street lamp, in the light of which he examines the rope before looping it around his neck... A miserable, endless day, the sun showing no sign of ever intending to sink behind St. Gellért's Hill, and all afternoon spent looking the pistol's barrel in the eye... The penitentiary, full of rats and close-cropped old inmates... Buried alive in the stench...

He felt utterly miserable.

"I'll make arrangements for your departure by daybreak," continued Diamant, and gritting his teeth, he swallowed a mouthful of beer after chewing on it as if it were some adversary.

Soon afterward Kálmán Ossuary left The Veteran's heart-lulling and soul-soothing vaulted chambers. He had experienced a miraculous transformation deep down in his heart. No more loitering around gambling casinos; on the street he would steer clear of his worthless, easygoing chums who casually fraternized with death; he would reconcile with his uncle, a prickly village gentleman out of whom he could no longer squeeze a single farthing; he would take his law exams and establish himself as a lawyer in the Inner City of Pest. Any life deficient in the family pleasures must, of necessity, be aimless and troubled. He would find himself a wife in the Josephstadt, where he had met Eveline. He would have the doors fitted with secure locks, be always on the qui vive, take his wife out only to the National Theater and for daily constitutionals on the Buda esplanade, soon with heads bent they would be leaning over a small cradle, enjoying the quiet life, no thought hidden from each other; they would have their photograph taken together, and on Sunday afternoons visit the Farkasrét Cemetery where the relatives rest in peace. Time to enjoy the pleasures of a fine kitchen, the rich roast, clean table linen, a soft bed and the alarm clock —quiet, happy days, with plenty of time to observe all the beauty of autumn and spring. No loud word would ever scare the silent bird of tranquility from their house. Only the sewing machine will whirr, the mailman will ring the doorbell to deliver a money order, and a retired old neighbor might amble over after dinner to regale them with tales of the Prussian campaign. The family doctor would make house calls, but mostly to discuss politics, and afternoon coffee would be sipped by his wife's dearest friends: old Josephstadt ladies who are never seen without shopping bags. The clock's hands would show the midnight hours in vain in a house where everyone sleeps through the night. The garbage collector's bell, or the dawn revelers' footfalls, would be heard from a great distance, as if from far-off lands. The oil lamp always lit under the holy icon, until the woman of the house begins to resemble the Virgin Mary herself, her face not yet broken by pain; if overheard talking in her dream, she would always speak of household and domestic matters, serving maid stuff: "Marie, mind the gentleman's caraway-seed soup..."

And since only sadness has the right to lie, they would never tell each other an untruth as long as they lived, Kálmán and Eveline, or whoever would substitute for Eveline (who would nonetheless be consulted and asked for her blessing).

Until now, each and every dawn had seen a similarly resolved, joyous and purified Kálmán turn in to sleep until nightfall, when all of the upright resolutions were again promptly forgotten. Chaotic dreams sprang at him their desperate madhouse surprises as soon as he shut his eyes in sleep, and helped to neglect those matutinal vows. When he periodically awoke from these horrible images, his heart beat like a syphilitic's who had stumbled upon the nature of his disease. Had he been a writer, he would have set down his dreams, the mendacious acts committed in his sleep, his conscious self-deceptions, his dreamland swindles—he would have had enough material for a lifetime... No wonder his dazed brain was reluctant to give serious thought to changing his way of life. One after another, his days flew by like migrating cranes across the sky's vault. At the age of twenty-five he still imagined that Eveline (if she actually refused to marry him) would find a wife for him, forgive him all his trespasses and also provide for his future. He believed Eveline to be a supernatural, goddesslike being whose generosity surpassed even a mother's.

Now, on this new morning of resolve, he stepped on the

sidewalk and set out half awake on the winding Inner City streets toward the small residential hotel where during the last season (ever since Eveline had left Pest) Ninon de Lenclos had more than once settled his debts. She had also replenished his supply of underwear and clothes, until at last Kálmán deigned to return to Ninon's miniature palazzo, to a bed on the mezzanine that was as capacious as any king or voluptuary's—without meaning any offense against Eveline's sacred personage, for the girl's marvelous face always floated before his eyes, like Jesus Christ's in front of the penitent on holy pilgrimage, giving strength and endurance on the endless march . . .

. . . whereas for Kálmán she took the form of heroines in romantic novels, and faith-healing saintly maidens who were indifferent to earthly suffering . . . Her face appeared embroidered on medieval ecclesiastic banners that flapped in the wind over the heads of the troop of unfortunates, among whom Kálmán marched, in the shadow of the banner . . . Only rarely did he see her as a tousled, scatterbrained schoolgirl (one of the students at an Inner City boarding school where Eveline had spent her youth)—and that had been a while back, when Kálmán was still at the height of his energies, and was capable of making decisions on the girl's behalf as well. However, the slender girl-child with the dreamy, far-off look soon saw through things—she could actually see what Kálmán did when he was alone, she could actually see Kálmán's thoughts, how he lived, walked the streets and whom he met. She began to see all of Kálmán's life in stunning detail when she was barely seventeen. That was the time she handed over to him the first thousand-forint banknote (how she had acquired it was unfathomable, since as a minor, she had no access to her considerable wealth as yet), which Kálmán took to the races and lost on a horse at the spring meet. Eveline received the news without a blink or word of regret. "I'll economize," she said, although Kálmán, in the old garden on which the windows of the Szerb Street girls' school opened, swore up and down that he would find no peace until he recovered the lost thousand...Eveline looked off into the distance and quietly implored Kálmán to spend his time more profitably than trying to make money. He needed to shift for himself only until Eveline finished her schooling, when she would take control of her finances...

Naturally from that day on Kálmán did not make the least effort toward obtaining gainful employment. (He had been born lucky. Once upon a time, when he was running after a rabbit in the autumn fields, the hunting rifle went off in his hands, and the bullet whizzed past his ear like death's express train. Only years later did it occur to him to give thanks to providence for this.)

Before he reached his hotel, an elegantly dressed, dolorous-voiced, black-gloved lady stepped out of a waiting cab and placed her hand on Kálmán's arm:

"Please don't go back to The Dove any more, my dear. You know you can always have a quiet, clean and comfortable room at my place. And I don't have to tell you that what's mine is yours as well."

It was Ninon, lurking in the neighborhood of The Dove, determined to keep watch even if she had to wait all morning for her beloved's arrival.

But this morning proved ill-chosen for the grand lady who otherwise had almost complete power over Kálmán—without, however, possessing his heart.

Kálmán now coldly dismissed her.

"Madam, it's all over between us. Find some other fool in town to satisfy your whims. I'm leaving Pest, and never want to see you or your neighborhood again."

"Why, were you unhappy while you stayed with me?" Ninon asked pointedly, and raised her parasol in a threatening way.

Kálmán looked around for an escape route from the over-wrought lady. He knew of a nearby house with a passageway through it—one of those mute buildings on whose flagstones only those initiated citizens' footsteps wore a path, who entered through one gate and wandered off through another, toward the distant unknown. This was where he intended to lose Ninon. But this experienced lady was no fool, and she, in turn, endeavored to herd the hesitant young man toward her closed carriage. She spoke passionately and nonstop, as if addressing an invisible confidante with the plaintive tale of her ups and downs with Kálmán.

"I tell you, there's not a man in Pest who had it better than this heartless youth. He had the prince's room all to himself in my house; all right, so he was occasionally obliged to go to a coffeehouse when the prince visited Pest for an assignation with one of his girlfriends. Other than that he was lord and master of the house; the concierge was forever running errands for him; he kept the tailors and shoemakers of the district constantly busy; why, the barber's assistant would wait on him in the hall all evening long, as if the prince himself were inside. Ah yes, the easy life, undisturbed, tranquil and refined; carriage rides out to Zugliget; introductions to all my genteel lady visitors; at night, a sensible and blessed peace and quiet behind the securely locked doors of my house, the pantry always fully stocked, and summer holidays in the country... all his to enjoy. My wine cellars, my livestock, my horses; my serving maids obedient as serfs, my chimneys gently puffing smoke; my overstuffed larders, my attics full of drying walnuts and fragrant apples; honey-sweet grapes by the bunch, and my homemade sausages and head cheeses; my local prestige: all his to enjoy. I presented him to my old, highborn friends who offered their lifelong patronage, and I introduced him to the vineyard master on my estate as the new proprietor whose orders are to be obeyed. Had he intended to repay me for all the wisdom and practical advice I gave him, he would have had to build a paper mill, and print banknotes night and day... Oh, the scoundrel!"

Here Ninon screamed, then swore like a sergeant, for Kálmán suddenly ducked into the passageway, and instantaneously vanished from view.

For a moment she stood there dazed as if hit on the head. Then a resigned smile passed over the face that kings had fought over.

"Let's go home, Friedl," she said to the handsome, silver-haired driver. "Looks like we're getting old."

The pair of matched Russian horses set off at a trot over the winding Inner City streets.

As for Kálmán Ossuary, he turned his steps in the direction of the Virgin of St. Roch's, whom he had long ago nominated as Eveline's local surrogate in providing miraculous help. That he had been strong enough to free himself from Ninon he owed to Eveline's, or rather Mary's, intercession. This most beautiful of Budapest ladies stood high up on her pillar, pure and divine grace, hewed out of stone. Her head was bent, but not because of the weight of her starry crown of gold, or because of her curiosity to see all the scoundrels and peasants trooping past on Kerepesi Road. Her hands were opposed in prayer, in a gesture of heavenly rapture, as if she sojourned here amidst eternal orisons for all Josephstadt women. "Ave Maria, Gratia Plena!" the gilded letters announced, and Kálmán approached the statue's iron grill with a faith bordering on certainty that others had already prayed here on his behalf. Possibly he had been commended to her safekeeping by Eveline, that exquisite creature, the last time she came here for matins at the Chapel of St. Roch, and knelt behind the nuns, among the mendicants, like some princess traveling incognito. Inside the fence lay a wreath of chrysanthemums, perhaps she had left it as a token, foreseeing that Kálmán would pass this way one doleful morning—a morning when she, in her country manor's window, contemplated the awakening of the land, while Kálmán, lost in the metropolis, had no one to turn to, to pour out his heart...Ah, the most tender thoughts in a man's brain cannot equal the sentimentality of a benevolent woman... Why, such a woman will tell a lie only (by her silence or her absence) when she wishes to spare a man the greatest torment.

Kálmán pressed his forehead against the cast-iron bars and prayed lightheartedly, wordlessly, like a pilgrim. His eyes saw Eveline up on the pilaster, and it was to her that his heart's murmurings went out, to her, lady of miracles, healing breath, caressing hand that brings oblivion.

"Eveline," he sobbed at last, as woefully as if this would earn him a special reprieve from the maiden who *saw everything*: his cold behavior toward Ninon, his flight, and now saw his ardent prayers as well. And for this reason would have to forgive him, even if icebergs rose up between them.

Far away in a Hungarian village Eveline's nanny, as usual, laid out the Tarot first thing in the morning.

The ancient crone squatting on the floor suddenly pointed at a figure that had long been absent from the lay of the cards.

"A traveler's approaching," she said, and Eveline trembled like a windblown leaf.

4. AN UNUSUAL YOUNG LADY
AND HER UNUSUAL BEAUX

MASKERÁDI—were he asked in the great beyond to speak truthfully about his earthly doings—would confess that he had especially feared those women who remembered his lies the day after; otherwise, he had preferred to pass his days at weddings.

Maszkerádi had lived in Pest back in the days when one could see on Chamois Street in the evening the white-stockinged daughters of the bourgeoisie sitting on benches under fragrant trees in the courtyards of single-storied townhouses, listening to the music of distant accordions, their hearts overflowing with love, like a stone trough whose water drips from a little-used faucet. In winter this part of town gave off the smells of the grab bags of itinerant vendors; in summer the predominant scent was that of freshly starched petticoats. Had he the inclination, Maszkerádi could have seduced and abducted the entire female population of Chamois Street. He was a stray soul, French or German in origin, variously prince in exile or card-sharp, refined gentleman or midnight serenader, fencing master or freeloader, as the occasion demanded. Married middle-class ladies cast down their eyes when he flashed a glance at them, while their husbands loathed the sight of his lithe limbs; in her book of hours every girl had a certain prayer picked out for her by Maszkerádi. Sometimes there were as many as four or five young misses bent piously over the supplication of a fallen soul at Sunday Mass in the Franciscans' Church. At night the occasional report of a firearm disturbed the tranquility of the quarter: a father or husband taking a shot at Maszkerádi who had been glimpsed lurking around the sleeping household. He sported a black beard and there was animal magnetism in his voice. He must have retained in his possession intimate letters from some extremely prominent Inner City ladies (for a while he had resided in that quarter)—to have avoided incarceration in the darkest prison of Pest.

One day this disreputable adventurer was found dead in mysterious circumstances in his apartment at Number Ten, where irate husbands had so often waited, posted by the front entrance, expecting to see their dear little errant wives. (Although the road to Maszkerádi was fraught with peril, women still ran off to his place on snowy afternoons before a ball, on spring mornings before an outing to the Buda hills, or after a funeral, aroused by the tears shed at the last rites. On rainy nights there were barefoot women lowering themselves on the drainspout—in short, no other man in town could lay claim to such traffic.) The coroner readily agreed to inter this dangerous individual without a thorough inquest; he didn't even insist on dripping hot candle wax on the fingertips of the deceased. Although the knitting needle stuck in the victim's heart and the nail protruding from the crown of his head were duly noted, the reprobate was not deemed worthy of much fuss. The sooner the meat wagon transported this carrion out of town, the better.

Not two weeks after Maszkerádi's demise the thunder of a gun was again heard late at night in Autumn Street. The newly-wed Libinyei had discharged his blunderbuss; he must have seen a ghost, although he swore up and down that he awoke from a nightmare to glimpse Maszkerádi jumping up from his bride's side and escaping through the window. Lotti was pallid, trembled from top to toe, and later confessed to her mother, in strictest confidence, a most peculiar dream that had surprised her like a warm breeze. "If I become pregnant I'll throw myself in the Danube!" the young bride swore, but later reconsidered the matter.

Less than two weeks later, Lotti's sister-in-law, the other Mrs. Libinyei, Helen of the springtime blue eyes, white shoulders like a Madonna, and the sweetness of walnuts, had to wake up her husband in the middle of the night.

"There's someone in the room," she whispered.

The husband, a dyer in blue, pulled the quilt over his face but even so he could hear the door quietly open as someone exited through the front entrance. His trembling hands groped for Helen's shoulder.

"Phew, you have such a cemetery-smell. Just like Lotti," blurted the surprised dyer.

Although this scene had transpired in the innermost family sanctum, the townsfolk still learned about the affair and began to give the two Mrs. Libinyeis the strangest looks. After all, it was most irregular that sisters-in-law should share a dead man of ill repute as their lover.

At the civic rifle club meeting, over a glass of wine, one tipsy citizen, possibly a kinsman, brought up this evil rumor in front of the two husbands. By then the story had it that it was the two Mrs. Libinyeis who had done away with the adventurer: one hammered the nail into his skull, the other plunged the knitting needle into his heart, for being unfaithful to them. Apparently he had gone serenading elsewhere in the night, attended the latest weddings and whispered his depraved lies into the ears of the newest brides. So now the dead man was taking his revenge by leaving the cold sepulchral domain of his cemetery ditch to haunt the two murderous women.

Did the Libinyei brothers give credence to the words of their bibulous companion? A nasty row ensued, in the course of which the Libinyei boys, befitting their noble Hungarian origins, and in homage to their warlike *kuruc* freedom-fighter forebears, broke the skulls of several fellow citizens. Swinging chair legs, rifle butts and their fists, they defended the honor of their women. For this reason the rifle association's get-together ended well before midnight, the precious ecstasy of the local Sashegy wines evaporated from under the citizens' hats, and the ragtag band of Gypsy musicians quit playing their discordant tunes among the early spring lilac trees of the municipal park. The grim and much booed Libinyeis hung their heads and trudged homeward on Király Street—the abode, in those days, of midnight-eyed Jewesses and dealers smelling of horsehides.

Reaching their house in Autumn Street at this unusually early, pre-midnight and sober hour, they stopped short, astonished hearts a-thumping, in front of the ground-floor windows. They saw, behind the white lace curtains, the rooms lit up by festive lamplight, while the sounds of music filtered out into the night, just like at certain Inner City town houses marked by red lanterns where even a stranger from distant parts could count on the warmest reception. The screech of the violin resembled a serenade of tomcats on moonlit rooftops.

The elder Libinyei clambered up on the quoin that was decorated by a carving. (It must have come under the scrutiny of every Josephstadt dog by late February.)

Having climbed up, Libinyei the elder peeked through the window into his own home.

Whereupon, without a sound, he tumbled from the wall and fell headlong on the pavement, stretched out very much like one who has concluded his business here on earth.

In a furor Pál Libinyei, the younger brother, sprang up on the cornerstone. His eyes immediately narrowed, as if he had received a terrible blow in the face. The wealthy blue-dyer glimpsed a sight he would not have thought conceivable. The two women, Lotti and Helen, in a state of shameless undress, were treating Maszkerádi to the pleasures of a fully laid groaning board. The ham loomed like a bulls-eye and the wine from Gellért Hill glowed as if a volcano had deposited lava in it.

Slices of white bread shone like a bed inviting the tired traveler. In the corner an itinerant musician's calloused fingers twanged the strings, with enough energy for a whole orchestra, while he witnessed the hoopla with the pious expression of a medieval monk.

Libinyei's murderous fist smashed the window.

In the last flicker of the guttering candles he could see the pilgrim-faced musician leap to his feet in the corner, raise his gleaming instrument and deal Maszkerádi's skull a deadly blow, fully meaning to dispatch him to the other world, this time once and for all. Indeed, the libertine collapsed like a whirling mass of dry leaves, when the autumn wind suddenly withdraws behind a tombstone in the municipal park to overhear the conversation of two lovers. The reveler with the bushy, overgrown eyebrows and black evening wear vanished into the flagstones of the floor. For years, the inhabitants of the house would search for him in the cellar, whenever they heard a wine cask creak, but it was only the new wine fermenting in the silence of the night.

By the time Libinyei made his way into the house he had grabbed an iron bar and was savoring glorious visions of murder as his sole road to salvation. However, both women (each in her own bedchamber) appeared to be as sound asleep as if there were no tomorrow. The itinerant musician had slipped away like a mendicant friar. Libinyei spent the night in his brother's wife's room, and attempted to convince Lotti that her dead husband lying under the window would arise and presently enter the house bleeding and gasping, to hold ordeal by fire over her. In a whisper Lotti confessed her mortal sins to her brother-in-law: she alone had laid Maszkerádi to waste, by means of the iron nail and the knitting needle, thereby earning the gratitude of every Josephstadt mother. Above all, Lotti had been outraged by the balding libertine's latest schemes to seduce the youngest girls awaiting confirmation.

"Oh, you witch," the blue-dyer stammered, sobbing and in love, "I'm going to take care of you from now on. And I'll skin you alive if you ever conjure up Maszkerádi from the beyond to come for dinner again."

Lotti solemnly swore, and at dawn they brought the corpse in from the sidewalk, where the itinerant musician had been guarding it as tenaciously as a ratter.

Such were the circumstances surrounding Malvina's birth.

Lotti died in childbirth; the attending doctors delivered the child of a mother who was more dead than alive. For the first fifteen years of her life she never heard a word spoken about her parents. She was raised by a black-clad, thin-lipped, dagger-tongued woman (Helen) to whom Libinyei, the girl's stepfather, never said a word. This woman spent her nights in a separate apartment of the house, with the taciturn itinerant musician on her doorstep, performing all sorts of hocus-pocus to keep the ghosts away. Libinyei, at times, addressed the girl-child as Miss Maszkerádi. (Later, after she had left her boarding school, Malvina used the pen name "Countess Maszkerádi" in her correspondence with classmates.) One day the monkish itinerant reported that Helen was in her last hour, whereupon his mysterious presence vanished forever from the household. By that time Libinyei had amassed such a fortune that he barely grieved over the death of his neglected wife. His possessions included mansions, land in the country, and real estate in Buda.

Good fortune and wealth did their best to console him. After Helen's death all kinds of relatives came to stay at the townhouse, but none of them won Libinyei's approval. Springtime visits to spas, quack remedies, barbers and doctors all failed to rejuvenate him. Soon enough he followed Helen, Lotti, and Maszkerádi into the great beyond. Malvina became the wealthiest heiress in Budapest: somber, frosty, intrepid, and miserable.

Malvina Maszkerádi was Eveline's best and only friend, entrusted with all of the girl's secrets, like a private diary.

A few days after the Tarot reading Miss Maszkerádi arrived at Bujdos-Hideaway.

"I sensed that you are in some kind of danger," said the solemn girl, her eyes downcast. "I wanted to be by your side."

Miss Maszkerádi had stayed at Bujdos before. She knew by name each dog, each horse and rooster. The migrating swallow and the stork nesting on the chimney of the servants' quarters both greeted the melancholy maiden. The servants dared not look her in the eye, but stared after her as they would at a creature from another world.

Eveline both loved and worried about her strange friend. But her vernal insomnia immediately passed as soon as Miss Maszkerádi joined the Hideaway household. Like one preparing for the grave, Eveline related her recent experiences in the minutest detail, including Andor Álmos-Dreamer's enigmatic demise and resurrection.

"He's crazy, but honest. This village Don Juan's going to be your downfall yet," observed Miss Maszkerádi. "And what about your gambler?" she inquired. "Show me the gambler's letters."

Eveline shook her head.

"He's afraid to write me. Sometimes in the morning I stand by the window and watch the mailman trudging along on the road far away. That gray old man always comes the same way, sad as autumn and just as hopeless. If he were to deliver a letter from Pest one day... But I don't even know if I'd like to receive a letter..."

"Your gambler's crazy, too... He thinks you're some otherwordly creature," Miss Maszkerádi replied scornfully. "I assume every man to be insane, and usually the events prove me right. Oh, there's the ass who believes you are a demon, an angel of death, and who wants to escape into death when he feels he's lost his freedom. Meanwhile another inane male will worship you like a saint or a holy icon, and expect you to perform miracles. Only I know you exactly as you really are: a scatterbrained, bored, orphaned young miss. Why, by now you should have married a first lieutenant or some young gent with a duck's ass haircut. But you believe life is more interesting this way. Well, one fine day some maniac will snag you by the throat like a fox taking a goose."

"Please calm down," implored Eveline. "Haven't you ever been in love?"

"Oh yes, with a dog...or a horse...or a wooden cross at the old Buda military cemetery over the grave of a young officer whose fiancée'd run off to work the cash register at a nightclub. Men stink. If I were to find one guy whose mouth had a pleasing aroma, maybe I'd let him kiss me. Or rather I wouldn't wait but kiss him myself. If, God forbid, I should find a man I like, I'd pick him like a roadside poppy. If I could only live...If it were really worthwhile to be alive, I'd show you how to live life. But I'm not in good health, and I'm not old enough to enjoy being in poor health."

"Just simmer down," Eveline repeated. "Can't you hear someone lurking around the house? Every night I hear him and my heart almost bursts..."

It was a spring night.

"Nah, it's just the unusual weather we're having," Miss Maszkerádi replied, unmoved. "It's all that meteoric crap—ashes and dust from burnt-out stars—the winds sweep into the atmosphere...It's only the night, plucking an old mandolin string in the attic that's been lying silent for years. No need to go mushroom-crazy, like some fungus that suddenly pops up, so glad to be among us."

"But I tell you, someone goes past my window every night. I tell myself, perhaps it's Kálmán, and my heart nearly screams out like a bird that's caught. Perhaps it's Álmos-Dreamer, and my tears soak the pillow... Or it's the night watchman, so I just sigh—but the candle still burns till dawn, I simply can't get resigned to living this way. But how else should I live?"

Sitting on the edge of the bed, listening to her friend, Miss Maszkerádi folded her arms.

"In old Russian novels people asked such questions, behaving like cardboard characters... But today it's totally different. Novels only show you how to die. I don't even know who my father was. One thing for sure, he never thought of me. My mother had no way of knowing, either, that I would be here some day. I came into being and grew like an icicle under the eaves. This is why I'll never have a child. I just can't recommend this lifestyle for you, Eveline, although I know you want me to. Well, each to her own... suit on suit, heart to heart," mocked Miss Maszkerádi.

"Malvina, you'll never be happy," prophesied Eveline, speaking as if from the pages of some novel.

"I must always look within myself, for everything. I believe only in myself, and myself alone, and don't give a damn about others' opinions. I view each of my acts as if I were reading about it fifty years from now, in a newly found diary. Did I do something ridiculous and dumb? I ask myself each night when I close my eyes. I think over each word, each act: will I regret it, come tomorrow? I am my own judge and I judge myself as harshly as if I'd been lying in my grave these hundred years, my life a yellowed parchment diary, its end known in advance. I will not tolerate being laughed at or cheated. I want to know this very minute what I will think ten years from now about today, about today's weather and about this night... Will I have to be ashamed of some weakness or tenderness? Is there one circumstance worth disrupting my life for, rising an hour earlier, or using more words than usual? I try to modulate my decisions and my emotions by looking ahead and seeing whether I'd regret it tomorrow. And I'm never nervous, it's simply not worth it.

"Had I been born a man, I would have been a Talmudist, an Oriental sage, a scholar who delves into decaying millennial mysteries. Too bad, I was not admitted at the university. But if possible, I would still marry a great, gray-bearded, immensely wise rabbi or Oriental scholar. Possibly Schopenhauer...or my first teacher, Gyula Sámuel Spiegler, if that little old Jew were still alive...Oh, you won't catch me crying on account of rival women, actresses, danseuses! The hell with the strumpets! What do I care if my husband sometimes sees them? As long as they stay away from me with their dirt."

Eveline heard out these words of wisdom with eyes closed. All her life repelled by women of easy virtue, she still envisioned them to be like the first one she had ever seen, in her childhood in the Inner City, near her convent school. A fat, ungainly, wide-mouthed, coarsely painted towering idol of flesh that passed by with petticoats lifted, like a killer of men, cruelly smiling. The little schoolgirls had nightmares about this otherworldly monster who probably roamed the town to entice inexperienced men to her cave in the mountains where she would devour them like a dragon. Ever after, the educated, curious and clairvoyant young woman still imagined fallen women to be like that. (She was most amazed at the Pest racing turf one summer Sunday when she attended the St. Stephen's Cup races with her lady companion, and Kálmán pointed out from afar a gentle, unimpeachably clean-cut angel, all blonde English-style curls, as one of the city's most depraved creatures who spent her days in the company of elderly counts.)

Miss Maszkerádi, all her Talmudic wisdom notwithstanding, loved to refer to women of easy virtue as wondrous creatures who lived off their bodies. She preferred French novels that described life in brothels, and would have given much to clandestinely observe the goings-on at some sordid club one night. She was convinced that the best way to get to know a man was by witnessing his coarsest words and acts.

"Had I a father or brother, I would send them to accompany my would-be fiancé on a visit to the *filles de joie*. I'd want to know how my future life-companion acted, how he behaved there..." Miss Maszkerádi insisted. "But I don't want to get married. Because then I'd have long ago become an expert in midwifery, and in all the seductive practices of loose women."

And on this childish note the wise Miss Maszkerádi closed the evening's proceedings. She went to bed in her room, smiling in quiet scorn at Eveline, who would listen all night long for the sound of footsteps coming and going around the house. She knew it was nothing but the spring wind fidgeting out there.

———

In the morning Miss Maszkerádi went horseback riding. (Actually, the real reason she liked to sojourn at Eveline's Bujdos estate was because it offered wide meadows and endless country roads for indulging in her passionate pastime. Back in Pest she rarely showed herself on the Stefánia Road promenade among the nannies, small children and the multitudes of happy or unhappy lovers. "Someone might think I'm trying to show off," she thought and was always annoyed whenever some man stared too long at her willowy equestrienne waist and her silver-spurred little riding boots. As if she were trying to impress anyone!)

At Bujdos-Hideaway a fat mare named Kati was Miss Maszkerádi's mount. This saddle horse had ears as long as a donkey's. She had a shifty way of eavesdropping on conversations around her, pricked up her ears at approaching footsteps, and assiduously whisked her short tail like a housemaid shaking a dust rag. At times she was as obedient as a trained circus horse. Then in one of her capricious moods she threw Miss Maszkerádi, and, maliciously satisfied, ran off. She was as old as the chief steward's wife, and as gluttonous, doleful and impetuous as a frustrated spinster.

Miss Maszkerádi rode over hill and dale, resting her eyes on the colors of the early spring landscape that alternated with the humdrum monotony of an aging chorus singer's costume changes. It is only human to be constantly astounded by springtime; sixty or seventy years are not enough to make you tire of it. Each spring a new card game begins with life itself; you may win or you may lose. Secretly everyone starts life anew each spring. Only thing is, no one has the courage to admit wanting to be born again, to start everything all over: love, marriage, lifelong projects. To throw off the shabby old clothes and those dented decorations. Oh to run, run naked and devour buds, trees, girls, pale boys in the woods, and quickly lay to rest the old folks wrapped in their lynx furs, still mumbling about winter.—Miss Maszkerádi had never in her life read a springtime lyric, and despised people who delighted in the weather. Wasn't it all the same, a screeching snowstorm or a mild lingering breeze, once you lay in your grave? Why bother to set out in life when it was over so soon?

So she whacked the melancholy mare Kati, and, flushed in the heat of excitement, cantered through birch woods, where the aftereffects of melted snow, blackened nests and globular growths hung from bare branches like so many hanged men slain by spring for being no longer fit to live.

The wily mare cantered on the wet road, past deep ditches as dark as grave pits whose dead had escaped to become ghosts; the meadows, convalescent after their long confinement, looked as feeble as a nonambulatory patient sitting on the edge of the bed. Birds: crows and magpies wheeled in the air as if newly acquainting themselves with the land below; spring was sprung with a vengeance, as if hardy hands were prying some vast door open a crack, allowing to slip back into this world those meteorological exiles, those playful roués and screeching, shameless hussies, clowns and paunchy rakes: the lock is creaking, there is a great rush as the stag-headed, mossy-bearded stable master sweeps over the land, horsewhips and expels winter's lingering leftovers, kicks the dead into the ditch, cracks the whip at wandering minstrels and unrolls the meadows' endless carpets for the upcoming catastrophic onrush.

On buds, naked little fairies seat themselves astraddle (till now they were mute shadows in hidden groves); in the air, snaps and creaks, voices of unknown origin, as if underground germs and seeds sang a grand chorale; gusts of air scamper like crazed wheels, whistling clouds whoosh by streaming overland, solemnly still waters for no particular reason stir now as if they, too, wanted a part in the Spring Ball; it is a miracle that strident, bleating billy goats don't flood the field where everyone and everything aches to play. And still, in abandoned little autumnal niches hidden among trees in the depths of sad copses that seem to be created for solitary ghostly reveries with bent head—someone must certainly be sitting there, in a clearing that no one ever sees. But even such solitudes are approached by young snoopers on tiptoes, eager to spy on saddish old folks' thoughts.

"Spring!" thought Miss Maszkerádi. "You are an idiot. I just don't believe in you!"

And yet she must have believed in it a tiny little bit, for she searched out the tree she had been in love with for years.

It was a dwarf willow up on the bank of a stream gone dry, highly solemn, determined to hold its ground like some watchman. Its twigs had long ago gone with the wind, like unfaithful, flighty women from an old man's side. But the ancient tree maintained a virile, calm, patriarchal equanimity. This was one somber, manly male who never showed any hurt, rejoiced not at Eastertime, nor did it celebrate the coming and going of evanescent life all around.

Miss Maszkerádi had sought precisely such a gruff, ancient

tree-like male all her life, to whom she could have been as faithful as to this rooted, bark-bound, impassive trunk that had a face, as in fabled forests of old, hands in pockets, and a waist aslant, in a bored pose. At times she fancied the tree as an aging vagabond who had weathered many a hardship in his wifeless life, tramped about aimless as a muddy dog, the kept lover of man-hungry females; he despised love's joys and woes, had plucked his share of triumph and hopelessness, taken quiet delight in success, had women on their knees to kiss his hand; passionless, not even pretending a semblance of emotion, he seduced the women in his path, then sent them packing, so many used-up playmates; they had loved and hated him, caressed him with trembling hands, then flung curses at his head, the way chambermaids in Pest toss trash out of a window... This manly one stayed calm and collected by living the inward life, thinking his own thoughts and always doing whatever felt good. He never kept a flower, a lock of hair, or remembrance of a kiss. He dealt with women as they deserved. Never did he wander with aching heart on moonlit nights, under anyone's window, no matter how much awaited... He might prowl about for a week or two like a dog in springtime, then, all skin and bones and weary of the world, he would return from his wanderings and never recall what happened to him, what women had said, what they smelled and tasted like... Miss Maszkerádi positively abhorred novelists who always write about old men remembering youthful adventures. Thus she could not stand Turgenev, whom Eveline would have read night and day.

The old rogue pretended not to notice last year's lover, Miss Maszkerádi. Indifferent and cool, he stood his ground by the vanished creek whose bed had perhaps drained off his very life, never to return, flighty foam, playful wavelet, rainbow spray.

"Here I am, grandpa," Maszkerádi whispered, sliding from her saddle.

She beheld the ancient tree's inward-glancing eye, compressed, cold mouth, thick-skinned, impassive waist, and pocketed hands.

"I am here and I am yours," she went on, after embracing the tree as an idol is embraced by some wild tribeswoman who can no longer find a mate that's man enough in her own nation.

The old willow's knotted gnarls and stumps, like so many hands, palpated all over Miss Maszkerádi's steel-spring body. The mossy beard stuck to the frost-nipped girl-cheek already quite cool to start with. Who knows, the old willow might even have reciprocated her embrace.

"I know you can keep a secret," she mumbled. "Please don't tell anyone I love you."

She hugged that tree as she had never dared to hug a man. Her arms and legs wound around the trunk, her incandescent forehead pressed against the ancient idol, this offshoot of Roman Priapus that had escaped being daubed in cinnabar by womenfolk.

"As long as I'm around, I'll visit you, old partner in crime," she said.

Kati, the shaggy yellow mare, wearily lowered her head, suffered Miss Maszkerádi in the saddle, and carried her homeward, morose head hung low, as if they had been beaten up at a wedding.

In the afternoon a fog settled over the fields, like gray souls assembled to rehash the mournful circumstances of their demise. Madmen made of mist occupied the upper galleries... apparently unable to recall how they had died.

Back at the country house, Miss Maszkerádi smoked one cigarette after another as she paced the rooms under the century-old vaults. She marched tall like a soldier, and appeared to be content, even happy. Yet when she spoke, her voice sounded weary:

"Good God, to think that some people live their whole lives unvisited by illness, accident, misfortune. Sometimes I think I'll be mauled to death by tigers."

Eveline sat in the rocking chair, reading a novel: Sir Walter Scott's *Ivanhoe*. From reveries of medieval knighthood she glanced up at her friend.

"You should read a good book, Malvina . . . We all die in the end . . ."

"But how? . . . You imagine yourself as mistress of a castle, because you have swallowed men's lies. Your death, too, will be theatrical, complete with the whole works: candelabras, priests praying, funeral bells, servants sobbing outside the door, a towering catafalque. A whole production with you in the leading role, you hope. But I just can't think that way, I'm a coward, a city bourgeoise, a *Bürgerin* of the Josephstadt . . . I am afraid of death."

Miss Maszkerádi stood on feet wide apart in front of the window, like some actress in tights. (She would have felt tremendously embarrassed if someone had told her this.) On her forehead a brown curl stirred during her cogitations as if blown by a breeze. Her slender body was like a solitary fencing sabre stuck into the floor of the *salle*. She swayed and quivered, as if the pulsing of her blood moved steel springs coiled within her body. On foggy days she was always tense and she anxiously racked her brain as if her life depended on thinking of something new.

"I can't resign myself to the fact that I live in order to die some day. I'd love to step off this well-trodden straight and boring path. To somehow live differently, think different thoughts, feel different feelings than others. It wouldn't bother me to be as alone as a tree on the plains. My leaves would be like no other tree's. What I dread most is a fate like my alter ego's."

Eveline finally gave up trying to follow the wanderings of the magnificent knight Ivanhoe in the Holy Land. The exotic mediaeval ladies flew up from her side like a covey of partridges, and Old England's oak forests receded, to murmur from far off, on the edge of the horizon.

"You mean to tell me you have alter egos?" she asked, as if discovering some dark secret here, of all places, on a boring village afternoon.

Miss Maszkerádi's steely-glinting eyes appeared as serene as an idol's or a maniac's.

"Yes, and I ran into one of them abroad, you know, the time I wintered in Egypt. This was a lady of distinction, a soulless vulgarian; she had both camel drivers and officers in red coats for lovers. She was sad only to the extent that a hotel orchestra's tunes remind you of sadness, and she was cheerful to the extent that life in Cairo, the nightly balls, the various entertainments devised against ennui, formal dinners and excursions into the desert are calculated to cheer you, with a hypnotic power that every rich and idle traveler surrenders to. She lived a life as inhuman, as empty of inner content as any of the society ladies who stay at the gilded white hotels down there, and can be seen tapping the caged parrot's beak with a finger that young men dream about. Perhaps her senses could only be aroused after she had gorged herself on rich, spicy dishes, danced at a ball, and listened to cold-blooded males calmly drawl incendiary words in her ear. She would settle into her seat at the theater with the indifference of an egret feather in a diamond hairpin. Sometimes she would leaf through a light French novel; among all those bald, grumpy, tired men she trod with silken footsteps. She had Creole or Gypsy blood, and she bore the name of a French prince who must have passed his days, advancing them like chessmen, in God knows what remote part of the globe.

". . . Back then I was in love with an officer who spent an occasional evening with me.

"Did I say I was in love? No, Eveline, I must confess I've never been in love, just like that French princess. I simply happened to spend the winter and early spring in Egypt; went to lunch when the bell rang in the hotel, and had an affair with an officer of the local garrison. Simply because that was how things were done in the *haut monde* I frequented for entertainment, just like a servant girl who goes out to a masked ball.

"One night the officer—and I can't for the life of me recall his face, or the camel driver's, who took me out into the desert—well, the officer had had a little too much to drink, and he confessed that on days when I did not require his services he spent the night with the Frenchwoman, and he swore upon his honor that he could barely tell the two of us apart. To him, our voices, bodies, hair, and gestures appeared mirror images of each other. What's more, while making love, the princess called him 'sweet young master,' the same term of endearment that I had picked up from a peasant woman here in Hungary. The princess, like me, begged to die at the moment of consummation. She loved the same feature of his face as I did, kissed his hand the same way as I, and watered him like a lady gardener her violets. And she, too, was supremely happy when this thirsty violet, parched by the Egyptian night, lapped up her blonde French vintage with loud slurps.

"The man was totally drunk, and insensitive to the fact that he was skinning me alive by ascribing my most intimate amorous behavior to another woman.

"I'm not going to go into what I felt and thought at the time. All I'm going to say is that on that night he lovingly implored me to let down my long auburn hair so that he could tie it in a knot around his neck. In vain. Like a naive little girl from the Josephstadt, I never really fathomed the purpose of this production at the time. Back then I had not yet visited prisons and madhouses. I only knew the life around me, worlds apart from the tragic depths, or the solemn mysteries—as far apart as our luxury liner and that Black Sea steamer full of howling slaves, that we passed near the African shore. Back then I still believed that no matter how I lived, acted, behaved and felt, I would still eventually await, clutching an old prayer-book, my heart at peace, the arrival of the Jesuit father to administer the last rites in my white-curtained Josephstadt house, with the consecrated pussy willow on the wall. Back then I still believed that from that tranquil island of happiness one could roam without hurt on wild sargasso seas, and that adventures and experience would not blind my eyes like droppings from a swallows' nest.

"I'll make this short. The next morning, after an anxious night, I thoroughly scrutinized my French princess, who until then I had found quietly repulsive, like most of the 'culture vultures' who spend every day of their lives in white ocean liners and hotels with gold trim.

"The princess undeniably resembled me. The saucy thing even imitated my style in clothes—or else I did hers. The only other thing I wanted to know was whether she had poor vision in her left eye, as I do. So I decided to test her. At lunch I sat immediately on her left and on my white lace fan I wrote in large, clear letters, 'I hate you,' in French. I'd already made sure that my left eye could not decipher the letters. During lunch we exchanged a few neutral words. Then I opened my fan and conspicuously waved it near her face several times. Had her left eye not been as poor as mine, she would have certainly noticed the inked inscription. But she merely smiled neutrally, bored and indifferent as a puma at the zoo. Her hair emanated the scent of Japanese gardens. She was as weird as an exotic bird. A ghastly chill ran through my soul when I considered that, under certain circumstances, I resembled her.

"After lunch I spoke briefly with the officer. I told him I wanted to rest that evening, so why didn't he spend the night with my rival. 'Besides, I'm curious to know what the princess thinks about this extraordinary similarity between us,' I told him. His eyes flashed like a knife in a scuffle. 'I'll ask her!' he said, licking his chops, the poor fool. Service in the colonies had degraded him, as it does most Europeans. Looking at him, I thought that once upon a time this blue-eyed young man had been a blond-haired little boy who went to school wearing a white collar, the taste of cake in his mouth and the trace of his mother's kiss on his forehead.

"Next morning the officer was found strangled in the corridor outside the French princess's room. My alter ego had committed the deed that would have been my lot. She had tied her hair in a knot around the show-off's neck, and suffocated him.

"What happened to the murderous princess? That I can't tell you, Eveline, because I left Cairo before the results of the inquest into the officer's death were revealed. I arrived home in a state of nervous fever and hallucination. I don't think I'll leave this country for some time to come. After all, in this land we more or less know each other, men and women, and surprises are unlikely; our sins are of the usual sort, the modes of thought familiar. Sometimes I visit menageries, and the eyes of caged exotic predators remind me of looks I have encountered in my travels abroad. So I am a native of the Josephstadt, after all. Even though in make-believe I have rehearsed a happy and serene death scene—oh, I don't think I'll rest in peace when I kiss the crucifix for the last time. Although at times I still think that my alter ego, the unhappy French princess, has suffered and atoned on my behalf. She has done my penance, by living out the life that I should have lived, by rights. I am the shadow that remains after she has disappeared. For where do they go, the shadows of folks who have gone underground? They must live on, somehow. So maybe fate will deal me a merciful death."

"Poor dear," replied Eveline, and embraced her friend with a heart as pure as only a village girl's can be. She smelled of old lavender and wore shirts of fine Upland linen. In cold weather she put on soft cotton flannel petticoats although she knew full well that this was no longer the fashion. She loved to linger in vaulted chambers, to dawdle in a May garden, and, come autumn, to sink into reveries wrapped in a Kashmir shawl. And she loved beautiful old novels.

"So who was your second alter ego?" Eveline asked.

"I'll tell you when we've forgotten about Egypt," replied Miss Maszkerádi, assuming the grave air of a schoolteacher. "Anyway, it's getting dark, time to light the lamp."

On this spring night the ladies of Bujdos found themselves serenaded.

It was in honor of the visitor, as always, whenever Malvina Maszkerádi sojourned at Hideaway.

When the moonlight rose above the canebrakes, where it had been brooding like an outlaw, it revealed, leaning against a linden tree, the figure of Mr. Pistoli, who had already gone through three wives, for he still hoped that he would conquer the Donna Maszkerádi, whom this incorrigible amoroso with the tinted mustache liked to dub the Dark Lady of the Sonnets, among other monickers.

Ah, Pistoli was a solemn and cruel-hearted man of the world except at Bujdos, where, the moment he set foot, he became a clown. He brought along a Gypsy band, and made sure to collect one half of the generous honorarium he bestowed on them from Andor Álmos-Dreamer the day after the night music— for Eveline, too, was a recipient of these moonlit melodies.

As soon as the two misses had turned in for the night, the huge watchdogs were let off their chains, the field guard discharged his shotgun and the spring night settled over the land like a maiden in her bed: here came the town fiacre on which Gypsies love to clamber as if it were Jacob's ladder. Ah yes, Gypsies love to ride a fiacre! The contrabassist, like a grandfather at a wedding, conducted the procession from the coachbox, where he had shivered, hugging his partner in crime throughout the potholed ride. The *cimbalom* was tied to the forage rack, and its player, a youth with a bowler hat and a frilly bow tie, stood on the running board of the carriage, jealously watching his beloved. Inside the coach violins in sacks lurched along with the nonchalant, brandy-tippling cheer of a red-faced road inspector making the rounds of his home district.

That ceaseless Gypsy prankishness, the horselaugh unique to this tribe, the chortling delight in each and every hour, the devil-may-care, self-indulgent, proud music of the moment, that buck-naked humor and animal delight in each breath of life: all of this appeared on that provincial hackney cab, as if Noah's ark had spilled forth these human beings from another world. The dark-skinned, gamey village Gypsy, raised on the meat of fallen animals, is worlds apart from his city kin. Although, like poor relations, they are well aware of their city cousins' living like lords in Budapest or Paris, and know the greats of the profession by name, they remain free nomads who possess nothing but disdain for an orderly world and laws of any kind. They live by their own lights, cling to their superstitions more than to life itself, see illness, the devil and death in their blue moods—yet among them suicide is rare as a white crow. They live in bands, the better to bear their poverty. Their boys are educated by older women, girls by older men. They use wild herbs to heal themselves, like stray dogs.

Mr. Pistoli was a patron of village Gypsies. He spent his entire life among Gypsies, returning home only to calm the wife of the moment, tint his mustache, clip the bristles sprouting from his warts, rub pomade in his hair, toss creditors' letters into the trash, and off he was again, in search of the band. If a wife became a burden to him, he eased her out as best as he could and took on a new woman. This half-mad country squire was a leftover from the Hungary of old, where menfolk even in extreme old age refused to be incapacitated. He waltzed merrily with willing women, like a dance instructor giving an apprentice girl a whirl. His big buck teeth, protuberant bullish eyes, lowering, growling voice, oversized, meaty ears, calloused knuckles and pipe-stem legs altogether produced a peculiar effect on the females of the region. For there are still many women around who will kiss the spot where her man has hit her; who will put up with years of suffering to receive a kind word at the last hour; who will cut off her hair, pull out her teeth, put out her bright eyes, clench down her empty stomach, ignore her tormenting passion, say goodbye to springtime, beauty, life itself—if her man so commands. Pistoli went about growling like a wild boar, and women wiggled their toes at him, to tease the monster. Thus he lived to bury three wives.

"Let's go see the beast," quoth Pistoli to his Gypsies, solemnly convinced that Miss Maszkerádi had arrived at Bujdos solely for his sake. He had prepared and pocketed his infallible tools: the meerschaum cigar holder embellished with naked lovers embracing, the silver cigarette case chased with bathing beauties. He made sure to bring his trick penholder (its glass compartment a peep show of nude dancers), nor did he leave behind those lithographs guaranteed to make females flush and blush and fantasize. He brought a tiny cap to pull on his index finger for all kinds of silly puppet acts. So, having earlier soaked his feet and cleared his throat, Pistoli set out "to conquer the beast."

In rollicking good humor, a song tickling his palate, whistling, he roamed with the Gypsies like a bridegroom who had a bride waiting in each village. His unruly animal spirits resembled the moods of convicts on certain days, or that of inmates at the Nagykálló madhouse where he had once spent half a year. He had abducted his first wife from there, a silent queen as beautiful as memory itself. From under her boyish haircut she had sent him many tantalizing looks, a temptress clad in white linen. Her name was Izabella, unforgettable as the mediaeval princess whose image comes to the dying mercenary on the battlefield. Back then Pistoli would still grovel on his knees, his hair grew thick and fast, his mood was like a young bull's.

He would gladly creep under the bed at Izabella's behest. This romantic heroine remained his lifelong true love. When one day she hung herself, Pistoli swore beside her corpse he would soon follow her to the grave. That had been twenty years ago. Since then, Pistoli had gotten drunk, married, buried wives, slept in muddy ditches and flower beds, his memory had stored the scents of as many women as the nose of a dog in a metropolis; he had loved ladies' shoes, flouncy skirts, shirts and exposed napes; had danced attendance like a madman around barefoot servant girls and saintly matrons; had howled his love's name out on the street in front of houses lit by the red light; had night after night climbed through the window into rooms where he surmised a female might be sleeping; there came screams, alarums, gunshots and wild escapes from stake-toting retainers, followed by triumph on the morrow in the bed of a kitchen wench, after his face had been bloodied by jealous rivals: such had been his life...And when he at last found himself alone, like a condemned man in his cell, by the moonglow of a candle or the sooty flame of an oil lamp, he felt the funerary wrinkles of the pillow, the deafening silence after the revelry overwhelm him with a drowning sensation...Startled, frightened of imminent death, he felt Izabella's hand pulling him into the beyond. So he no longer slept at night, but only in daytime, near lit candles, surrounded by wardrobes, chests and drawers he had emptied. Snakes slithered past on the carpet and he felt like howling, but he was stopped by the memory of his former roommate, the colonel who would howl all day, confined in a straightjacket.

So this was the satyr Pistoli who rolled about in the Gypsies' laps, cackling so loudly that the crossroads, momentarily empty, resounded with the ghostly echo of his laughter. The mute trees stood somber, like gibbets awaiting some escaped criminal. Shadowy hedges, that must surely shelter Death stopping to write down the lottery numbers he dreams of, ominously pricked up their ears, as if waiting for Pistoli to leap, tired of laughter, over them at a single bound into the wild blue yonder. Roadside wells, so many taciturn accomplices, were passed one after another by the Gypsy-laden coach. Women had thrown themselves into these wells, women to whom Pistoli in his manic moods had irresponsibly promised the world, as nonchalantly as he pledged payments to creditors. The ladies had adored his extravagant promises, and became unhinged when none were kept. The wells in the fields, like passive abettors of the crime, persisted like so many monuments to monotonous existence. No inquest would ever hold them responsible. Meanwhile Pistoli needed constant giggles, nothing short of sheer raving manic glee, just to make it through the night, just to see another day. Once he rejoiced exceedingly when he broke a leg jumping from a window. He considered it a small payment on Izabella's account.

But let us go in the moonlit spring night, along with those dusky Gypsy lads, their silent melancholy instruments, the contrabass that had danced at silver jubilees, and let us leave the disappointed roadside trees behind, trees ever pining after wanderers, like so many deranged old women . . . yearning for a traveler who would stop to eat his supper under their shelter, drink a bottle of wine, sing the song dearest to his heart, then tie his belt on the sturdiest limb, to go into the long night undisturbed, in peace. (Pistoli had always detested, as much as he did the tomcat-whiskered, avuncular bailiff, each jutting branch of every tree spreading its boughs his way, offering a suitable occasion to carry out his long-standing resolve. He would much rather have looked at the bedsteads carved from these trees, and the women who sat up on the beds, forever waking, ever watchful, caressing and sheltering Pistoli while he battled the wraiths from the nether world that frequented his dreams.)

The ghostly company at last arrived at Bujdos-Hideaway.

"Let's have Miss Sonnet's songs," Pistoli commanded the

Gypsies, after they took their positions under the manor house window that shed blue light into the night. The oil lamp was lit under the holy icon, for the house had always belonged to those of Russian Orthodox faith, folks who were ever ready to sacrifice lamp oil and wick to implore the Holy Virgin's mercy for the miserable.

When the music struck up Eveline was reading a novel as usual, and, as usual, she was comparing the men she knew with some figure conjured up by the letters on the printed page. She loved these nocturnal hours, this removal from daily life, the stories of people whose lives and fates had been set down on paper... Perhaps someone had already written her story, too, some time ago. "Young Miss," the fortune-teller had once told her, "all your childhood dreams will be fulfilled. But you won't like it when these dreams come true." She dreamed of men who would gladly suffer for her, of a magnificent life as a woman of the world: theater, balls, entertainments, good horses, the independent life, country quietude alternating with the metropolitan buzz... passions, fine words, unforgettable days. Life had always fulfilled her desires as easily as a magician producing roses from a hat. And now here came a midnight serenade under her window, just as in the Spanish novels she was so fond of. The señora on the balcony, her caballero below.

Miss Maszkerádi grabbed a full-length fur coat and burst into Eveline's room, swearing.

"Did you call in these Gypsies?" she asked peremptorily. "I hate these fifth-rate village bands. You have no idea of the kind of music I love. I am a modern woman. I don't even remember the old-time favorites any more. Listen, I'm going to empty my revolver at them if they don't shut up."

"Be a good girl now," was Eveline's quiet response. "Your beau is here again."

"That provincial stumblebum! Phew! If he ever took off one of his boots I'd run away and never come back to this place!"

"It's Pistoli," Eveline explained, with some heat. "Don't you recognize he's playing your songs?"

"Oh, you precious thing!" Miss Maszkerádi's tone dripped venomous disdain. "If we were in the city, I'd set my servants on them for disturbing the peace. I was just starting to doze off, thanks to a triple dose of Adalin. And now this scoundrel shows up, with his Tartar manners, his insane nomads and their Asiatic instruments, and slaps me back into reality. We are in Hungary after all, in a godforsaken little village. We'll be lucky if the bastard leaves our windows intact. Why, last year he tossed stones into my bedroom. Why can't the gendarmerie lock up this wild beast?"

"Now try to be nice to him," said Eveline, with a certain amount of hostesslike solemnity, getting out of bed and pulling on some petticoats and silk-lined, lacquered slippers. She pinned up her long tresses and smoothed out her forehead. Forgetting the hairpin between her teeth, she pensively listened to the outdoor serenade.

"You better make sure right away it's Pistoli and not some highwaymen here to rob us under the guise of a midnight serenade," Miss Maszkerádi continued, red as a turkey and as furious.

"Nothing easier. Just open the window, shove the shutters aside, strike a match and ask the darkness outside whether it is Sir Pistoli, the excellent chevalier and most noble seigneur, whom we should thank for this exquisite midnight surprise."

Maszkerádi cursed on, like one of the Gypsies ...

"I'd rather die. I'd rather go blind than face this ragged old rattletrap."

Eveline snapped the red garter around her knees, and dug up a bulky and warm crimson house coat. She bustled about like a colorful pollen-laden moth above the midnight flowerbeds. Her face was fresh, determined and enterprising, like a traveler's who rose at dawn to set out for cities full of promise.

"I happen to be a local landowner. I can't afford to offend any of my neighbors, Malvina. So I ask you to please respect the customs of my house."

"I swear, I'll pour boiling water over that cur!" threatened Miss Maszkerádi. "I'd never known a more insolent character. Gets soused and that's his excuse for going around, molesting decent womenfolk . . . Don't you have gendarmes in these parts? Haven't you got watchdogs in your yard?"

"My dogs are as well acquainted with Mr. Pistoli, as doormen at the Orpheum with a spendthrift count. We can't help what's about to happen. Squire Pistoli is lord of the neighboring estates and must be entertained as a guest in the dining room until he feels like rolling on toward some other archipelago. You know, Malvina, we are dependent on each other in these isolated parts. No one comes this way, only the tax collector, and we do our united best to keep him permanently drunk."

Miss Maszkerádi shrugged, then tore open the window, although for a moment she entertained the notion that the wild squire might send a bullet her way from down below.

"Come on in, you wretched dipsomaniac!" she yelled into the darkness. "But you better shave off your beard first, because we'll glue it to the table with candlewax."

But Pistoli was not quite done with his preparations. He approached midnight serenades as solemnly and ceremoniously as a small-town quadrille organizer his duties. Have you ever seen a master of ceremonies at a quadrille willing to forego even one of the figures in the customary repertoire? The young misses and their partners are raring to go, their eager feet ready to dance the *csárdás* till dawn—while the pompous quadrille director leads, like Moses did the Jews, the entire company through a labyrinth of one elaborate old figure after another. Why, figure number six alone has thousands of tricky variants. (As for me, I was always happy just to be able to find my partner after all those artful dodges, and continue the kind of tantalizing conversation that used to be initiated during the quadrille by most young gentlemen of the better sort in the Hungary of old.)

Pistoli was a past master of the midnight serenade.

He knew every single dreamy melody that had ever been played beneath a shuttered window by a Gypsy band in Hungary. He was familiar with the Lake Balaton songs, the fantasias of Boka, Lavotta and Csermák; nor did he neglect the waltzes of József Konti. The ladies he had conquered through his serenades had instructed him thoroughly in what a woman likes to hear in a half-dreaming state. Last but not least came Mr. Pistoli's favorite song, the one that had so often served as overture as well, a nocturnal signature as it were, sent up toward those silent windows: "*Cloudy sky above the forest...*" This was the song Mr. Pistoli crooned, posted under the linden trees. He had a rather pleasant, resonant baritone; after all, in those days in the provinces one had to have some musical accomplishment to win over a woman's heart. When the song ended and the undertones of the contrabass had vanished into the night like the final note at a wedding, Pistoli, hat in hand, approached the window where the shutters had been thrown open. First of all, Eveline lit the customary match (much to Miss Maszkerádi's annoyance), then spoke a few words thanking the excellent gentleman for his thoughtfulness.

"I just wanted to pay my respects," Pistoli solemnly replied.

The manor house had a verandah that was still unused this early in spring. Upended garden chairs, wickerwork tables, flower stands, white stakes topped by iridescent glass globes, hammocks and swinging chairs lay heaped on this verandah, as if summer were in permanent exile. Eveline invited Mr. Pistoli and his musicians to step in here. A table was set right side up, and Eveline returned from the interior of her house with bottles of wine and glasses, while Miss Maszkerádi dragged forth a ham from the larder. The Gypsies received plum brandy, which they knocked down from a black jug in their corner, keeping track, on the sly, of how much slivovitz passed down each gullet. The garden candelabras lit up part of the courtyard. Sleepy servants peered out through windows and the huge hounds paced growling in the yard, forbidden to nip at the Gypsies' legs. Mr. Pistoli, swaggering and strutting between the two girls, asked them repeatedly how they were able to live without a man. Maszkerádi looked away; her writhing lips seemed to be uttering silent curses, while Eveline affably replied to her guest that until this day she had not thought of marrying, but from now on she would consider Mr. Pistoli's wise advice.

"To the best of my knowledge, thus far every woman in your splendid family has married," Mr. Pistoli somberly observed.

"I am the last surviving member of the family," said Eveline. "The last one to bear the name of Nyirjes de Nagynyirjes."

"Oh, that can be helped, as long as one stays on good terms with the king. You must know the ways and means, which axles to grease, and if you're not afraid to take some trouble, the honorable family name can be saved for posterity. For all of us, here in Northeastern Hungary, live for the sake of history. After us there will be no more Hungarians of the ancient sort, our kind. Our morality, our customs, the noble traits of our lineage will be extinct. Hungary, as we know it, will not be here much longer. The newfangled, modern types will displace us from the land of our ancestors. This is why I feel so sad on account of every unmarried Hungarian maiden. Children, more and more children must be born to Hungarian women, to ensure the survival of our kind."

Pistoli declaimed his words in the form of a toast. He clinked glasses with the girls, and waited, expecting to be contradicted, but the two young ladies preferred to remain silent. Miss Maszkerádi, eyes downcast under long eyelashes, patiently held her peace, although the visitor's eyes did not leave her for one second.

"I happen to be a widower...And a widower is a wretched man. In his cold bed what can he do but remember the way it used to be, under the former dispensation. Everything in his house reminds the miserable widower of woman's almightiness, her splendor and her joy of life—and this after he'd just about learned how to make a woman happy. A widower never beats his new wife, for he knows all too well how much that hurts. If he gets irate, he takes out his anger on the pipe stem, for memories wafting from the graveyard make him forgiving amidst the troubles of this world. All day long the widower stays silent like a snail in its house. Twirling his mustache, brushing his boots, inspecting his pockmarks in the mirror, he winks an eye, like the wise man he is, not wanting to catch his servants in the act of stealing. After a bad night, a widower, at the very most, might scold his boots. Otherwise his face is wrapped in a perpetual smile, like an actor's, while he keeps his clenched fists out of sight under his vest. Nor does he intend to flourish them ever again after the funeral. He'll hold his peace forever now, silently wagging his head over the transience of this world, and he feels unspeakable contempt for those men who, desperate to sound cheerful, are constantly boasting, praising the graciousness of their deceased wives. Every girl worth her salt ought to marry a widower, for he will appreciate her, spoil and pamper her, be as gentle with her as one taming a wild dove."

Miss Maszkerádi swallowed as lightly as a dreamer, wary lest her lovely dream fade.

"Just what I need," she breathed, raising her eyelashes, the blade of her knife-sharp glance flashing against Mr. Pistoli's white vest.

"Life," Pistoli went on, in rather measured accents, weighty, halting, like a wise old county magistrate, "life is no joke, my dear young lady (who could be my daughter). For the farsighted, the folks in the know, life is a deer park, where gentle breezes and fragrant grape leaves keep you company, complete with afternoon foot-soakings, peaceful snoozes, fine hounds and desirable wenches, the hell with all care; a long life, a nice pipe from time to time, mellow dinners: that's the way to spend life, life that digs your grave even now, steadfastly, like the ever-burrowing mole. To want nothing, and ask only for peace and quiet. Hope for nothing besides fair weather on the morrow. Trust no one, believe no one, think no extraordinary thoughts, just live, live, and love; fall asleep, and wake up healthy... Wear comfy slippers and pass the night in a feather bed. Live out a happy and long old age, the best part of life. To get an honest night's sleep, and then a snooze after lunch, let out a few whoops, fight and make up. Will you marry me, you glorious rosebud?"

He reached out and took Miss Maszkerádi by the arm.

The stern young lady did not resist. Dreaming, she sat on, only her eyelashes glowed, darkling as spent stars. When she spoke, it was almost as if she were talking to herself:

"Life is a great masked ball, my good sir," she spoke musingly, as if picking her words from somewhere afar. "I can't really tell: are you actually asking for my hand?"

Pistoli did not wish to rush matters, for he had learned around women that a judiciously even and sedate comportment always works better than rash, impulsive behavior. Enjoying his moment in the limelight, he took his time stuffing his small pipe. After a prolonged and painful sigh he motioned at the Gypsy band to step forth and play his favorite song. Hearing this tune, his eyes bulged like old maids crowding in a window. His foot, tapping, created a racket like ghosts riding roughshod under the table. He raised both hands repeatedly, a paterfamilias trying for a moment's quiet among unruly offspring. Finally he slammed his fist on the tabletop like a highwayman. The Gypsies ceased. Pistoli's head swung left and right a few more times.

"My life...is at your disposal," he said, in a husky voice. "I'm ready to jump from any church steeple at the crack of dawn, if that happens to be your wish."

"Then you really love me? When nobody loved me till now," Miss Maszkerádi murmured.

"I'm past the midpoint of my life, I've eaten the better part of my bread, like they say, and I've never loved anyone but you," was Mr. Pistoli's solemn reply.

"But Mr. Pistoli!" exclaimed Eveline.

"Let's stop fooling around. Miss Eveline, I'm here to betroth the young lady, your guest. I beg you to give her to me in marriage."

Mr. Pistoli, having said this, lowered himself onto one knee, much to the amusement of the ladies of Hideaway. The Gypsies underscored this with a tremolo flourish of strings, meanwhile nearly smashing the sides of the contrabass, whereupon the dogs began to howl, waking the haystack-embedded watchman, who was already approaching at a run.

"I am in love like a common vagabond. I implore you to forgive me." Mr. Pistoli turned clasped hands toward Eveline.

"Let's not get all mushy," Miss Maszkerádi interjected dryly. "In this house it's always Eveline who winds up the musical clock to play the tune from grandma's time. I happen to be a seriously world-weary woman, my fine young man. Let's talk turkey now, like traveling salesmen in the waiting room at the train station. What will you give me if I marry you?"

Pistoli dusted off his knee. In his frustration he gave a twist to his thick mustache like a pork butcher left holding the knife while the squealing pig runs off. Women he very much preferred to address in theatrical tones like a wandering comedian, ranting and raving, "slain," only to move on, without wasting one serious word all his life. As a rule he bestowed his favors on women only as long as they believed his lies. Like lunatics, these women stared goggle-eyed, nostrils flaring and quivering, ears pricked up at his never-before-heard avowals, and gazed out through the window in a prolonged brown study. Yes, Mr. Pistoli's favorites were women prone to hysteria, whom he would sniff out seven counties off. He would rub his hands together in ecstasy hearing news of a woman who had had her hair shorn because she fancied it singed her shoulders. He capered like a billy goat when a woman confessed to him that she had swallowed her child. And he was utterly elated meeting a young wife at Munkács, who confided in a whisper that ever since her chin sprouted a man's beard she's been afraid to look in a mirror. He dealt with these women like a lion tamer, and packed up as soon as he tired of the fun.

"What will I give you?" he mumbled and surveyed the scene. "First of all, I give my name, which only locals mispronounce the way they do, as Pistol. It is an ancient Florentine name brought by my ancestors to the court of Louis the Great. In these northeastern parts a noble coat of arms still means something. The closed crown above the shield carries some weight in these parts. Mine contains pelicans, seven of them, the mother feeding her brood with her own blood. For the Pistolis were always known for self-sacrifice."

"As for me, I'm a freethinker," replied Miss Maszkerádi. "Let me repeat, in this house Eveline is the one who respects all those ne'er-do-well, windbag forefathers, dropped from peasant wenches' wombs, or all those granddams that lay down with every drunken retainer or purring pageboy. I live by myself and for myself, like a tree, alone in a field. I've always been proud of being companionless. But let's drink, my good Mr. Suitor, for all this talk gives me the dry mouth."

Maszkerádi grasped the goblet, kicked away her chair in the manner of a traveling circus equestrienne, and leaning close to Mr. Pistoli, locked the winsome twin blades of her eyes into his. Draining her glass, she tossed it into the garden among the shrubs.

"Let no one else ever drink from it again. For I drank your health, Mr. Pistoli."

"I won't mind if you call me Pistol, like the women around here," said the overjoyed gentleman, rollicking with laughter. "I can already see that you don't wear tin pants like the feminists."

"No sir, mine are lacy and dainty, fit for any man's eyes," was Maszkerádi's rapid riposte.

She pulled up her fur coat a ways. Her two shanks reminded him of the forelegs on the noblest breed of rat-catching terrier. Her two feet pointed straight forward, clad in diminutive fur-lined slippers. Her black stockings stretched taut like youthful desire. There was a flash of lacy underpants that made Mr. Pistoli snatch away his gaze, as if he'd looked at the sun.

"Not so fast," he growled, all sly reticence, "there's nothing wrong with flannel underwear, either. Those were the days, when women stayed hale and fair in flannel."

"Why then, take my word for it, Eveline's the one for you, my good sir," warbled Maszkerádi, oriolelike. "That esteemed young lady still wears linen purchased by grandma from the itinerant Uplands cambric vendor."

Eveline's soft laughter resembled a gentle breeze in a tree's swaying boughs.

"And my heart is calm, not crazy like yours."

"A crazy heart!" shouted Pistoli, forgetting himself. "That's what I've been looking for. Wandered and roamed all over the world, to find a crazy heart at last, the right one for me. For you'll find me a jolly old soul. And my house merry as if the devil himself'd got into it. I don't keep sad servants, nor receive melancholy women. In my household all must be bright and merry, for nothing lasts forever, least of all life. My watchdogs know the craziest routines, just like clowns in the circus. My chairs might have three legs and when the beds collapse, the cellar echoes the crash. The armoires have a way of toppling on visitors. And my mynah bird knows how to swear like no one else in Hungary. My big stoves resound with laughter and all the walls are covered with illustrations from the funny papers. The one thing I've learned at the madhouse is that you mustn't be depressed. Because depressed people are capable of clawing out each other's eyes."

Elbows on table, chin propped up, Miss Maszkerádi listened to Pistoli wide-eyed, like a customer to a sales pitch.

"So what else have you got in that wonderful house of yours?"

"Peace and quiet. For I never open an envelope, be it letter or telegram. If anyone has any business with me, they can drop by. I read no papers, save for *The Country Tattler*, because from conversations on the train or in the tavern I can catch up on the news of the world. But when the circus or a theater troupe visits Munkács or Patak, you'll find me in the first row and I like to send flowers to the leading lady so she'll think I'm crazy about her. Miss, you'll just have to get used to my treating all women as if they were past or future lovers. So you mustn't ever be jealous, for I've had occasion to observe in the madhouse how jealousy can make people bite each other's nose off."

"So how would we live together?"

"Like musicians. In the morning it's up to me to devise some prank, while at night it'll be your turn to think of something to make my belly shake with laughter, for that's absolutely essential for good digestion. We'll consume abundant dinners, I'll prepare the salads myself. On holidays I'll cook a leg of mutton in white wine and cognac. You won't have a care in the world, other than making sure my bed is nice and soft, with a warm brick always nearby in case my feet get cold, and an ample supply of bicarbonate of soda on the night table, for I take no other medicine. Thus far I've managed to be sultan in my own home. I've always required that my wife take on the form, manners, nature, body and clothes of a different woman each day. But henceforth I am prepared to be a slave—your very own slave."

Maszkerádi nodded enthusiastically.

"I bet this sort of talk made those crazy women keel right over!"

"Yes..." replied Pistoli softly. "They believed every last word, because I always made sure to look them in the eye."

"Well, look me in the eye and let's clink glasses."

After a little while Messer Pistoli had to inquire:

"Tell me, what kind of wine is this, it's like kisses on the throat..."

"It happens to be a five-year-old vintage from Badacsony, my fine young man. I always drink it here at Bujdos, where no one else drinks wine."

Pistoli now rose and his unknowing, obstinate, walnut-sized eyes scanned the two ladies as if appraising the effect his words would produce.

"I empty this cup..." he began, as if his words were awaited by the entire county assembled with bated breath, "here's to the dove-hearted mistress of the house, her saintliness Miss Eveline Nyirjes de Nagynyirjes, whose hands shower on this miserable Hungarian countryside blessings as abundant as the lily's pollen. I drain this cup to this sad island-dotted land's snow-white egret whose return softens the barren soil of local hearts, like springtime rain quickening the hard crust of the field..."

"Watch it, Eveline, next he'll have us cosign a loan," Miss Maszkerádi stage-whispered in her friend's ear.

Eveline patiently lowered her eyelids.

"Well, if we must..."

"Don't worry, I'll free you of this Freddy the Freeloader, once and for all. Just have a small cask of my wine rolled up from the cellar."

Hearing the rest of Pistoli's toast, Eveline had to blush and avert her eyes, for it teemed with allusions to her parents and uncles of blessed memory, "friends after my heart," the good old times, the patriotic duties of Hungarian women, local flood control and love shod in white silk slippers—at which point Pistoli flourished his handkerchief embroidered with the ducal crown to dab his eyes while his voice tremolo'd village cantor style; in short, he played the entire repertoire of the provincial orator, the perennial toastmaster at funeral, wake, or wedding feast—whenever wine loosens the tongue, and heated fantasy fondles tomorrow's hopes. In Hungary each country gentleman is a Cicero. For centuries Hungarians have been channeling their superfluous energy into flowery toasts, touching indeed, enough to make you cry, were it not for the subsequent thrashing and highway robbery that so often befalls the very person extolled by these toasts.

Eveline, slightly sniffling in the manner of a grande dame, deigned to clink wine goblets (and maybe even believed one or two of these avowals, since the good man leaned so heavily on the table). Then she excused herself and vanished into some other part of the house.

Miss Maszkerádi now gave her guest a glance such as a white-clad temptress that haunts back alleys might bestow on a troubled wanderer.

"And tell me my young man, what sacrifice might you be willing to make for my sake?"

"I'd jump from a tower..."

"Drop the tired clichés. What I want to know is: could you, full of love and trust and faith, lie yourself down in a casket, as Álmos-Dreamer did for Eveline? You know, us women are children and like to envy those sisters for whom men make great sacrifices."

"Upon my sacred word of honor..."

"And would you be able to drink my health till daybreak, match me drink for drink, and then not be ashamed to walk stark naked down the marketplace like some poor raggedy vagabond who'd been chucked out of the whorehouse without a stitch on?"

"You're asking a lot."

"Could you look into my eyes all night and next morning put everything up for sale, let it all go, everything you possess? Your respectability, your reputation, your manhood, let it all vanish like smoke? Be the village fool, the joke of the county, laughingstock of the nation, just because your jealous lover Malvina Maszkerádi asked you to? Just because she wished to destroy you for other women, the way you'd smash an Alt Wien cup, so they'd never again fool around with the man she's made her own. Never again would a sly, lustful strumpet stretch her claws toward my man. He would be nobody's, like the raggedi-est contrabass player in the land—except mine and mine alone. Would you be able to do that for me, my Prince Bluebeard?"

"At the madhouse people sometimes played pranks on each other. One postal official barked from morning to night, just like a *kuvasz*, and justified it as an attempt to get a rise out of the constantly shrieking colonel. You wouldn't be laying some kind of trap for me, would you, lady of my heart?" inquired Mr. Pistoli, who thought he had long ago done with probing feminine mysteries. Shivering, he buttoned up his vest and yelled to rouse the slumbering Gypsy band. "Give me 'Down the Street in Pápa Town!'" he commanded, and continued to gaze attentively at Miss Maszkerádi.

The Gypsies played softly, as if accompanying a dead colleague to the cemetery.

"I've decided to do away with you," announced Miss Maszkerádi's cold voice, even as her eyes wormed their way under Mr. Pistoli's vest like an exotic dancer's snake. "I'll rid this region of your obnoxious personage and moral contagion! Why, in these parts one finds mostly fine, upright folks, just like in Crimea. On name days and anniversaries people like to hug and kiss, as if this watery region lay somewhere in Russia, if you will. Wide-eyed women, their willpower as fragile as birch twigs, undefended and defenseless, inhabit this land alongside melancholy, fraternal men ready to forget any let-down if you give them a single friendly word. I believe you are the one and only outlaw running loose around here, wily as a serpent and cunning as only the most venomous troublemaker can be. Have you ever in your life gone for the kill? Ever smash a goblet, stone sober, over somebody's head? Ever kiss a red-hot stove, if that's what you felt like? Here among men who weep when they fight, weep when they're merry, and weep when they make love, you stick out as the frosty-footed rat that you are, in spite of all your masquerading. What we have here is a sober rake who never blurts out what he thinks. A coldhearted tor-turer who watches with quiet satisfaction when his *pálinka*-soaked Gypsies go up in flames. A tigerish, bloody-handed man capable of ripping off a woman's breasts, who privately judges each woman to be nothing but a whore. A tin cup that cares not a whit whether wine or blood is poured into it. A foul-mouthed, disgraceful bag of filth with a jailbird's opinion of womankind."

Pistoli's smile was as broad as if he'd been listening to houris warbling for his ears alone.

"Around here, every woman's been my lover," he said calmly.

"Me too?"

"Not yet, but you will be, by dawn."

Maszkerádi shrugged.

"Perhaps."

Now two elderly servitors appeared, rolling a small cask the size of a baby hippo onto the verandah. Hats held in hand, heads bared, they looked like Prince Rákóczi's faithful serfs. They poured wine into a floral-ornamented jug, then sound-lessly exited as if they were going straight to their rest in the nether world.

"I happen to know you well, Miss," Mr. Pistoli began, his hands rising to his temples as if to put his thoughts in order. "You are the most proud and arrogant woman I have ever known. You would like to crush me underfoot like a maggot. And you're perfectly right. I am the most worthless man in Hungary... So now you think you'll get me drunk and humiliate me. Roll me in tar and feathers and send my carrion back to town on the meat wagon."

"That's exactly what I intend to do," Miss Maszkerádi replied, her lips pressed together.

"Maybe so. But to me, you're worth it. So, let's drink up this devilish wine of yours."

"Sip it, don't swill it, buddy... You're drinking my special reserve. Hegyalja's best Tokay. It comes from a hillside the sun likes to make love to."

Miss Maszkerádi bumped hers against his, almost smashing the goblet.

"I detest your eyes, they drive me crazy." Her voice was a low murmur. "They're full of shadow women whose hearts you've laid to waste, devoured, torn apart. I see them, the blondes, naive and innocent, the silly brunettes, sloe-eyed and birdbrained, the sanctimonious faces of sensuous hefty ones, the Slovak Virgin Marys and the doghaired, rough-and-tumble Hunnish descendants of The Birches. I can see my sisters clutched in your executioner's grip, and then, after a kick from your brutal, shapeless boot, chanting prayers in the iron-barred nave of the prison church, or in the madhouse, wrapped in wet blankets, wildly craving death and suicide; or else solitary, sleepless companions of the moon, who consult fortune-teller's cards. Yes, I can see how you turned them into witches, wild beasts with scraggly hair, foaming at the mouth. You are a tremendous scoundrel, Pistoli—but I love you."

Pistoli placed his hand on the girl's shoulder.

"I'll tell you something that I would never admit to the pretentious, stay-at-home, down-at-the-heel squirelings around here. My ancestors happened to be mercenaries. And me too, I'm just another vagrant soldier of fortune who happened to pick this region for his theater of operations. I love no one. I could howl in pain and joy, for I am a solitary, I make no confessions or concessions, walk through life stubbornly alone, need no one's friendship, scorn anyone's hatred; shoulders back, chest out, I am all alone. The most they can take from me is my life...And madam, I sense that you, too, are proud of being able to be alone for long periods, and often."

"Always..." The word escaped Miss Maszkerádi's mouth, in spite of herself. She quickly regretted it, for she went on: "What business can you have with me when I refuse even to tread on you, when I avoid you like a dead cur lying belly up in a ditch..."

But Pistoli pretended not to have heard the young lady's razor-edged words. He merely hummed and nodded at his wineglass:

"I drink wine to find my friends. They're all here. My youth, my courage, my skepticism and superstitions. They're all right here, everyone I've ever loved and hated. All those dear faces look at me from the glass of wine. They beg for mercy, but I still drink them up. Here they are, the women who went insane and now wait in the madhouse for the chance to steal a knife to plunge into their hearts—or mine. They stare at me, and call me, and promise me everything. My three crazy wives. One lies abed all day and her hair is shorn as short as a boy's. She has no gray hairs—the hair of the insane does not turn gray. Her eyes never leave the window, she waits for my face to appear. She just lies there and never opens her mouth to speak, like an angel in eternity, the angel that carries omniscience in her apron. I become dazed, as if I gazed at a distant star, whenever I think of her. Whatever became of her, where did she go? For she never comes back to haunt.

"My second wife was unfaithful, that's why I had her put away. I couldn't stand to hear every skinny, ragged bird of passage bragging aloud about my wife's indiscretions. Yes, one of them happened to pick me as his confidant. Well, I let'im have it, madam, and beat him up good and proper, like a shepherd beats his donkey. These two fists slammed his head and face and eyes, so that my knuckles just about cracked. (I think I loved this woman best of all, although I'd be hard put to recall her name now...) Then I went home and wept and howled for mercy and shuddered with the ague when I lay down next to my wife. If she'd been nice to me then, I think I would have forgotten and forgiven her everything, destroyed the very memory, like an anonymous letter.

"But she persisted in her vile, cold, sinful, brazen ways. So I resolved to pay her back in kind, and wrenched her from my heart, as you would uproot a sapling from the soil. For I am a heathen...I've had my share of suffering, the rain and the cold, I whistled in my misery and hopped around on one foot. Yes, I've contemplated the deepest, yawning wells and I've dug up old bones in the graveyard in the dead of night to tell my troubles to when my torments got so bad I was afraid that if I started to howl, no human power could make me stop. She had betrayed me...I would crow and run around in crazy circles like a rooster when the barn's on fire. My left hand had to grab my right wrist to stop it from reaching for the knife. I had to be rid of her, at any cost. So now she, too, is at the Nagykálló insane asylum, and if her shadow came back to haunt me, I'd shoot it."

Maszkerádi, saucer-eyed, heard out the squire's say, as if the turbulent ice-drift of his words carried a smoldering lava flow in its wake. She was well aware she was playing with a deadly trap, yet she could not keep her fingers away from the steel jaws. What was the secret of this crass and fatuous man that drove women insane? A drawn-out train whistle sounded somewhere in the great depths of the night beyond the hills, like life itself fading into the distance. Her imagination evoked the grim building, its saltpeter-stained yard-thick walls and arcades sequestering those women whose heads, bent like sad cypresses, brooded over this man—hale, sanguine, and filled with cruel intent—who sat facing her. Those great bulging eyes fixed her with the hypnotic gaze of an animal tamer. Perhaps it would be a good idea to summon Eveline...But she was probably absorbed in a romantic novel like a somnambulist. The tipsy Gypsies frolicked in the dark, like so many executioner's assistants. They wrestled the dead-drunk contrabassist to the ground, straddled him across the face and belly, and watered him in his besotted state. Like ghost images of an otherwordly night, these village Gypsies milled about in the pitch-black yard. Pistoli's calm and forceful voice called out from time to time, as if they were rambunctious dogs: "Down, boys, down."

Whereupon they toppled over, squatted or lay down, assuming the shapes of frogs or beggars kneeling by the roadside. They lay low in the shade of midnight's sooty fireplace.

"And what about the third one?" asked Maszkerádi.

Mr. Pistoli took a tremendous swig from the jug, as if putting out an underground fire. It took him a moment to regain his breath. He looked around, dazed.

"This Tokay wine is the best painkiller. It turns you into a veritable Hindu fakir. Even if a woman's knitting needle penetrated my heart, the wound wouldn't bleed."

"Drink up, Pistoli, if you're drunk I won't feel ashamed listening to your obscenities. You're allowed to do certain things when you're drunk. Yesterday you would have disgusted me, but today the weather's different...Spring nights can be strange and unpredictable. They make you think we have something in common with the stars." With that, Miss Maszkerádi pushed a newly-filled jug at her inebriated companion.

"Ah, the third one: she loved me so much. She was called Mishlik, but she might have had some other name as well. Once I had a dog I called Mishlik...Anyway, her eyebrows grew together, thick and uninterrupted like somber memory itself. Her face was unapproachably severe, like a façade with shuttered windows, where no crimson-clad girls ever lean out over the windowsill. Her mouth was always pressed into a thin line. It was a well in a castle keep that had run dry forevermore. Her chin was as sharp as a nun's knee. Her mania was trying to choke me in my sleep, night after night. She said she loved tranquility, and meanwhile the slow caresses of her pliant, cool, delicate fingers would insidiously, barely perceptibly turn into a choking death grip around my throat. It was like a serpent winding around my windpipe. I had to jump up and run. But she was powerful, lithe and limber. She would wrap her arms and legs around me, and press her lips against mine in a fatal kiss. Her mouth was like a vampire's. Her kisses left crimson spots all over my body, like the sting of nettles. She kept her eyes closed, so I wouldn't see the fires scorching her within. Maybe she was worried she'd frighten me away. Wordlessly, without a sound, she loved me to death. Poor thing, probably she had no inkling that she was out to kill me. Yes, I was definitely afraid of Mishlik. I started staying away from home at night, for I soon noticed that her courage renewed in the dark. If I beat her, it was like hitting a rubber ball. Her footfall was so soft that I never heard her stepping behind my back. She would sit, motionless, and calmly gaze off into the distance. Oh, how often and how bitterly I regretted marrying this madwoman from the Uplands!

"My sleep came to resemble the groaning of a ghost in a lonely windmill. I tossed and turned like the damned. Each creak of the door woke me, as if I were a prisoner awaiting death. My health, my hearty appetite and carefree moods evaporated. Why, even my Gypsies gave me a scare when they insisted on sending me home toward dawn. Perhaps they, too, were in Mishlik's service, like those great big maple trees whispering in the night, the sight of which always made me swallow hard. Trees to hang yourself from . . . I spent most of my time in the company of a blind piano player who was never sleepy, and was forever drunk, somber and black, and kept playing funeral marches for days on end. I dubbed myself 'Don Sebastian', and on the highway always scrutinized the stately black horses pulling the hearse toward the cemetery.

"One night it occurred to me to go and check on Mishlik. At least I could do away with her, if I found her cheating on me.

"I rapped on her windowpane at midnight, softly cajoling, as in the old days when the tapping of my ringed finger was well-known to the daughters of each and every house in this wetlands region.

" 'Who is it?' Mishlik called out.

" 'Don Sebastian,' I replied, in a changed voice. But there was no way of fooling Mishlik.

" 'I'll bring the key to the front door,' she said from behind the shutters, without the least surprise, as if all I ever did was drop in at midnight.

"We had funny weather that night. The wind lashed the chimneys, howling like a hound in a cemetery that comes across strange dogs digging up the graves.

"I huddled near the front door, wrapped in my overcoat, as if to hide my bones, my white shanks. I felt a light-headed wish for death to ruffle my hair, like the giddy rush of passion you feel walking past a former lover's garden on a spring night. If I were to die here, to be found by women like a soldier at his post ... I stood and waited like an unlucky gambler scrutinizing his cards. Indeed, what would this night bring?

"Mishlik opened the gate.

"She looked at me without a word. She didn't seem to be amazed or gladdened by my midnight homecoming. As a matter of fact, her face was usually as expressionless as a snake's. You never knew what went on inside her head. The rare times when she spoke always made me glad, because she never lied.

"The dining room was lit up. I did not like the idea of Mishlik awake at night. Who knows what she might be scheming, staying up till dawn? Women should always have something to keep them busy. Nursing the baby, doing the wash, or going to sleep. If they stay awake, with nothing to do, it can only mean trouble.

"I asked her: 'Why aren't you asleep?'

"She flipped her hand.

"'I knew you'd be coming home. I knew you'd get tired of your painted women, and return hungry for the touch of your wife's clean hands. Here, let me massage you. I'll knead you like bread dough.'

"I might mention here that I always loved to have my wives rub my back, my legs, my gouty knee. Sooner or later every man worth his salt develops gout. Past a certain age taking care of one's health becomes as important as making love. So I expected any woman who loved me to find the aching parts of my body, and rub and pinch them with her rose-hip fingers. Then I could fall asleep like a tomcat whose neck is caressed. But Mishlik had something else in mind. And I abhorred being choked.

"I threw off my coat and stepped into the dining room.

"Good God! I'll never forget that sight!

"There they sat at the table, my two former wives, the ones I'd thought were at the insane asylum. Sitting at the head of the table was my first wife, Sári, her hair shorn, her demented eyes enormous, and reeking of *pálinka* brandy. Now she was sipping a sweet liqueur and chose to ignore me.

"My other wife, Mári, laid her head on the table, as if she'd just returned exhausted from a long journey. Lord, how fat she'd grown, her belly as big as if she were expecting a child... Her face was so sad and wasted that I could not harbor any anger against her.

"'Won't you sit down with your wives,' said Mishlik, who also took a chair at the table, and crossed her arms across her chest like some magistrate.

" 'What's going on here?' I shouted. 'How did these poor wretches get here?'

" 'They came to see you one last time,' Mishlik replied.

"My first impulse was to jump for the door, and Mishlik smiled quietly at my useless exertions. She had already pocketed the key."

Pistoli paused, grabbed the wine jug, and imbibed such a draft that his gullet nearly burst. Maszkerádi could only look on goggle-eyed at the stout man's astounding prowess.

"So what did the madwomen do? Why didn't they claw out your eyes?" she murmured.

"They demanded their conjugal rights," Pistoli replied, and paused, his unblinking eyes fixed on the tabletop. "You are a lady of breeding and refinement, so I shall say no more.

"But, as you can see, I survived, although they could have killed me just as easily. The three of them could have torn me apart. But they turned out to be manageable.

"I caressed them, soothed them, calmed them down. In the morning I had all three of them carted to the Nagykálló asylum. And that's where they've been ever since. But each night I check under the bed before I climb in. In dark alleys I always look behind my back. To this day any sudden, loud cackle still startles me. And I hate to look the moon in the eye. For I am Pistoli, the local maniac. Do you love me?"

"Drink up," Maszkerádi replied. "Drink so you won't remember a thing, so you'll forget me, this night, springtime . . ."

As if drawn by a ghost, she rose and set out toward the garden that sprawled, moist and lurking, around the house. She kept stopping and looking back.

Pistoli, red-faced, rolled his eyes left and right in contentment. He let Miss Maszkerádi wend her way toward the garden alone. He raised the empty pitcher to his mouth and blared laughter into it as into a horn. His fists pummeled the tabletop, he danced seated in his chair. He ruffled his hair. And Maszkerádi waited in vain, watching him from the garden. This unaccountable man refused to stand up, and go after the confused young woman.

Pistoli downed another mouthful or two of wine; then, like a whirling ghost, he ran out and, together with his Gypsies, vanished into the night.

A melancholy day dawned on the manor at Bujdos.

Miss Maszkerádi never said a word about the events of the night.

5. OUR LADY'S FOUNTAIN

The WILD duck quacked in the reeds.

It was springtime; day by day more of them returned to the land, more of those invisible beings from their far-flung wanderings, the ones who come again to teach the long-stemmed grass by the ditch to hum and sing, who play with insects that crawl forth from the soil, the creatures that swing on bare birch twigs and screech at the highway traveler.

It is these invisible hands that flap the white blouses women set out to dry in the meadow; they also dig quick runnels for spring freshets, squat in a ditch to teach frogs diverse *cochonneries*, grab ahold of the cows' tails and flick a light fillip across the snoozing shepherd's face under his tilted hat. They rip moss from the manor house's eaves, ascend like so many bubbles in the ancient drainpipe's dark bowels to emerge near the chimney, on which they plop down and sit, swinging their legs. They slap young wives on the back, pinch the rooster's spur, feed the hounds baneful weeds to make them run around all day. They are mischievous kobolds, smoke rings, balls of air in sunlight; in a drizzle they flatten themselves under leaves, squeeze behind the bedstead, crouch on the threshold, hide in the back of the cart, tangle, like invisible bats, in the peasant's matted hair, latch onto his wife's chemise and tug his daughter's pigtails. You might call them breezes that arise in the raspberry patch, or warm drops of rain beating against the windowpane so loudly that they wake the dreamer. They pick on the graybeard, press his head into the straw, and ride his neck with legs flung apart. And they chivy young men as if they were starlings.

In pouring rain or curtain-tugging sunshine life went on in its customary monotonous rounds at the old manor house of Hideaway. Eveline found a trunkful of old novels in the attic, books read by her grandmother in the last century. The faded green volumes exuded an air of romanticism dear to her heart. Jósika, Dumas, Sue, a Rocambole... Oh, why wasn't it winter again, with the snap and crackle of large logs in the fireplace to accompany her reading! As for Miss Maszkerádi, she stopped at times by the carved gatepost and pensively surveyed the landscape. Had she caught a glimpse of Mr. Pistoli, that worthy joker would not have gotten away unpunished.

Andor Álmos-Dreamer, being the romantic bachelor that he was, had naturally stayed away from the Bujdos manor ever since Miss Maszkerádi had been in residence.

Each human life possesses certain sensitivities, dove-pecked injuries, that are never noted by the casual observer, like invisible cracks in amber.

Words uttered unthinkingly, absentminded glances, careless gestures on the part of our fellow humans, somehow manage to avoid the wise or cynical man, bouncing off his outer wrappings, whereas they seem to follow in the tracks of other people, seeking them out from afar, like cats do certain women. You may be in the company of a certain lady, promenading or sitting in a garden, or even aboard a ship, in a reverie—not a cat in sight within miles—yet after a while you suddenly notice a feline lying at your lady's feet, grooming itself. Where this cat came from, you'll never know. Yet there it is, having sensed the presence of that certain woman who will appreciate it.

It's the same way with words and other phenomena in life.

Miss Maszkerádi, about two years previously, in the course of a conversation had pronounced the word *kronchi*, meaning "crown" in the argot of Budapest. Andor Álmos-Dreamer, who happened to be present, immediately smelled a rat. Not much later Miss Maszkerádi in the same Bujdos manor house referred to certain "provincial hicks" in such a scornful manner that Andor Álmos-Dreamer nearly lost his temper. Yet Miss Maszkerádi was merely following the current fashion among the educated upper classes of using Budapest street slang. It was cool to flaunt your knowledge of thieves' jargon. Another passing vogue, just like that summer when every Budapest lady carried her hat in her hand. Álmos-Dreamer, romantic bachelor that he was, naturally believed the epithet "provincial hick" to refer to himself. He said not a word about his being offended, he simply stayed away from the house. Miss Maszkerádi was too proud, and Eveline too naive, to inquire about the cause of Mr. Álmos-Dreamer's withdrawal. The next year, when Miss Maszkerádi again sojourned with Eveline at Bujdos, it was accepted that the bachelor would stay away from the house for the duration. There are certain doors that open only from the inside. Such was the door that Andor Álmos-Dreamer's sensitive nature made him lock himself behind. He was the kind of country gentleman who is as touchy as a gouty heel. (As opposed to the kind of provincial whom nothing can offend, and who loudly, eagerly devours life, ever ready to quarrel, make up, fight again and hold a grudge, then love, only to forget everything on the morrow and resume gobbling life again at the very same table to which his beard had been so cruelly stuck with candle wax the night before.)

So what sort of ideas does such a romantic soul entertain when the wild duck begins to quack in the reeds and every night he dreams of Eveline?

One overcast afternoon, when the house became as stuffy with pipe smoke as if every one of his forefathers had clambered down from the framed portraits to light up, and antique medals, Maria Theresa thalers and Roman coins failed to keep him entertained; when pacing back and forth with arms behind his back became as dreary as the endless rainfall, and he found himself sending up a surprisingly prolonged sigh, as if some great sorrow had scurried just then through the door, to hide quickly under the old raincoats only to shamble forth in the night and crouch by the sleeper's bedside like a silent old man...On such an afternoon Andor Álmos-Dreamer visited his former lover, Madame Risoulette, to confide in her all his troubles and heartaches.

Risoulette, too, lived in the wet lowlands, in a château that had been a Franciscan monastery once upon a time. Tiny white windows gave on the arcaded corridors, and in the circular courtyard the poplars soared high above the roof. It was a clean and cloistered environment, redolent with the scent of innocence and resonant with the chimes of a musical clockwork. Risoulette's husband, a retired captain, suffered from gout, and surrounded his aching limbs with barometers and weather glasses. For him the two questions in life were: what's the weather like, and what's for dinner. He cared not a whit about anything else. Over the years Risoulette had been the sweetheart of every worthy man in the neighborhood. And each believed she would never forget him, for she was able to recall each amorous date, each momentous hour, the very dress she had worn on the day in question, and what's more, even the words that passed, only to eventually crumble into dust. The lady had a remarkable memory, she never mistook one man for another. And she never embarrassed them by letting on that afterwards she had given herself to another. Each and every man parted from her sure of possessing her heart forever after, certain that from then on Risoulette would be lost in tearful reveries...And each man knew her by a different name. Whether out of superstition or because of the novelty of each fresh love affair, this woman had given herself a different name for each lover. For Andor Álmos-Dreamer she became Risoulette, because she noticed that he was attracted to her combination of a dusky Oriental complexion and lighthearted Gallic elegance. "Risoulette" suggested both the Orient and the Occident. Risoulette was goodness personified, ever the ready plaything of her lovers' debauched whims, and she never complained. After a breakup, she might pale slightly, and frequent the church for a while; usually she weathered one or two minor illnesses, but she never clung to a cart after the ride was over. She sat down by her Captain's side to eye the barometer with a lifelong devotion. She smoothed down her unruly curls and cinched a black leather belt around her waist. She took stock of the estate, and burned any compromising letters—after having kissed them. She was not overly fazed by the telltale mementos lurking here and there in the neighborhood: a hair wreath (made of her tresses), or a souvenir slipper, or a memorable shirt. "My husband believes what I tell him!" She never worried that any man would be base enough to betray the precious moments she had bestowed on him.

It was almost ten years ago that Andor Álmos-Dreamer sailed through those happy days when he could call Risoulette his own. At the time, the affair carried every sign of a great and deathless love. The emotional young man had nearly gone out of his mind: without the least thought or hesitation he had placed his fate in Risoulette's dazzlingly white little hands. Miseries, joys, overindulgences and ever novel, life-giving sensations composed this love affair, and while it lasted, Andor Álmos-Dreamer walked about half-dazed, happy and oblivious. The way he saw it, the world existed only because his love willed it so. Later, he would look back on these years as individual burial mounds in the dark graveyard of his life, tumuli where the oil lamp's flame still flickered. Back then each day had been as momentous as the Battle of Austerlitz. Even the watch stopped ticking in his vest pocket. Life lay ahead, a long and leisurely meander like the River Tisza in summertime. Each morning began with the invocation of Risoulette's name.

And every dream's curtain was lowered by Risoulette's hands in the night. Yet eventually all of this passed, like the clatter of a cart receding beyond the hills. Risoulette had developed considerable expertise in letting the bird of passage fly on without his even noticing the feather or two left behind in the strange nest at the forest's edge where he had passed the night. By the time Andor Álmos-Dreamer had come to his senses, the woman he had held in his arms only the day before, and the love that had both of them breathing in unison, thinking and feeling as one, now loomed like memories of an ancient church, where he had once chanced to linger awhile admiring a rare icon. Risoulette benevolently guided her men across yawning chasms and dizzying rope bridges. It made her proud that not one man had ever tried suicide on her account, although over the years there were many who would reminisce about her in the evening hours when a crackling fire and mulled wine offer some solace in one's solitude.

This was why elderly gentlemen referred to Risoulette as "Our Lady's Fountain": for she had given drink to multitudes of thirsty men.

But Risoulette always returned to her Captain's side, and ex-lovers saw her again only in their dreams.

The Captain received their guest with hearty hospitality, and right away inquired about his gout, for by now he socialized solely on this basis.

"Does it still reside in your heel? If I recall correctly, you used to have a touch of gout in your waist as well as your knee..."

"There's no getting rid of it," replied Álmos-Dreamer in the resigned tones of times past, when he had regaled the Captain with tales of his own affliction.

"Springtime is the most critical time of year. It's that in-between time—neither winter nor summer. A dangerous season. I don't even dare stick my nose outside, but the rascal has a way of sneaking in through the cracks, every time the silly maid opens the door. I tell you, my limbs feel like they're made of glass. No wonder the crazy English turn the onset of gout into a family event. Truth is, it does keep you endlessly occupied. But don't let me detain you—I know you're a fellow sufferer."

With that, the Captain took his seat in the easy chair of his own design, nestling amidst shawls and fur coats of a peculiar cut. His mustache twirled to a point, his face coppery red, there he sat, the local weatherman, his voice rasping on:

"Go, talk to my wife, poor thing's always bored because of my malady. Please, be gentle and chivalrous with her. Not many women have suffered as much as my poor wife. She's an angel sent from heaven. Alas, her hand is not as delicate as it used to be. All things grow old in this world, Andor. My gout is getting to be twenty years old soon. Say, is it true some German's found a cure for gout? . . . But I better let you go. Anyway, what on earth would I do if I were cured? I'd have to start everything all over, whereas I no longer want to change anything. Change is for others, the folks who'll come after us. That's why I prefer to read only ten-year-old newspapers: I surround myself with people and events, all dead and gone. I just don't understand this newfangled world."

The Captain proudly sat back in his chair, stiff as a statue. By now he had grown fond of his affliction, maybe because it prevented him from rashly setting out on a new life.

"Everyone's a Socialist nowadays. Only me and my gout are left over from the old dispensation," he said, and once more he shook Álmos-Dreamer's hand, as if this handshake were his farewell to everything that was pleasant and desirable in life. His head, topped by an otter hat, sank a little lower. Next he struck up a conversation with his own foot, evidence that he had not renounced social life for good.

The only change in Risoulette was that now she wore a white scarf around her neck. Perhaps she did so on account of the wrinkles that had sneaked up on her through the chimney one fine day. Her eyes, her maddening, silky soft, humbly smiling, gently entreating visage, always beaming such utter surrender at her man that he felt like some superior being—her eyes seemed to hover hesitantly, aimed at some distant point. Could she have glimpsed a cloud that no one else had noticed? Her features assumed an expectant expression, similar to those women who stand around at stations endlessly waiting for the train bringing the long-awaited traveler.

"Is it really you? . . ." she faltered, getting over her surprise. But she quickly recovered. "I recognized your footfall at once. Your steps have a way of approaching from room to room, so that I find it impossible to sit still. They bring the promise of something extraordinary, something grand—like a feast day on the calendar. Where have you been all this time?"

"I've come for your advice regarding Eveline."

"Your great love?" replied Risoulette without any surprise, just as the best nurses never seem surprised by the patient's wishes. "All right, I'll invite her over . . . Right away . . . The two of you can meet here undisturbed. No one ever visits us any more."

Eager to please, as if she had been waiting for years just for this errand, Risoulette (a subdued, compliant smile on her lips, like a grandmother eavesdropping on her frustrated, grown-up daughter's ecstatic tryst next door), set out her pen and stationery. Using violet ink, and the spiky handwriting taught to upper-crust young ladies in convents, she penned a letter to Eveline, inviting her over for a cup of tea and a little chat. Her delicate fingers, their ruby and emerald rings not as flashy as before, used to write quite another kind of missive in days not so long ago: lengthy, delirious, sophisticated letters, any one of which would have made some man happy to wear it next to his heart all his life. But men are so fickle . . . Sealing the letter she softly laughed at Andor.

"Not even the most exclusive dame is immune to the eternal feminine wiles. In our old age we take pleasure in bringing men and women together. My husband would readily hear out the case histories of every gout-sufferer in the world. As for me, I could never have my fill of attending to lovers' petty everyday affairs... It was all so beautiful... Alas, I had no one to give me advice. That's why things didn't always go as well as they might have. I'm just a frail, sentimental creature. My heart is filled with all kinds of fantasies, like the ones itinerant musicians play under one's window... And I get to thinking. The truth is: I'm getting old. But I still love you, just as the groom's best man loves the first locust blossoms. I have always loved you, for I dream of you, and with you, often. I dream of keys, roosters, beds, bathwater, and you... In the dream you go far away, and then you return. Forgive me for being so superstitious. Fortune-telling is my only amusement. But Eveline will be here soon, and I'll retire to take care of my old man. My hands know how to soothe his aches, as if I really were a witch, like rumor has it about me."

Andor Álmos-Dreamer kept turning his hat in his hand, like a troubled client at a faith healer's. He cast only a cursory glance around the old room where in former times he had sat so often, showered with caresses, or else knelt on the light green rug, his heart as full of bliss as a pilgrim's. His old friends, the tin soldiers on the antique grandfather clock, were still there, leaning against their mediaeval town gate, in the manner of bored mercenaries. Up on the walls the hawk-nosed, priestly-looking, apoplectic ancestors, and ancestresses about whom the only feminine thing was their costume (for their faces were shaven and their jowls were broad, as if they had always been pressed against their men's chest)—these portraits could have told many a tale about Mr. Álmos-Dreamer's doings. These mute, immobile elders had witnessed all those eternal vows, pledges and professions of faithfulness that, although completely unasked for, are still uttered by men in the course of their interminable blubberings, when they reach a point where no other words can be found than those of the vow that binds unto death and keeps the nether world at bay, words that clank like everlasting manacles.

Yes, Andor Álmos-Dreamer had knelt there, in front of this humble-eyed, blushing woman clad in white, her face always transfigured by happiness and pleasure, who raised her white hands as if to fend off her lover's confessions. "Please... don't... You know I don't deserve such a bounty, all this happiness. It's enough that you put up with me, that you think of me at times, as long as I can see you every now and then... You should save your heart's ardor, the hot lava of your emotions for worthier women. I'm only a roadside tree in your life, here to fan your face with a cooling breeze while you stop for a snooze in my shade." Risoulette might have uttered these words... Or maybe she said nothing. Her two hands merely stopped the flood of words gushing from the young man's mouth, although it meant the fountain of life for her... "Anyway, one day you'll abandon me like an aimless vagabond does a *fille de joie*. And you'll recede into the distance, like a memory of one's youth. Hush now, don't explain, for my heart will break yearning for you..." But we have yet to see the man who will hold his peace when about to deliver a declaration of love. Next to ornate toasts, amorous declarations offer the greatest relief for men's need to talk. The feminine hand raises the floodgates holding the swollen river, and there comes a rush of words, from east and west, from fairy tales and dreams, like a colorful caravan that assembles at the caravansary from the four corners of the world. It's no use, trying to prevent men from knocking their foreheads against the ground when this gives them the greatest pleasure! Only make sure to send all crusty old men out of the room when the moment of a lover's confession has arrived. Their know-it-all, unlotioned, leaden, otherworldly complexion does not belong on the stage of gorgeous declarations. At the most, a superstitious ancient nanny might be allowed to huddle in a nook, to note the words and to parrot them later when the rainy days arrive.—Lovers' confessions! The happy hour, that always gets omitted from funerary orations by the graveside. Whereas that is all we should ask of the departed: hasn't he forgotten to declare his love during his days on earth?

Whatever Andor Álmos-Dreamer knew of life and love, he had learned from Risoulette. At intimate moments, eating and drinking, during long walks, while the fever of love took a brief respite, Risoulette taught Andor all that was worthwhile and amusing in life. Her store of knowledge included not only what she had learned from her old aunts at Szatmár; she was familiar with the notorious Marquis's book of recipes, as well. Her exterior was as wildflowery as a wandering Gypsy woman's, and her eyes flashed at times like a knifeblade honed at night near a nomadic campfire; and although she sometimes cried out like a wild bird before surrendering herself to her mate, still, her lips exuded the fragrance of French perfume, her raven locks were redolent as Carmen's on the operatic stage, and she groomed all parts of her body as well as a princely bride for her nuptials. She had mastered amorous enchantments of such sophistication that this petty nobleman of The Birches would have gladly split open his breast merely to have Risoulette dip her miraculously petite foot in his heart's cascading blood. This woman was truly remarkable in every respect: her mobile, expressive nose, her dark eyelashes and noble nape, her sensitivity to cold, her gullibility. In her whimsical moods she was the lady sung by poets, who found her intoxicating. Like a taciturn magician, she had her secrets. Her tears, her laughter could have sent men to the gallows. But she was mild as a dove...And like springtime itself, you could never get enough of her. Her conversation was always worthy of attention, it was like leafing through the pages of a fascinating travelogue. She played with her voice like a child with a ball. She existed in order to put you in a good mood. She was joy personified.

Andor Álmos-Dreamer, glimpsing his graying head in the Venetian pier glass—in which they had stared at each other so often like provincial couples engaged to be married—now wondered, amazed, how could he have ever left this woman? Here he had been kept as spoiled as a pet hedgehog, and still, he had wandered away from this household. He had gone away, to chew pumpkin seeds in his solitude, like an obstinate child.

At last a light spider cart wheeled into the courtyard, as in some period piece where the gentry are always carousing and no one has time to live an ordinary life.

Next to the coachman, who wore a beribboned hat sat Eveline, dressed in a dove-gray outfit. The short-tailed gray dapples that had gaily trotted along, while her hands held the reins, were now shaking their jingling accoutrements, as if this had been their sole raison d'être.

Watching from behind the white-framed window, Mr. Álmos-Dreamer was moved to see the two women greet and kiss each other under the red awning of the verandah. Risoulette, solemn and deliberate, gently embraced the maiden as if coveting her innocence. She kissed Eveline on both sides of her face. Now that they met, they were no longer rivals. Side by side, the woman in her forties and the girl in her twenties banished the thought of competing for the same man. Eveline's bearing was noble, refined, and condescending, rather in the manner of a lady of the *haut monde* being amiable toward an acquaintance who must spend her life in a provincial village.

The Captain slapped his legs as one does an unruly horse, and advanced to receive the young miss at the front entrance.

When the white door opened, Eveline's eyes took in Mr. Álmos-Dreamer with equal portions of surprise and distraction, as if the last grains of fairy dust from solitary reveries were still dropping on her eyelashes. She turned around to look behind her. Risoulette, teary-eyed, nodded at her with boundless benevolence and made herself scarce.

"You wanted to see me?" Eveline asked.

She took off her deerskin glove and offered her hand like a flower to Mr. Álmos-Dreamer.

"Yes, I, too, should have thought of the Captain and his wife. But believe me, Andor, I've been as inactive as a lazy cat. Days go by and I hardly even have a thought. Life for me has receded into the far distance like the mountains on the horizon that I shall never get to. It doesn't even occur to me that there are cities, humans, and other lives in this world. I've made myself cozy on a pile of ashes. And as long as it stays warm, I'll be all right."

Andor replied the way he had once spoken to Risoulette:

"I'm the kind of man it is easy to forget. But I had never wanted to attach any importance or significance to my person. So I live on, a man who is far prouder than he has any right to be. Life is a mere flick of the hand...It is not important. And not very interesting, either. Time goes by, meandering like an impassive wanderer who never sees new landscapes, different cities, fresh or hostile faces. I'm merely a watchman in the corn-field who observes, from under a hat pulled over his eyes, the passage of unknown and uninteresting strangers on the high-way. They're all marching toward distant destinations, their eyes on the far horizon, their thoughts on foreign marvels. One will be shipwrecked at the Cape of Good Hope, another will be garroted in a Hong Kong opium den, the third will circle like a hapless bird of passage over alien lands...Everyone is on the go, dying to live, see, feel, and run amuck; wanting to inhale new scents, touch the hair of unknown women, taste strange cuisines, to make love and forget like sailors...this is what most men want. I alone seem satisfied by sitting on my hovel's threshold—haughty, frozen, stubborn like a rock in my voluntary and conceited renunciation—while over my little rooftop life flies past, insanely clattering, deranged and carefree. Could it be I am a gopher without a mate, or a melancholy blind crow at the forest's edge? For a human being I am most certainly not, no, no, I don't enjoy, I don't want, I despise what most men do. Possibly I am one of the dead who can see and look on, amazed by nothing and detesting everything that the living do. Or else once I was a pipe-smoking Turk on a shopsign in Munkács, and now I'm off on vacation. Truth is, I want nothing, my worshipful lady."

"But you did want to see me, no?" said Eveline, who blushed a little, lowered her eyes a little, and adjusted her skirt a little, as women are wont to do, when they are unsure of themselves.

"Oh you, perhaps, are the only one for whose sake, at whose memory, I sometimes feel like bursting into a drunken or crazy sob so loud that it would be sheer pleasure...You are the one I think of, lying in my bed, you with your birdlike sadness, your eyes reflecting an otherworldy light...you are beautiful and alien, you are a whole different world...You contain archipelagos, Spice Islands full of unknown scents, joyous frenzies tumble from your eyelashes, many-colored shadows chase each other on your forehead, and hemp bursts into flower at your feet...For me, you are a mystery, although at night I scream out that you are simply a woman...You are a disheveled terror opening the door a crack in the middle of my reveries, like a murderer clutching a knife...you are a dead woman, a pale wraith hugging the door and summoning me to the netherworld...You are death and you are life."

"Poor man," said Eveline, and caressed his forehead, as any woman will, truly touched by hearing a man cry.

Now Álmos-Dreamer again addressed his words to the absent Risoulette. It was the final exam in all she had once taught him.

"I know it is cowardly to confess to a lady what we think in

135

our weak, vulnerable moments…I'll have to drink enormous amounts of alcohol in my solitude to forget the things I'm saying now. I'll have to commit foul deeds to rid myself of these agonizing memories. I'll have to travel far, and in foreign cities buy myself brides at midnight from their cabdriver fathers… Have myself robbed in clandestine houses kept by procuresses with eyes like beasts of prey…But I have to tell you that I despise and hate you and still I cannot live without you. You are despicable, for I know you love another. He is probably some young Budapest cabby or gambler, or a carousel operator in fancy pants whom you, instead of some older woman, provide with spending money. I detest you for finding yourself a gigolo in your youth, when you are so fine that one night with you would cost a hundred sovereigns in Shanghai…And I abhor you, for you remind me of my grandmother—like a song that bubbles up from the throat—you kill me, you daze me, in my dream you suck my blood, you are a woman who has driven a man wild, a man who until then had only known the manly, spirited, self-sacrificing kind of love…You are ever new and foreign, and I cannot find you behind the skirt flounces of desirable women in the cities of the night. And yet I've looked for you so long that my feet went lame…Looked among whores and nuns."

"Poor thing," said Eveline, lowering her arms like a wounded bird her wings.

"You resonate inside me like Negro jazz…When there's a wedding at the sugar cane plantation and the slaves blow their mouth harps to produce a storm of dance music that makes everyone lose their minds…At other times you are a Hungarian folksong, heard on the Tisza's bank in the moonlight at a fishermen's tavern, when the heart is wounded, a suicidal hour…Grandfather's waltz or a Sunday afternoon at my piano…the squeaking of mice and circus music. You are an unending howl rising from the insane asylum…You are love."

"Please don't hurt me..."

"Don't be afraid. I happen to be the kind of forty-year-old man who is dying to make love, maddened by thoughts of orgies, but whose body is a centenarian's, and has to import a street singer to satisfy his lady, while I sob in the next room...I am sick, old and mad. A used-up, tattered old hat that had once upon a time been worn at a crazy tilt by some girl at a boarding school and left behind in the corridor of the hotel where she rushed unthinking, riotous, crazed on the arm of the triumphant male...The night watchman stops to muse, as his old walking stick pokes at the hat with a numbered tag sewn in at the orphanage or boarding school...I can only crave you, crave you like sunshine that cannot be held."

"I shall cure you. For I am a springtime woman. I admire and love you. I'll be the cricket in your house, who'll play the violin for you in your solitude. Please stop suffering."

So said Eveline and she placed her hands together.

But the self-lacerator could not be stopped in his heart-rending séance. The cello that had lain silent for so long, and which was now brought out from a corner nook, poured forth songs of woe, like Baron Münchhausen's frozen post horn emitting melodies by the fireplace.

"Why have I summoned you here? Because in this house once I was young, like a wandering musician who, young and hungry and aimless, sings below the window. This is the house where I spilled all emotion so that there is not a drop of blood in me to take to the other world, so that a flower might grow on my grave. This is where I once knelt, like a happy jack of hearts that had somehow escaped from the pack...This is where I played the Ram, the Bull and the Lion...Here I once was a star on the ceiling that lit up the sleeper's dreams...I was the wind that blew in under the doorsill...clattering ghost rummaging among the dried hunting bags in the attic...I was the tomcat snoozing on the roofridge, gathering fresh strength for the morrow...Here I was love. And you, you could be Risoulette's own daughter, you dear love."

Risoulette, when she heard mention of her name, entered the room quietly, humble and joyful like a serving woman on Christmas Eve.

"Wouldn't you like some tea?" she asked and cast a reproachful glance at Eveline, who sat, chilly and moved, in an ancient armchair. (She still had her shoes on—whereas Risoulette had always made sure to place her bare foot in her lover's hands.)

Mr. Álmos-Dreamer cast down his eyes like a guilty man caught in the act, while Eveline gave Risoulette an Eastertime smile, like a woman to her lifesaver on the riverbank after repenting the attempted suicide.

"Please sit down, Risoulette, and play the piano for us," she said in a wheedling, cajoling voice that can never be attained by someone choking with emotion. Eveline spoke in calm and deliberate tones. Meanwhile Risoulette stood in the door, bewildered, like a woman who has spilled kerosene on her skirt but cannot find a match to set it aflame.

"Well, if you don't want to be alone any longer..." she replied compliantly, somewhat saddened. "Do you like Tchaikovsky?" she asked Eveline, and coolly turned the sheets of her piano music.

Mr. Álmos-Dreamer excused himself and left the room. Next door he listened at length, without stirring, to the Captain's litany of gouty symptoms, until he suddenly sobbed out loud. He yanked out his handkerchief and laid his head in the Captain's lap.

"You are my best friend," he wept and kissed the Captain's hand.

"You mustn't act in haste," said the Captain, after Andor Álmos-Dreamer confessed his misery, like a drunkard to the *cimbalom* player. "You must never, ever, take women seriously. I have traveled much. Here, there, everywhere. I've been to India, I've been a dance master in the Caucasus, a musician in a prominent household where American girls received wealthy foreigners. I have passed for a Frenchman, a German, and a Dutchman. I have lived on the donations of cardsharps and have been kept by women. Once I killed a man with a champagne bottle in the house where I was dance master. No, you mustn't take women seriously—even though in the Austro-Hungarian army they hold a different opinion on this matter."

It was so unexpected to hear the Captain address a topic other than his gout that Andor wiped away his tears. He looked in surprise at the gruff gentleman who sat grim and disconsolate in his armchair, like a cross over a grave.

"If people listened to me..." the crypt-dwelling knight went on in thoughtful, arcane accents, "there wouldn't be so much giddiness around...so much senseless behavior...stupidity... People's life stories sound to me like tales heard in the restaurant of a train station. The train stands snowed in and people tell each other their experiences and observations. In hindsight everyone knows where he made his mistakes. I have yet to find a traveler at the train station who is content. One has to be very stupid to find life bearable. You, too, are a lost soul. Instead of remaining here in my dear old house, you had to run around chasing skirts worn by women of unknown emotional capacity."

"I am truly sorry now."

"Why, you had everything you wanted here. We always tried to please you, coddle you, we thought you were the most intelligent man in all of Hungary. I always have to sigh over human obtuseness when my guests leave for unknown, distant destinations...Why get on a train if you don't have to? Only deportees and wandering Jews travel by train. Any normal person stays at home, smokes his pipes, and picks out his otherworldy resting place well ahead of time. I am going to sleep my long and restful sleep under my walnut tree. And where did you go off to? Why, you went and climbed up on the high wire at the traveling circus and now you can't come down. Why go in for this goggle-eyed torment when you can live your life painlessly, without as much as a sore throat? The way I see it, everyone in this country is stone drunk and I am the only teetotaler, for I have never loved anyone."

"I have horrible nights."

"Because you behave just like a woman. You must have a doll or a baby in your lap, you can't imagine life otherwise. You are unable to tell a funny story without giggling. You are not solemn, calm, severe like a convict who has been sentenced unjustly, yet you consider yourself proud and clever. Living life to the hilt is for jokers. You put your faith in women, whereas you ought to know that a woman is merely a nightgown, a feather from a bird of paradise. They are beautiful and kind, and we need them. But no decent man has them on his mind at the hour of death. Listen, old comrade...Go climb an oak tree, like a long-whiskered oak beetle, and listen in silence from under the leaves while others cry for help in the woods. Just take it easy."

The Captain said no more.

Half an hour later Risoulette appeared, after the piano had fallen silent, like an unhappy mazurka at a time of young love. Eveline had departed without a farewell through the garden. Evening was falling the way death creeps up on a solitary man.

"Come here," said Risoulette to Andor Álmos-Dreamer, drawing him into a side chamber. "I have to give you something that was entrusted to me."

She embraced him and her kisses were as drawn out as a honeymoon, as joyous as a reunion and as submissive as a harem. She quivered as if every bone in her body were sobbing, like a maiden on her wedding night.

6. TOWARD EVENINGTIME

THE DAY was fading like a weary heart.

The birds left off their daily doings; the Lord's diminutive laborers flew off in silence toward their little homes, grown quiet, just like humans toward eveningtime.

The region known as The Birches gradually wrapped herself in a dream-misted shawl, like an ailing lady who, after passing the afternoon in reveries, at twilight concludes that, after all, she must go on living alone. The rays of daylight steal away past the distant row of poplars, like a dearly beloved who keeps waving back from the distance, but departs nonetheless. His place remains empty in the armchair by the fire, where with understanding nods he had listened till now to the most diverse daydreams, turning the sheets with tranquil devotion while the soul played various musical numbers . . . Evening fell, the music was over, the invisible musicians, hunching their shoulders, ambled off outside the window, taking the roundheaded musical notes under their overcoats, to set these next to the wine glass at the tavern, for their own amusement. Those warm currents around the heart have turned into cold smoke, the way the paper strip turns into smoky flakes under one of those squatting bronze figurines, to the amusement of the party crowd. The young virgin who earlier that afternoon stood in sunshine among the forget-me-nots on the banks of a seductive spring stream, now retires, as abandoned as Gretchen, into her little house where, head downcast, songless or disappointed, she huddles until the little dream-mothers, bright and merry, with kindling bundled on their backs, return from the woods to blow a flame into even the saddest fireplaces, and from that flame mix some sparks into the exhausted heart falling asleep.

Everywhere this lugubrious twilight announces an end to pleasures, indicates closing time for the garden in which we had planned our lives and loves to be as ceaseless as the distant waterfall's murmur. Everywhere shadowy cares tug at our bootheels, cares that until this moment we had not even noticed, cares that now find us at sunset, the way a lost lapdog finds its owner after the fair ends. Everywhere desolation flutters around human souls as angelus sounds and singers begin to save their voices, the rich tints of the wine in the glass turn color, the smiles now playing on faces fade like silk discolored by the sun; we listen, and wonder if the beating of our heart might not be slowing, this wanderer having taken in such a large chunk of the world in the course of the day, and we involuntarily look back on the still sunny meadows of times past where we would be so happy to return, to be young once again, in our full maturity; but the wandering journeyman cannot change course, and must advance toward nightfall's vague mountains that numb the heart. Everywhere, all over the world, people now think those tragic twilight thoughts about the pointlessness of days past—loves and songs dying away without a trace—happy hours, like so many grains of sand, trickling away, irreversibly —smiles that will never return—lights falling from heaven to earth, caught for a moment in the eye only to drop toward the grave; everywhere those painful farewells (such an unfair human gesture!); everywhere, reaching out to us, a pleading hand we can no longer clasp:—but saddest of all, on any day, is twilight in the Nyírség, the region known as The Birches.

Oh, don't let me die at eveningtime in this land!

Let the last moment come on tiptoe, peeking through the keyhole one mute, deep night when not even stars are visible and it is an easy task to cross over from one pitch-dark hovel to the next. Or let the guest arrive in broad daylight, after lunch, when not even the strangest vehicle appears menacing, and not even the stoniest-faced messenger appears scary. Let the knock come when one sits, dusty and sleepless, awake, weary with tomorrow's hopelessness, a miserable night's knot in one's throat, ready to renounce everything in favor of attaining rest at last: one wretched dawn, as women of the street slink homeward, carrying their ragged souls, whipped to tatters; when, more dead than alive after their all-night revelry, drunkards slip off the sled to sleep and freeze in the falling snow; when feeble-limbed gamblers and soul-spent, exhausted musicians creep homeward in back alleys—then, may the black herald reach me after the long night's journey. But spare me at eveningtime, as you would a young doe.

Twilight in The Birches has its own strange creatures that are only found in these parts.

Like conscience itself, they run alongside Eveline's carriage. Daytime's bright magpies fly up on hedges to greet you like gossipy old women wearing bonnets. The tangled, leafless grove sticking its head aboveground, a plaything of the winds, now grows quiet and hides those frog-headed, owl-footed, twittering shadows that could any moment ooze away from the tree trunks, to give menacing chase, sticking out their tongues at the carriage. Lingering crows still inscribe wavering circles overhead, in hopes of a feast—it's all the same to them if they make a meal of a neighbor or kin. In the misty fields wandering Gypsies' fires flare, as if they were preparing for some great work, these quaint strangers, panting, passionate, with their dramatic locks of hair and their voices like wild birds', who vanish unnoticed from one day to the next from fields where they for some reason had camped out for a while—leaving at most a colored rag or a few twisted stems of grass to indicate their stay here and the direction they left in. On another side lie canebrakes and rushes, hovering like the dead in midair, capable of coming to life any moment. High above the reeds, where the air is as empty as space floats a nameless solitary bird, musing about the aimlessness of life on earth. The clods on the road, serf-souls many centuries old, cling to the carriage wheels.

Bare birches, like chilly maidens, quiver in this landscape, their twiggy arms crying out that life is unbearable. It is not advisable to travel this way, for at eveningtime the crossroads accost the traveler to tell her speedy horses are no use, the moment, the hour will never be recovered. The desolate roadside crosses offer their services, spreading their Veronica's kerchief of wilted grass to kneel on for one last prayer before taking leave of life... Here and there by the roadside, somber, heavenward-reaching, sturdy-trunked trees turn morosely wrinkled brows after the passerby, implying they had seen finer sights in their youth; from forlorn treetops the kestrel screams like a banshee banished from this world. Ditches brown with dead leaves and vines squat sprawling alongside the road like people with faces so hideously deformed they must lead a crepuscular, underground existence. And like the lonely plainsong of an outlaw on the run, there is some exhalation in the air that squelches the heart's joys. It turns one's mood as dismal as the unseen fisherman's solitary oarfall among the marshland rushes. It wraps the soul in a desperate futility, as if the scarecrows, exiled into the wasteland, and the haunted, dried-out trees had spilled their venom on the passing traveler.

At the crossroads a man in an overcoat leaped in front of the ambling horses and grabbed the bridle of the near horse.

Eveline was startled from her reverie. Her ancient, liveried coachman jumped down, swearing, from the rear of the spider-cart.

"Kálmán!" Eveline shouted as if roused from a dream. "How did you get here?"

Ossuary stepped up to the girl seated on the coach box and placed his hand on her driving glove.

"I've been waiting here for hours. I decided to come after you because I can't understand why you're staying away from Pest. I'm not the kind of man you can just drop like a worn boot on the highway. For I get up and come running after you like a hurt, wounded, angry...Anyway, what are you doing here, why haven't you thought of me all this time?"

Eveline eyed Kálmán, and sensed that her fate was at a turning point. Bewildered, frightened and confused, she shut her eyes. She was a woman. She did not cherish moments of crisis. She merely wanted to live in peace, like a bird on a branch.

But Kálmán clutched her wrist forcefully, like a highwayman. The eyes in his dusty, lean, wolfish face stared, bold and steadfast, into Eveline's eyes, with the look of a bloodhound that had been chased here by Budapest dogcatchers. He was waiting for the girl's eyes to flinch. His fingers felt her pulse, trying to guess what went on in her mind. He scrutinized her with eyebrows raised all the way, then watched her with lowered eyelids, like a gambler intent on the fall of dice. She seemed ailing, weary, unhappy. A hundred days' and a hundred sleepless nights' remorse showed on her face.

"Easter Sunday it will be four months since you've been gone, Eveline. The last time, winter whistled in my chimney, and now spring fills the world, like the tunes from a military band on a Danube steamer. So I surprised myself with a wish to see you—though I should have stayed in hell: back in Pest, in the coffeehouse, or at the horse races, rather than put up with this cold, snooty look from you. What's with you, girl? Have you totally forgotten me?"

Frightened and curious by turns, Eveline stared at Kálmán's soldier of fortune visage. It was a face she had dreamed of many times, always trembling with heartache. Kálmán's eyes had grown larger, like the saucer-eyed dog's in Andersen's fairy tale. The hair on his head stood up stiff in spikes. She had so often heard his cocky, defiant voice in daydreams, emerging from behind the tapestry of a brown study. She was afraid of him. And yet, when the daughters of melancholy descended on her, and sat down at the foot of her bed to knit unending stockings from endless balls of yarn, she never failed to think of Kálmán, who surely must have power over these otherworldly beings and the mournful moods of the soul as well, for this man, like a warrior, never shoved any fear. His ruthlessness she found as imposing as a bulldog's ferocious set of teeth. And his audacity reassured her, like the fidelity of a trustworthy Negro giant who watches unsleeping on your doorstep throughout the night.

"Have you nothing to say to me?" Kálmán burst out and gave her hand a mighty shake.

Eveline sighed.

"Where am I going to put you up? You can't stay at my house!" She sighed again.

"So, you would have preferred never to see me again . . . You like living here among the village beasts of burden, where there isn't one knowing eye to observe flirtations and couplings. I can well understand why you wouldn't want my presence here. I have a wicked, but honest nature. I don't hide the truth from you. I'm not one of your half-witted devotees you can send out to stroll on the street while inside, in the booth of the fashion boutique you are having a tête-à-tête with some other gent. I happen to be your good friend and I bite; I'm always ready to split open the skull of anyone who would spread evil rumors about you. But I'm not afraid to tell you to your face what I think of you. One thing you can be sure of: I would have walked all the way here, even if there hadn't been a train to this godforsaken place."

Eveline closed her eyes, listening to this tongue-lashing. In her heart of hearts she was gratified by the harsh tone, as an adulteress is by the beating she receives at home. She felt she was doing penance for this afternoon, for basking in the torrential downpour of Mr. Álmos-Dreamer's ardent words.

"I have a friend in the neighborhood, you can stay with him," she said, fluttery.

"You know I don't think much of Mr. Álmos-Dreamer, that total lunatic," Kálmán scornfully replied. "Sooner or later I'm going to drown him in the river."

Eveline was taken aback.

"You are crazy...I would so much like the two of you to be friends."

Mr. Kálmán wrinkled up his eyebrows severely and stood tall.

"Listen, Missie, I have more than once warned you not to make me play a role from some French novel. I am a beast, and will kill any rival, with tooth and nail if I must, instead of carrying on intrigues. So get those novels out of your head."

"Please forgive me," Eveline faltered, as if she were on her knees in front of him. "I didn't mean any harm."

Just then she thought of Mr. Pistoli who lived within rifle-shot from here, right off the highway, in his solitary badger's den.

"Get up!" she commanded and made room for Kálmán on the coach box. She firmly grasped the reins, like one setting out on serious business, and the dapple grays, after some consternation, went into a loping trot.

Evening had fallen.

The candles went out in vagabonds' hearts; the lights went on in solitary houses. The moon surveyed the scene over the marshes, like a sheriff who decides to leave the outlaws in peace tonight.

Mr. Pistoli spent his days perfecting his ennui. Being the wise and crafty male that he was, he thought it expedient for a while to hang up in the attic his amatory game bag, from the loops of which he had in his time dangled so many silly starlings and timorous water hens. He could truly confirm that, for bagging women, all you needed was plenty of time on your hands, and persistent, patient lying in wait. Yes, he had lain hidden under bushes watching the daughters of the soil, their faces bathed in sunshine, flexing their limbs in the breeze, bending their waists in their labors around the haystack; foxlike he sidled in the neighborhood of spinning rooms, husking bees, feather-plucking fests, wherever girls' songs rang out with amorous yearning; he had observed stealthily and steadfastly the young washerwomen on the riverbank; on highways he would keep company with market women heading for a fair, and chatted them up, sampling their goods; and it was seemingly without ulterior motives that he chanted the hymns and litanies along-side female pilgrims, when on Our Lady's Feast the simple folk of the land wended their way to Pócs.—When he grew tired of simple-minded serving wenches, fed up with their naive benev-olence that wanted to make him hale again in all his sickness and indolent lollygagging, he would cast a bored look at the newborn babe and mumble through gritted teeth: "He'll grow up to be a bandit, no doubt." And he would drag himself to his feet like an ancient reaper and move on to another scene and other women, without ever looking back. He squeezed his way into dance classes for girls apprenticed in the trades, who were still learning how to apply makeup, and on his way out tram-pled the compacts of ladies' maids; he gave midnight serenades for actresses of the traveling troupe, offered his arm to accom-pany widows returning home from the cemetery; attended coffee-klatsches where ladies lamented men's infidelities; he sized up feminine gullibility as precisely as a grocer weighing out saffron. Like most rustic Hungarian males, he was not choosy in amatory matters; and, if asked to give an accounting on his deathbed, would not have recalled a single female. Possibly his only recollection would be that the choral society of X had elected him its president and at his funeral their deep basses and nimble tenors would perform the song "Why So Gloomy Now?"

This primordial lifestyle went hand in hand with the ennui that would seize him from time to time, like somnolence the hounds, once springtime is past. He would hide out in his lair like a groundhog that had met with a mishap. He would chew on a tender new leaf and play the violin for his own pleasure. He took delight in prolonged yawns, hapless groans, spent hours in bed staring at his big toe, and finally rose only to set a billy goat capering, as aimlessly as a whittling man who fondles the sticks picked up on the road.

He received Kálmán Ossuary as impassively as he would a mendicant beggar.

"For Miss Eveline's sake I'm willing to sacrifice house and home," he said, and at the lady's request he designated the garden cottage as Kálmán's abode.

This garden cottage, built on sturdy posts, stood near the riverbank. This was where Mr. Pistoli had kept his mad wives in his married days. But the cottage had also sheltered girls who ran away from home for Mr. Pistoli's sake, thereby causing that fine gent much aggravation in smoking them out once he had tired of their lamentations. The place had witnessed the crack of the dog whip as well as the melting, lilting tunes of Gypsies, depending on circumstances. These days it was mostly middle-aged women who had cause to recall the garden cottage, to curse or bless Mr. Pistoli, to the stout squire's total indifference. He had however a black mourning band sewn on his stiff black hat, even though he had had no bereavement in some thirty years.

"Mr. Pistoli, now that you're a widower, you won't be needing the cottage," opined Eveline, who was well versed in local lore.

"I understand perfectly," replied Mr. Pistoli, sage acquiescence personified. "You'd like to visit the young gentleman from time to time, without disturbing me. But I was never one to tattletale about women who confide in me. And just in case the wind should blow my way some wayward Gypsy gal, why, let'er camp out in the corn loft. In my youth I had no qualms about climbing into smoky hovels after' em . . . But you shouldn't take seriously everything you hear from old Pistoli."

"Please take care of Kálmán," Eveline implored the master of the house, before taking her leave. "Dear neighbor, you are a man of considerable experience. You know the ways of the world, how people are, the dangers . . ."

"Leave it to me. In any case I'll get rid of Blonde Maria, who visits me occasionally, still unwilling to accept that I've given up women for a while."

"Thank you," said Eveline, and, accompanied by Mr. Pistoli's solemn, pitying, empathetic nods, she drove off on the dirt road into the darkness, like the closing accord of a tragic concert.

"What's the beard for?" asked Mr. Pistoli on his first evening with Kálmán, eyeing the latter's semilunar side-whiskers.

(In a paunchy, smoky wine jug, from which highwaymen on death row might have sipped their last mournful drink, a vinegary local wine had been set on the table. Pistoli's frequent deep draughts from this vessel had the effect of making his mood more and more dour. He signalled with his eye, inviting Kálmán to follow his example.)

A dismissing flick of the wrist was Ossuary's answer to his host, who paced the room with hands linked behind his back.

"You should ask my barber. Probably this is the current fashion in the capital."

"Me, I've never had a beard," continued Pistoli in an insinuating tone. "Though I guess I could have had one. Yes, in my youth my beard grew reddish, like the Duke of Orléans's. Later it turned black and thicker. It would have grown together with my mustache, eyebrows, hair, just like Robert Le Diable's. But I never tolerated even the slightest little tuft under my lower lip, even though every gentleman worth his salt in this county used to have one."

"It's not the beard that matters," Kálmán replied appeasingly. "Not every woman likes a bearded man, anyway."

But Pistoli resisted.

"In the Orient only slaves shave, free men all sport beards. Not your kind of half-beard, the significance of which I can barely comprehend, but full beards that cover the entire jaw and lend definite character to the face. I recommend you grow a full beard at the cottage."

Kálmán shrugged. He did not feel like arguing with this village squire. But Pistoli, so long a loner, now grew voluble, hearing the sound of his own long-silent voice.

"In the old days all over Hungary the fashionable thing for a man on attaining a certain age was to let the beard grow. An ancient tradition, this. Lad took a bride, and once married, he'd sprout a luxuriant beard. Why, a beardless county judge or deputy would have been unthinkable in those days. Women were expected to appreciate a man's beard. It's all a matter of custom.—Only itinerant actors and waiters shaved their faces back then. Nowadays most modern males forego facial hair. They imagine themselves more interesting and cleaner that way, and somehow even more intelligent than their fellow men sporting mustaches. It seems to be some kind of badge of freemasonry among contemporary males. But I despise modern men."

"Take it easy, your honor."

"Why does modern man look down on tradition? What gives him the right to think himself different, brighter, more enlightened? Especially here in Hungary, where the very survival of the nation seems to demand men to be conservative and old-fashioned. For I see no evidence of real virility in the younger generation. Women have no moral sense, and expose their nakedness, their physical and spiritual shamelessness just like their chic underskirts hung out to dry in the sun; young men are unreliable, weak, cowardly and spineless, though they act as cocky as if they had some special, hidden talent. But that's just it. The new generation is far shallower and feebler than the old. Nowadays you can hardly find a specimen of the steadfast-as-oak, ascetic, upstanding, straight-arrow Hungarians of old. Everyone's characterless, without convictions, and ready to switch allegiance... Anything for the promise of an easier life. I feel sorry for this country, watching it slip into the hands of scoundrels and men without character. Soon there won't be a single honorable man in the land. Only the blind can't see the demoralization of our society and public life. A nation of thieves, the home turf of pseudopatriots, brazen, selfish, cold-blooded liars. Why, honor was laid to rest here before the revolution of 1848. This is why the nation's downfall won't be such a great loss. Could this all be because Hungarians gave up their beards?"

"I repeat, the beard isn't everything, my good sir," replied Ossuary, who although he was no great scholar, nonetheless read the occasional newspaper. "Life cannot stay put, it would soon stagnate. New men arrive, who don't want to stay on the beaten paths. Everyone carries in himself some concept he would like to realize. You mustn't be angry with men for striving toward new goals. The old stations in life have all been occupied by our elders, and they have littered the scene with their greasy papers. We can't stay put where we were, back in '48, when men still had such dreamy, otherworldy eyes, that you can't look at an old portrait without being moved. They barely ever smiled, they barely even lived, they were always suffering and sacrificing, for homeland, or for some woman. Since then we have discovered that neither is worth butting your head against the wall for."

"But if this country should perish, if the Hungarian nation should die out, it will be this accursed generation's fault!" shouted Pistoli and slammed his fist on the tabletop.

Then he looked around and smiled like a dead man.

"I am an ass, for talking politics," he said in a soft voice, and with hands linked behind his back retired to bed. Deep down he was probably convinced that the precious Miss Eveline would have been most satisfied with his performance. Not one obscenity had been uttered in the course of the night, although women's sexual habits usually formed Mr. Pistoli's favorite topic.

"So modern men don't drink?" asked Mr. Pistoli on the following night, when the young man again ignored the eyebrow's invitations to imbibe.

Ossuary flicked his wrist again:

"Our ancestors guzzled enough wine for generations to come. For centuries everybody's been wine-drunk in Hungary, for our hills have always been richly blessed. Why, at times wine had to be poured into pits for lack of barrels. Wine was drunk in the early morning and late at night. In the light of the foggy, red-bellied winter sun, rowdy or resigned, life went on. No one ever considered suicide, because wine was a compensation for everything. We'll have to see many a sober generation come and go, before all heads are properly aired out, and the last remnants of a race of drunkards die out . . . How could a nation accomplish anything when everyone was on a permanent drunk, even on their wedding night?"

"Hot diggety-dog," grumbled Pistoli. "You, sir, have indeed been indoctrinated by the enemies of this nation. I would surely emigrate from here if your kind should become too numerous. Luckily there are still a few decent folks left who respect our ancient virtues."

Pistoli placed a hand on the wine jug and spoke in a most solemn tone, as if what followed was a matter of life and death:

"Sir, I'll tell you who shouldn't drink: those whom alcohol turns into swine. Let'em swill water from the trough, like farmyard animals. For there's nothing more digusting than a drunk.

(Though I did come across a certain kind of woman who favored only drunks, she could make'em satisfy her every last kink.) Yes, wine can be full of ghosts, or else lissome, high-life chorus girls. A sinister sign marks the forehead of the man who imbibes only the ghosts.

"All those staggerers with bloodshot eyes collapsing in a tearful heap by the ditch; pillaged hearts clutching a knife; those hollering at their reflection in the well's suicidal depths, or laying themselves down across the cities' thoroughfares; those who rend women's hair; the jealous ones who stink of bitter mineral water; those trembling hands ready to commit murder; all those unfortunates who must guzzle wine to find the courage to stumble through life's vast night—well, they had all better plop down by the puddle, because this is one party you won't be recovering from on a prison straw-mat, or in the confessional cage of conscience's accusing *agenbite of inwit*. The drunk that regrets drinking, and in his sorrow scrawls German verses on the white planks of the summerhouse, kneels at the foot of the wronged woman, and must pawn his lynx jacket after an all-night binge, vows promises to lonesome trees, and spends half his life trying to make up for the mistakes he made—he should stay at home, within the confines of his four walls, toss the doorkey into the river, and never leave the house, not even if he wakes dreaming that the place is on fire. The solitary drinker should tie one hand to the bedpost, so he'll find instant refuge among the eiderdown quilts when the good Lord's golden vintage turns dark inside his wicked guts. That would be the finest farmers' almanac, in which the rhymester would immortalize the solitary drinker's thoughts and feelings in this land! The desolate village manors ready to collapse, and only that last jug of wine to light up the gloom inside! The way the prematurely old and lonely man talks to parts of his body when the wine goes down the hatch and you must converse with your own broken leg, since there's no one else to talk to!

The lugubrious glug of the solitary swig, and that meaningless crooning when the head crashes to the tabletop in a room! Women long since dead calling out from carefully saved photographs and ghosts of friends lurking in corners! Small and large coffins, packed full of memories, now returning on the surging flood of inebriation, bobbing and dancing like a gatepost carried off by the springtime Tisza's high water! That would make a fine almanac, if you wrote down the thoughts of the solitary toper! I did try once, when I was still able to suffer."

Kálmán listened with distaste to his host's words. By now, he had had almost enough of the eccentric village squire. He liked to look on life with dry eyes, as a strict business proposition.

"No matter how your lordship entices me, I'm not interested in drunkenness. I don't intend to clamber up on the kettle-drum like a circus monkey. I want to breathe free, and seek favorable passage on life's river with a cool heart and sober mind. I prefer to calculate, just like a businessman."

Pistoli smiled inwardly and thought, "This young whippersnapper thinks he's so very smart, but I'll show him his place!" And he took a prolonged draught from the smoky jug, just like a thirsty forest in a May downpour.

"Well, a solitary man needs his bit of ecstasy to put up with life," he mused on. "Take for example me, who always believed that in the matter of brains no one in the county could come close to me. If need be, I could always muster the wiliness of a snake. And still, there came nighttime hours when, in spite of all my wisdom, I didn't relish my solitude. The company of people bored me, for I had the misfortune of always detecting their true selves, their real voices behind the false front of small talk. Oh, I never fell for people whose fluting voices warble nothing but white-gloved courtesy, kind flattery and fraud. I always knew their innermost thoughts. Filtering through the pious, holier-than-thou psalms, I could always hear the dull thud of the drumroll at the execution ground. And so I was never crazy about the company of my fellow humans. Even women I desired only as long as I didn't tire of them."

("Why, oh why does this old fool insist on boring me to death with the story of his life?" Kálmán secretly wondered.)

After another hearty swig as soothing for Mr. Pistoli's throat as a glass of water at dawn for the feverish invalid, he went on: "Let me repeat, I have never craved the company of men, but still there were times when I couldn't do without it. Therefore I had to conjure them up, lure their shadows here, their sunken footprints, their veiled voices. I seated their disembodied forms around my table, and we conversed about life and death, as well as works and days. The good old wine jug always brought them here, no matter how far away they were. The wineglass pulled them up from the bed where they lay with a hand on the wife's belly.

"Each swallow of wine brought out their innermost feelings, clandestine thoughts and never-before-confessed misbehavings. They told me what they do at home when they believe no one is watching. They had opened up the blind windows of their souls' dank cellars, and let out the cold blast of egotism that filled their miserable lives. After these gatherings not one of my acquaintances remained unfathomed. I had reconsidered all their voluntary actions and reviewed the deeds they had committed without themselves knowing the whys and wherefores. I inspected them from all sides as one would a bullock at the marketplace. Did they possess any redeemable human value, and what was it? What was the key to their makeup? Did they really merely dangle from the hair of women's private parts, like rancid little crumbs, while claiming they were connected umbilically to the eternal feminine, the Mother of us all? And so I examined them like an apothecary does his poisons. I often laughed out loud when I discovered new sights. In my solitary investigations I had to slap my forehead when I came upon the key to the behavior of one of my friends. I calmed down and made peace with myself. The life I had lived thus far, like a surly badger, was surely the best, for I had lost nothing by avoiding men. I became as cheerful as a fallen girl after her confession. My heart filled up with the joys of life. And the wine jug welled up with women who were never unfaithful, never evil. They were women who gave me joy. So I played cards with them till daybreak, the stakes were nose-tweaking and making love. The winner would receive my dream for the day, for dreams were all I ever paid to women."

"The scoundrel," thought Kálmán Ossuary, from whom a woman was lucky to receive, at the most, his condescending agreement to accept her presents.

"You think I didn't see Eveline leaving the garden earlier this evening?" Mr. Pistoli asked with a sudden flash of his eyes, and gave Kálmán Ossuary a penetrating glance.

The latter, a bit discomposed, bit his lip, and racked his brain for the ugliest epithets regarding Mr. Pistoli.

"But let's return to the women in the chalice. (Alas, Miss Eveline has never complied with my summons, even though in my boredom I had more than once appealed for the young lady with the doelike tread who happens to be the chatelaine of this neighborhood. Naturally she bathes far more often than the chateleines of old, about whom I had once read that on Good Friday they washed the feet of beggars, but never their own. They used to wear egret feathers in their hats, although their necks were not exactly immaculately clean. Those heavy, brocaded skirts and leather undergarments concealed unwashed limbs, that's why itinerant peddlers hawking perfumes did such roaring trade. Still, the scent of ambergris and frankincense was often overcome by the natural body odors of those ladies of yore. That's why I could never go in a big way for women of earlier times. I never welcomed guests from the other world, for I happen to be blessed with a most sensitive olfactory organ.) My women were always live ones, hot, full-blooded, full of zest for life—although they would usually turn up in the dead of night. They stuck their bare toes in my mouth, grabbed ahold of my hair, straddled my shoulder and rode me, and stuffed their hands in my pockets. They would shift me around and knead my muscles, banish me under the bed, chase me with flashing teeth, and nibble me like puppies. The hefty ones danced around on the tabletop; the skinny ones stood on their head.

"The petite ones tumbled about like sleepydust on eyelashes. The big solemn bony ones cracked my waist as if they were in love with my bones. I can't understand why I never became conceited, since my women stuck by me even when I returned from one of my binges infested with vermin. Why, they even helped me get rid of the bugs. No, no, I never would have believed they'd keep me company all my life, and not get tired of my speechifyings, my ailments, my whims, my ravings. On the contrary, I was always expecting to be stabbed to death in the constant sparring... But at night, when I settled down by the wine jug, all my women proved to be most accomodating. They never threatened to murder me."

"And tell me, your excellence, how far did you get with these fantasy women?" asked Ossuary, quietly sarcastic.

"They made me love and desire the live ones. I began to search for their imaginary scents and ungraspable limbs. But in real life I never found the salvation promised by the imagined figure.—But let's go to bed. Tonight I made an appointment to meet Miss Eveline."

7. PISTOLI GOES ON A LONG JOURNEY

ONE DAY Pistoli made a peculiar discovery around the garden cottage. He saw the imprints of horseshoes on the wet black path that meandered in the far end of the garden like a clandestine love affair.

"Heads up, Pistoli," he cautioned himself, and swung his head back and forth like some Asian monk. With eyes apparently closed, he stood on his right foot and rubbed the sole of the other foot against his right knee. In his preoccupation he opened the door to the cupboard, then gazed for a long time at his boots lying on the floor—he preferred to take them off during the day. After this he began to finger a swelling that sat like a second, smaller head on top of his cranium; old Hungarian tradition held such small melonlike growths on the head to be a sign of wisdom.

"Watch out, Pistoli," he growled, while he ambled down the celebrated moldy steps to the cellar, in order to take a great deep breath and in a glass siphon suck up some wine from the barrel. The wine trickling into the stone jug unexpectedly evoked Miss Maszkerádi, who was actually never far from his mind. The trickling wine sounded a feminine note, and Pistoli's eyes bulged.

"You're nothing but a poor little homegrown wine," he addressed the wine jug in a scornful tone. "And Maszkerádi's made of fire and the noblest *aszú* grape. How dare you, a humble local *vin ordinaire*, dare to imitate the regal Tokay vintage?"

Next he stood, mouth agape, in the middle of his courtyard as if he had never seen the migratory birds that now approached above the rooftops: it was as if rapidly shuttling aerial omnibuses had poured forth the swallows, like so many white-pinafored convent girls let out for summer vacation. Soaring storks inscribed huge circles and giant pretzel-shaped paths in the sky. The wild geese squatted down in the reeds, just like their relatives, the wandering Gypsy girls at the forest's edge, when they cast their spells with twisted stems of grass, leaving behind signs for their lovers—or as it often happens, for the gendarmerie. Along with the birds of passage, it was time for the vagabonds to appear, for, with the thawing of the season, they saddled up shank's mare to hit the highways in their seemingly aimless, tireless peregrinations from one end of the horizon to the other.

There stood Mr. Pistoli as stunned by all this as if he had been hit over the head and unable to find the culprit.

He was suddenly jealous, and as downcast as an ancient sumac tree whose sunlight is cut off by a new wall. He went and sniffed like a keen-nosed vizsla the horseshoe imprints on the loamy, earth-scented, cherry-blossom-strewn path, and thought he could pick up a whiff of Miss Maszkerádi's unique perfume. This exotic and eccentric lady was to be his last great love, and he intended to take her with him to the other world as pure as a rosary wrapped around his wrist in the coffin.

The doves were tumbling in the air above the manor house like distant springtime memories of youth, and Pistoli, in a tragic gesture, interlaced the knobby fingers of his two hands, like branches of a lilac bush. How could Miss Maszkerádi possibly desire some other man in the neighborhood? And of all men, this clean-shaven, cheerless whippersnapper whom Mr. Pistoli secretly despised as thoroughly as he would some fledgling tenor... Pistoli was like a naive housewife past her silver anniversary, who one day discovers straw from a Gypsy girl's pallet on her respectable's husband's shoulder. Yes, those men who never stop talking about women's unfaithfulness are the ones most surprised by it.

The springtime air was as sweet as the waists of young girls bending over their flower beds, seeding, and Pistoli was ready to sob out loud in his desperation, like an old Gypsy, whose brats had got him drunk. The very saliva turned bitter in his mouth when he recalled the scene in Eveline's garden with Miss Maszkerádi in the role of the temptress clad in white linen and the only thing he regretted now was that he had not given a piece of his mind to the confused girl who, with the characteristic unfathomability of womenfolk, had been ready to offer herself that night to any roadside hobo. At least he should have shouted in her face that he condemned her behaviour—and here his throat choked on a very ugly word—and that he despised, detested and disdained her . . . Instead, he had saved her, put her by like some Easter egg he could crack open whenever he felt like it. And so now he felt cheated.

As if sent by fate, on this day there appeared in the vicinity of the house one Kakuk, a drunken hobo who had crisscrossed Hungary many times, had spent nights in jails of all types, and chalked the customary signs left by beggars and vagabonds on the gates of households where the poor wanderer is welcomed, or where the dog bites. In his old age he had settled down in these parts and was wont to rest his wine-saturated, red-as-the-winter-sun, cobwebbed head for hours at a time on the stone wall surrounding the manor until Mr. Pistoli condescended to toss him a word or two.

Originally Kakuk had settled in Pistoli's neighborhood with a different agenda in mind: he claimed to be an ex-hussar and notorious brawler, but the stout squire crushed all his ambitions. He made Kakuk mount a fiery stallion, and the famous hussar was thrown screaming right in front of the tavern called The Eagle; subsequently he had Kakuk beaten up so badly that the poor man was laid up in bed for weeks. At last the tramp confessed to being an itinerant cobbler all his life, patching and soling as he rambled the countryside. His real name was Ignatz, he had done time at the Veszprém jail as a suspected highwayman, and he ended up in Pistoli's permanent service, as if he had sworn fealty to a gang leader.

After a while Pistoli deigned to notice the cabbage-shaped, shaggy gray head resting atop his crumbling stone wall. It was a head that had groveled oftentimes in front of Pistoli's feet when the squire, lording it, made Kakuk kneel in the dust, or after returning from unfamiliar kitchens and servants' quarters where he had been beaten up with stakes and poles. Just now Pistoli was deeply moved, for he thought he caught strains of funeral music approaching from the direction of the birch grove where the highway bends. The violins sobbed and wailed, the contrabass growled, hollow like fate itself; the coffin must have enclosed some bride, accompanied on her last voyage by black-clad men holding gendarme swords tipped with lemons. Pistoli imagined it was his own true love being interred in the distance.

"Don't you want me to take a letter to some old lady or young miss?" Kakuk humbly inquired, and out of force of habit he chalked a hat on the stone fence, a vagabonds' sign for an unfriendly house, to be avoided.

It was with uncharacteristic kindliness that Mr. Pistoli received his shirtless serf, who in his time had delivered so many billets-doux in Pistoli's hand, enough to earn him a hundred deadly beatings. Lecherous widows, servant girls sent home from the big city, small-town waitresses, procuresses and noble ladies had received letters via this vagabond, letters that were sometimes totally uncalled for—Pistoli had simply picked the recipient as a potential paramour. This was cause enough for Kakuk to set out posthaste, clutching the message entrusted to him. He would lurk like the autumn wind around solitary houses. On bitter cold winter nights he would amble in godforsaken small-town alleys where women who had gone astray camped out in ramshackle hovels. A landlady named Stony Dinka would treat him to mulled wine, whereas the dove-souled Risoulette entreated him with clasped hands to persuade the saucer-eyed Pistoli not to harrass her any more. Both the messenger and the ladies had aged somewhat in the meantime. The owl hooted on storm-tossed nights, complexions had lost their apple-blossom pink, and fingers that used to rake through masculine hair now clasped only the prayer book.

"No, I'll never write another letter," replied Pistoli about a quarter of an hour later, having behind carefully closed doors instructed Kakuk in a soft voice at length about what was to be done.

The very next day the tramp was back, and tugged Mr. Pistoli's leg which was dangling from the bed (for the squire could only fall asleep by swinging a leg).

"Back o'the garden," Kakuk said, cryptic as some spy, before vanishing like a bad dream.

It was sunset: the trees in flower were listening for the foot-falls of someone coming to pick their blossoms, while shadows, like exhausted hounds, stretched across the path. The hedge sent up a little bird, God only knows what business she had there, brooding the spring afternoon away...

There, where the lime trees huddle together like revolution-ary generals before their execution, awaiting the crash of light-ning with arms uplinked, there stood a memorable little garden bench, a secret spot on the grounds surrounding this red house, as private as the purity of a youth and the nobility of a heart. Formerly, when women had still travelled on clouds over this land, and a female foot was worth a kingdom, Pistoli spent hours seated there next to his soul mate, uttering never-to-be-recalled fine words; or else brooding alone like some knight whose unbalanced bride jumped from the castle ramparts the night before;—but he was never bored.

In later years, whenever Pistoli approached this small bench, he envisioned women who would quietly rise as he neared and vanish into the birches like a delicate mist withdrawing under fallen leaves beneath a frigid moon. Women he had yearned to meet sat there, and women he had tired of, but later wanted back with all the pain of a middle-aged man missing the joys of his youth. And since a real man holds no grudge against the women who robbed him of his youth, merely to pin his wings on their hats, Pistoli thought he saw seated on that bench mostly those ladies who had drawn blood.

And now, once more, a dearly beloved took her place on the little bench. The hat decorated with a pheasant feather shaded the face averted in surrender, like a bird being taught to sing. It was Eveline, sitting where Pistoli's former loves had sat, and she was listening to what Kálmán Ossuary had to say.

"Just look at him jabber!" reflected Mr. Pistoli bitterly, as he hid to eavesdrop behind the hedge, pricking up his ears like a horse.

Alas, Mr. Pistoli was too far away, though he would have gladly given a fine fur coat to overhear the lovers' conversation. But it was enough just to look at them: the eyes said it all, it was so obvious. A glove pulled off the hand might feel the way Mr. Pistoli felt. The russet brown cloak's undone buttons might have sensed his keen disappointment. Those soft curls lurking about her ear quivered like young maids when they find out the whys and wherefores of their coming into this world. The swan neck, the adorable mouth, the long lashes: they were all unaware of the hourglass and time's flight. The finely-shod foot, the liquescently smooth stockings, and the amulet heaving above the panting heart all imagined this was the first instance of love on earth, wherefore their sudden all-importance. The tender curves of the shoulder, the phenomenal lines of the arm, the miraculous shape of the hips: no way did they foresee lying someday in the grave pit's damp depth and infinite solitude, with no one to praise them. And the splendid cheek might be leprous after a few years—while this moment, this heartthrobbing hour, imagined by bird-bodied, bird-brained love to be eternal, would have become a matter of indifference.

All Pistoli could do was wriggle his big toe, as if it were a gopher, inside his boot. He regretted that not once did Ossuary kneel, during his endless warblings. Then the moment of farewell arrived. The exchange of abiding looks. The arm gliding off like foam down Niagara Falls. The departing lady's subdued, lingering, pensive footfall, as if she were leaving for good, for the infinite beyond.

Soon afterward came the clatter of a carriage, stealing off past the garden's far end, like a Gypsy kidnapper's cart.

"Tomorrow I'll sacrifice a pig to celebrate that it wasn't Maszkerádi with that joker," resolved Mr. Pistoli, and made an effort to sneak back to his house without being seen by Ossuary.

By nightfall he had remembered all kinds of old songs he believed he had long forgotten. The ditties descended like a spider from the roof beam, and he snapped at them like a dog at a fly. Of some songs he recalled only a single line, but he still hummed through the entire melody. He laid his head on the tabletop, absorbed in woolgathering. From time to time he flung a ditty, as one would a bone, at Kakuk crouching in a corner. But he had little patience for another's singing. It didn't take long before he shouted: "Ah, nonsense!"

And whinnying, he struck up a new song, only to get stuck halfway through, like a rickety cart full of drunken wedding guests.

Ossuary was loitering in the moonlight like some terminally bored ghost.

Suddenly Mr. Pistoli stood in front of him with raised forefinger and declared triumphantly:

"I was a tougher kid than you...And I'm still the better man. The girls were weeping and wailing when they left me. For I am Pistoli, that's who I am."

The moonlight over The Birches advanced hugger-mugger in the sky like a shepherd hiding a lamb under his coat.

And, wrapped in black veils, night crept away, like a woman's once undying love.

Kakuk spent all day lolling in a ditch, for the grass was growing in; he chewed grasses like a hound healing some ailment. And, anyway, he had been dropped into this world to lie about in ditches, while the flouncy-skirted, flowery-embroidered, rowdy marketing women pressed ahead to pass each other on the highway. Life does have its do-nothings who welcome as a matter of course each successive morn. They trudge, slothful and passive, into eternal darkness, for they never imagined that dawn would ever displace the night. All those daytimes must have been a misunderstanding, as was the aimless wind, rustling rainfall, wall-clawing torment, and bitter dementia. The truth lies in the great night that stretches from one end of the sky to the other in motionless eternity, where rockets devised by humans will never penetrate.

Kakuk clambered forth from the ditch, tiptoed up to Mr. Pistoli, whose wide-open eyes stared at a demijohn of Bull's Blood while his left hand inscribed all kinds of sigils in the air to his familiar spirits. He was dour and woebegone, a wax figure at the waxworks. His mustache was curled to point up. His worn lacquered dress boots proclaimed to the visitor their superiority to everyday footwear: these boots would never trudge in the dust of the highway.

"The equestrienne," Kakuk announced, as if he had been

hanging out around a theatrical troupe, and had picked up the actors' accents.

Pistoli slowly shifted his weight to his feet, shoved himself and his chair away from the table, tore his eyes away from the wine bottle and gave a deep sigh like a prisoner on death row. The half-blind pier glass on the wall had long forgotten what womenfolk looked like, how they would once upon a time stop for a quick peek at themselves or to pin up their hair in a top-knot. Nowadays the mirror always reflected Novemberish faces. Pistoli looked into the mirror, and twirled his mustache like a gray rodent.

"Ah yes, the equestrienne," he murmured. He opened his mouth and spat at the mirror, practically reeling with bitter-ness. "The trollop!"

Had he a weapon on hand, surely he would have grabbed it. But firearms and even sharp knives had long ago been banished from his house. Pistoli feared suicidal schemes and death-craving moments. He wore only the flimsiest belt that was guaranteed to snap under his two hundred pounds. Many a dawn found the droll, carefree boon companion, the life of last night's party, ardently yearning for death, sprawled across the worn rug that served as a coverlet on his bed. He sank his teeth into the pillow, for that's how it was in a novel he once read. Suicide approached barefoot in the snow, and lurked around his property like some pushy beggar. He could never enjoy love unless it was totally hopeless.

And so, hands in pockets, it was with an impassive face that he noted the saddle horse tied to a sapling in the birch grove. He knew that yellow mare from Eveline's stables. Kati was her name. She flicked her short-clipped tail like a lady her fan, and trotted as obediently with a lady's saddle as if she were in collu-sion with her rider. Pistoli squatted down next to the saddle horse. In a fevered flush of humiliation he repeatedly resolved to take refuge in the shrubbery if and when Miss Maszkerádi returned from the garden cottage, but her visit was still very much in progress.

Pistoli's face flamed as he counted the minutes spent under his roof and shelter by this lascivious lady—in the company of that detestable youth.

"How could I so debase my lifelong pride, my manhood?" The reproach welled up inside him like a poorly swallowed dumpling. At the Ungvár theater he had seen the itinerant troupe perform a melodrama in which a woman was murdered. "Jacqueline, see you in hell!" the actor had declaimed. Pistoli never forgot these words. Drinking his wine, during lovemaking, or in his despair he had often uttered this exclamation until his heart nearly broke, for ultimately he came to feel sorry for each and every woman because of the frailty nature had given her...

At long last Maszkerádi emerged from the garden cottage. (Pistoli was most amazed at not seeing a dozen female hands clutch the departing lady's tresses—the fingers and nails of women who had in that cottage sworn him eternal faith and love unto the grave.)

Brightly and merrily swaying, like an April shower, came the young lady.

Perhaps if she had been sad and conscience-stricken, like certain dames of old who left the site of their illicit love as woebegone as the passing moment that never returns; if the lady had approached in full cognizance of her frailty, ready to forego a man's respectful handkisses of greeting, and trembling in shame at the tryst exposed in broad daylight, like Risoulette, sixty-six times, whenever having misbehaved, she hastened back home teary-eyed to her Captain; or if a lifelong memory's untearable veil had floated over her fine features, like the otherworldly wimple of a nun...Then Pistoli would have stood aside, closed his eyes, swallowed the bitter pill, and come next winter, might have scrawled on the wall something about women's unpredictability. Then he would have glimpsed ghostly, skeletal pelvic bones reflected in his wine goblet, and strands of female hair, once wrapped around the executioner's wrist, hanging from his rafters; and would have heard wails and cackles emanating from the cellar's musty wine casks, but eventually Pistoli would have forgiven this fading memory, simply because women are related to the sea and the moon, and that is why at times they know not what they do.

Ah, but Maszkerádi's confident stride made the footpath seem like it was made of rubber. Her face mirrored a calm satisfaction, as after a successful revenge. Only the best of friends can cheat on each other without qualms, unspeakably glad of the secret not even the best friend can be told now. Curiosity, the impulse to imitate close friends, the oftentimes identical fashions shared in hats and clothes: these will guarantee certain rogues unhoped-for successes at both the dance academy and near the sheltered family hearth. Women fond of each other drink from the same cup with a will, wear each other's shirts and clandestinely kiss the same man's lips. Later perhaps they'll fall at each other's throat if the secret is out before the flames of amorous passion, like shepherds' campfires, gutter away in the ever-receding distance.

"I kiss your hand, Mademoiselle," chimed Pistoli in the birch-strewn grove, catching Maszkerádi in the act of untethering her mare. "The weather's turning hot-blooded on us. Any day now we'll have to have ice brought in from town."

Maszkerádi was not surprised at running into the Peeping Tom. She smiled like a queen.

"How good of you to watch my mare, Pistoli. Please hold my stirrup," she replied, light and easy, like a waltz. Never had he heard her voice so fluting. And she was all furtive and happy smiles, like a honeymoon diary kept by a young wife.

"You may help me, Pistoli," said she with infinite conde-scension, like an angel from heaven meeting a mendicant on the road. For alms, she cast an absentminded glance at Mr. Pistoli. Quite possibly she thought the perfume emanating from her clothes would suffice to gratify this stout gentleman.

Pistoli began in a bleating tone, as if he had trouble finding his voice.

"Don't, please don't for a moment think, dear lady, that I would dare delve into your comings and goings. Although the attic floor in the cottage does have a hole I once used for spying on women, to see what they did when left to their own de-vices... I remember seeing many a terrified or pensive face on solitary womenfolk. They would put their room in order, spread the towel out to dry, smooth down the pillow's creases, scrutinize themselves in a hand mirror as if they feared that kisses marked them like the yellow patch on a mediaeval Jew's robe... But my memory retains nothing of you, my dear lady, for I consider your action so low, so ordinary that it's not worth burdening my brains with."

"So what do you think of me?" hissed Maszkerádi, raising her head, serpentlike.

Pistoli advanced two steps, as on a fencing strip.

His voice no longer shook, though it still sounded as alien as if it belonged to a train conductor:

"I think, my little flower bud, that you are the lowest of the low in all of Hungary."

Maszkerádi raised her riding crop and struck Mr. Pistoli twice—two full blows. The chastisement had its effect: Pistoli turned tail and fled. In his room he took to his bed and remi-nisced about a Count Stadion, a lieutenant whom Mrs. Rózsa-kerti had once slapped in Nyíregyháza. That quondam lieutenant blew his brains out the next morning.

"Ah, to be kicked by a mare's no shame," said Pistoli that evening to Kakuk, when the latter squatted down by the bedside.

The tramp waved a disdainful hand:

"She'll be back to make up with your honor," he opined, waiting for Pistoli to fall asleep, so he could guzzle the leftover wine.

That night, with its besotted, harried ghosts and bulgy-eyed goblins, dragged on interminably, like a midnight train wreck, the morning after which the survivor takes stock of his remaining limbs.

The whiplash's sting sent Mr. Pistoli to seek refuge in one of his favorite activities: composing his will, perhaps for the twentieth time. He apportioned his extant and nonexistent belongings among women he had known or would have liked to know. The Stony Dinka of former days, "whose hair was like Sultan Flor shag-cut tobacco," was assigned entire herds of goats, whereas there was only one lonesome billy goat to dispose of, by the name of Pista, who exercised his horns in the vicinity of the manor. To Rosa Máli he bequeathed his best bed, which had the distinction of once serving the "Hatted King" Joseph II for a night's rest on his Hungarian travels. Risoulette inherited the awe-inspiring roosters that would come down from the dunghill when summoned by a whistle, to put on a cockfight that Pistoli found more entertaining than watching circus wrestlers. To the sanctimonious Mrs. X he left the nude photographs of which the lonely bachelor had quite a collection. For Mme Y, who was well versed in the insignia of officers from all branches of military service, he set aside a book of hours dating from the days of Prince Rákóczi. To Mrs. Weis he willed his fur coat, Mrs. Fehér his boots, Mrs. Pussenkatz his hunting rifle. Only the wines and sausages in the larder were left out of the will. For Pistoli did not intend to pass away as long as a single glass of wine remained to be drunk in the house.

His pipe collection had long ago been promised to

Eveline—so that her future husband would have something to smoke.

And now Miss Maszkerádi, too, was inducted into his list. The letters produced by his goose quill grew fatter. Curlicued appendages embellished his capitals, and his sentences ended with braided flourishes suggesting baroque imprecations.

"My lady Maszkerádi must not be omitted, even though she is responsible for the most infamous day of my life. In the name of the Father, the Son and the Holy Ghost I declare that I am no longer angry at her, for I now realize that it was entirely my fault that that young lady grabbed the handle of a whip instead of something else equally suitable for her delicate little hand.

"The sky is getting cloudy. I no longer feel like setting down the whys and wherefores of how much I have loved her. She will not forget me for quite some time. For this reason, after my death she may have my embalmed right hand. Let her cut it off and take it as her plaything."

And he kept nodding his head emotionally, as if he had been some old outlaw on death row, at last speaking the truth.

Next, he reviewed all of his female acquaintances one final time, to make sure he had not forgotten a single one who would make him anxiously toss and turn in the grave. He replayed in memory all gullible smiles, tearful female eyes, marriages on the rocks, disrupted tranquilities, and grief-stricken faces, temples that ended up looking like careworn old shoe leather; recalled all, down to the farewell smiles that women sent after his cart, women he had promised to visit again the next day, whereas he avoided their neighborhood ever after; down to every trembling hand that did not want to let go of his, just as the drowning clutch at a straw; and those women whose bashful legs longed to run after him, but were constrained by modesty to stop and with closed eyes receive sorrow's bludgeon on the back of their frail necks; all of his women, whom basically he felt so sorry for (because they had believed his lies) that his heart nearly burst for them ... Just like a sentimental cardsharp running his fingertips over the deck of cards. And he fell into a long reverie.

Snapping out of it, this same gent cackled mockingly as he slashed on the Diósgyőr foolscap a signature befitting a Prince of Transylvania. Using a carnelian signet ring he pressed his seal on the paper sprinkled with writing sand, managing to burn his fingers on the sealing wax.

Kakuk now stirred behind his back like some clattering kitchen clock. Staggering and swaying, he announced that this afternoon's guest at the garden cottage was Miss Eveline—"that Virgin Mary of Pócs"—and the tramp's eyes grew red, like a murderer's who is convinced he is merely executing fate's decree.

"Easy does it," replied Pistoli, whose legs trembled as if he were being taken to be hanged.

He felt the lust and horror of the amorous betrayals around him, just as in that French novel he had once read, where the chevalier brought into the sanctuary of respectable families the contagion of his depravity, so that the grandfather, a man of hitherto untarnished character, sought his ultimate carnal thrills in his granddaughter's debaucheries.

"Easy does it," he repeated, as if he were approaching, hat in hand, a resting butterfly at noontime.

"I've got to climb up in the attic to get my game bag," he announced in a husky voice after a while, whereupon Kakuk made such an ignorant, doltish face that no one would have believed that he had never missed a chance to spy through picket fences or windows left open on men and women at intimate moments. One reason Mr. Pistoli liked Kakuk was the latter's ability to play dumb, cunning scoundrel that he was.

The tramp helped to pull off his boots and scurried about Mr. Pistoli like a midwife, while that gentleman tiptoed barefoot toward the garden cottage. There Kakuk grasped the bottom of the ladder like a fireman assisting his chief, and humbly blinked at Mr. Pistoli who was sneaking up into the attic.

"Go," waved Mr. Pistoli from on high, as if the ill-favored old tramp's proximity would desecrate the cottage, inside which the precious Eveline was having her enchanting, delightful, tormenting tryst. He lay down on the attic floor, found his old peephole, and felt an exquisite thrill, as if naked fairies, female torturers had tied him into knots, drawn him up to the rafters, and meted out the bodily chastisement that Mr. Pistoli believed was his due for sins never confessed. "Keep it up, harder, for I am the greatest sinner," Mr. Pistoli's soul cried out inwardly. His bones cracking, his sinews stretched to the breaking point by the self-inflicted torment, like those martyrs' who received the Inquisitor's whiplash on their naked bodies with a beatific smile directed at heaven. An aging man may find pleasure even in the ability to suffer.

Eveline knelt in front of Ossuary like a little lambkin gently laying her head in the shepherd's lap. Kálmán's fingers fondled the girl's curls, those precious strands of hair on which life's joys and sorrows had played, like a sonata's melody on the violin's strings. Arm extended, he held up one of her braids to count the knots tied on it by Eveline with the regularity of stitches in a stocking. There were thirteen loops on the braid of hair, for the thirteen unhappy years she would have to spend as penitence for this blissful hour. Then came the silken ribbons tied at the end of the tresses. And after that, nothing. Cold solitude and nights of oblivion. Life remains beautiful only as long as one can still suffer torments on hopeless nights—a suffering that will surely merit the prize of redemption.

Eveline raised her head and looked into Ossuary's eyes with such an otherworldly smile that up in the attic Mr. Pistoli's

hands involuntarily groped for a knife. He had apparently forgotten that once upon a time even his own ragged features were
thus searched by feminine eyes looking for heavenly salvation.
How far was the memory of those women who would have sacrificed their all at such moments of self-forgetfulness . . . But he
had been modest and never asked them for anything other than
what they bestowed so freely.

Eveline stared, as one who sees a miracle on a treetop: the
appearance of the Virgin Mary or Jesus Christ in a lamblike
cloud. Her eyes did not need to shed tears for they were misty
already, as if she had already heard the otherworldy voice assur-
ing her that her prayers were not in vain. This was the greatest
love, the kind no one believes in until they experience it. The
hour that trickled by would forever tower over Eveline's passing
life, a red tower visible from the greatest distances. Life may
race by over hedge and ditch like a pack of foxhounds. Yes,
other lovable riders may come to join the party, the pursuit of
the silver fox of happiness, but no matter how far she would
gallop, the memory of this hour would never fall into oblivion.
The tower stood on the horizon, its thirteen steps no longer
unknown for the reminiscing lady. There is the step of the first
handshake, then the steps of the eyes, voices and kisses. The
steps spiral around this fairy-tale tower turning upon a duck's
foot, always in the direction of the sun's heat—the sun of love.
The step of the feet, the station of the hands, the balcony of
embraces, the momentous landing of the respite between
kisses; the gallery of nameless desires, the arbor of whispers and
sighs; and at last: the tower's peak . . . Love, that brought all of
us into this world.

Eveline beheld her idol. Pistoli well knew this kind of gaze
on women's faces. This is the gaze of the insane who in their
solitary cells, cast an entranced glance after the feathery-hatted
knight. It is also the gaze of fetish worshippers, who expect
miracles of their diminutive Asiatic deities. Eyes that are a hair's

breadth away from madness; eyes that would terrify, if on a lonely night one were to behold them reflected in the mirror...

This is what Ossuary said:

"Baby, I have a problem: I want to leave this accursed house and return to Budapest."

"Please forgive me..." Eveline faltered. "I had guessed your thought before I came here."

She rose on her toes, and strutted to the table like a child with mischief on her mind. She snapped open her handbag and pulled out a stack of banknotes as her timid offering. Blue and pink banknotes, neatly folded, as only women know how to fold brand-new, crisp bills.

Ossuary, to end this scene as quickly as possible, with one bored gesture scooped up the gift, and sank it out of sight so quickly that Pistoli was unable to make out which pocket the money went in. All of this proved sufficient to make Pistoli rise with a rumble, and leave the attic on thunderous, thumping feet.

When he reached ground level he broke into the *verbunkos*, a traditional soldiers' recruiting dance, and embraced Kakuk.

"I'm getting drunk as a lord and I never want to be sober again," he shouted. "Go get my cart. Move it, Kakuk, if you hold your life dear. Wine, I want wine."

Growling and staggering, he leaned against the gatepost and waited until Quitt arrived, the one-eyed Jewish carter who hauled Mr. Pistoli about whenever the urge to roam seized him. Bells jingled, hanging from the necks of his horses. Sad little jingle bells, that rang out over the highway like the entreaties of a mendicant friar.

Pistoli hoisted and squeezed his hulk onto the cart's forage rack. He was determined, tough and energetic, like one setting out to commit murder. He whistled for Kakuk, who hotfooted it after the cart like some canine.

The cart flew, as if blown by the breeze. It swayed and

reeled, heaving Mr. Pistoli's bulk from one side to the other. He cackled or cried, as the mood seized him. At last he started to snore like a wounded wild boar. Even the man on death row has to sleep.

8. LIFE'S PLEASURES

FOR THE third day now, Pistoli had been riding across the landscape of The Birches.

During his time he had visited all of his old hangouts, the taverns where he had once brawled, administered and received beatings. At the same time he said his farewells to former lovers, as if preparing for a very distant destination.

This journey revealed that Pistoli had not had more lovers than any other man who had spent his life in this sunflowery, tranquil, impassive land crisscrossed by highways. Just as in autumntime when women winnow, the wandering winds sometimes carry off both chaff and seed alike... Pistoli's lovers were the same as any other man's. Except other men forget these women as one forgets a song after the carousal is over; at the most, a bitter taste remains in the mouth on the morning after, as one contemplates with distaste the muddy boots. Whereas Pistoli never forgot the women who were kind to him. He would recall their words and gestures even three days later, when he would be already well on his way to recovery, taking the cure via the back alleys leading to out-of-the-way pubs where the beer tastes best, or else he would sit around in front of roadside taverns musing and admiring the red glow of wine in the sun, taking his delight in the birdlike song of the wench dipping water at the well. And he would go about wielding a crooked cherrywood staff on which he skewered fallen leaves like so many uncomprehending hearts. He would stop from time to time and laugh his horselaugh when he recalled some quaint oddity in his late drunken nights, on the back roads meandering toward taverns with names like The Linden Tree or Green Tree, or toward some girl's room reeking of cheap patchouli.

For he even got to know the kinsfolk of these loose girls, some of whom had asked him to be godfather to their child. He acted as sagely as the roadside crucifix that absolves the highway wanderers' every trespass. The music played at fairground barbecue stalls, the flutes at midnight serenades, a familiarity with feminine foibles, contempt for the world, which he shook off like rain fallen on his hat's brim—all this had made him acquiescent and resigned to the way things were. Rarely did life whoop it up inside him; he mostly went about purring like a cat rubbing against your feet. When something pained him unbearably, he would run off, until like a lost dog, he picked up the right scent, the trail of wisdom.

He found Stony Dinka in the same place where he had left her ten years before. Nothing changes in these parts: women either look like Mrs. Blaha ("the nation's nightingale") or else like Queen Elisabeth. And hearts are as alike as inscriptions on headstones in the graveyard. ("One lived 72 years, another 83. Isn't it all the same, where one spends that extra decade: in hopeless love or on death row?" mused Mr. Pistoli, skulking around recently widowed women in village graveyards.)

Stony Dinka owned an inn overrun with wild grapes out near the limits of a small town, the *csárdá* known as The Rubadub. In the past Pistoli had crossed the threshold both at cock's crow and to the howling of dogs in the dead of night; he had arrived here to the thrumming of clangorous *cimbalom* music, ready to take Stony Dinka to a wedding—or else as cautiously as a construction worker climbing high up on a tower. At The Rubadub, Pistoli could always count on a hearty reception. "His heroics live on in memory," as Pushkin sings of Zaretzky.

He had especially distinguished himself in bowling—he was the best in the entire county—winning vast quantities of kegs from folks on outings from Nyíregyháza, tradesmen sporting Kossuth-style hats and bureaucrats of the county water regulation bureau, who affected checked pants. But he won Stony Dinka's favors only after "beating out" Pista Puczér, editor of the weekly *Awakening*. Editor Puczér, a man of short stature with a big bushy beard, the peppery, fiery village prank master, had from times long past staked some claim to Stony Dinka's heart. His rowdy behavior, his constant brandishing of the *fokos* (ax-headed staff), and his peacocklike screech had more than once turned what started out as a most promising May picnic into general mayhem. To Dinka's reproaches all he said was:

"But I'm faithful to you. And keeping the faith is golden."

Whereas Stony Dinka knew for certain that Pista Puczér had approached and propositioned not only her serving maids (who wore red slippers on their bare feet with a purpose after all), but all of her girlfriends as well. But she could never catch the wily editor in the act, and send him packing. All those henhouses, kennel bunks and haystacks knew how to keep their secrets. And so Pista Puczér persisted, rolling his hypocritically faithful eyes in the grape arbors surrounding The Rubadub, much as Pistoli rolled his iron bowling balls, whenever the outcome of a match was in doubt. For the very same reason, Pistoli was the only man Editor Puczér had never thrown out of The Rubadub, although in the kitchen he had repeatedly grumbled in front of a flushed Stony Dinka:

"Are you cooking again for that windbag? Sooner or later he'll run off to America."

When the journalist Puczér began to swagger around The Rubadub, wearing a skullcap and smoking a long-stemmed *chibouk* pipe, Pistoli at last decided to get rid of him. His decision was followed by action. He sent one of his village familiars, a red-skirted Gypsy gal, to seduce Pista Puczér in the pantry, leaving the door ajar so that Stony Dinka stumbled upon the pair at the critical moment. Her screams brought the whole bowling party running, and P. P. had to flee in partial undress toward Nyíregyháza, pursued by broom-wielding serving women.

After that Pistoli was lord of The Rubadub. But he no longer participated in bowling tourneys, in fact he hardly showed his face among the guests. Instead he sat by himself in the innermost room playing the flute, talking to wine bottles, toasting Stony Dinka (née Jolán Weiss)'s aged parents who, in the medium of sepia-tint photographs, graced the walls of this quince-scented room. These onetime furriers in the town of Szerencs had labored with unceasing diligence stitching untold numbers of lambskin vests, jackets, coats, for they had fourteen children to raise. This made him meditate about life and death, and he came alive only when the clatter of smashed plates signaled a fight among the clientele in the taproom. Then Pistoli took his iron-studded, lead-weighted bludgeon and began a god-awful thumping on his inner room's door, bellowing oaths he had learned from convicts on the chain gang. Other than that, he kept as quiet as a hospitalized invalid. Normally he would turn up at Stony Dinka's only after having been ejected from twenty other pubs, after at least a dozen women had derided him, kicked him in the forehead, deceived him, rolled him in the tar and feathers of various torments, flashed him what the village madwoman flashes at the jeering children, poured water on him from upstairs windows, and finally put him out of the house. At times like that he went to bed early, before Stony Dinka called for the last round at The Rubadub. Half asleep, he would still hear the guests bawling, only to feel infinite scorn for those good-for-nothing carousers.

"Shall I make some caraway-seed soup for you?" asked Stony Dinka when Mr. Pistoli showed up at The Rubadub and reclaimed his place in the innermost room among the embroidered tablecloths, quilt- and eiderdown-laden beds, Hebrew blessings and wardrobes stuffed with many-pleated skirts—as if he had left here only the day before (although years had gone by).

His expression mute and tragic, Pistoli stared off into space. He had pulled his hat over his eyes, clasped his *fokos* in front of himself, without even bothering to loosen his belt. He fidgeted back and forth, implying that he meant to move right on, that he had merely dropped in to see his former lover for a moment, for a quick drink, and a kiss. But this time Stony Dinka did not take him by storm, to remove his hat and boots as she had in days of old. By now the lady was forty-two years of age, and instead of bangs, she now wore her bleached hair pulled back and in a coil on top.

"If you were still a brunette, you'd look just like Queen Elisabeth. What happened to all your dark hair?" Pistoli inquired with raised eyebrows.

"Never mind about me, you old scoundrel. You tell me, where have you been, what bitch in heat have you been after, since I last saw you? In fact I've seen you passing by whenever some devil-sent business brought you to these parts, but not once did you take the pains to show your wretched mug in here."

"Simmer down," replied Pistoli, who was taken aback by this tearless reunion. Stony Dinka usually took him in her lap and kissed him like a child that had been lost and found.

"Watch who you're ordering around," the woman responded. But her voice had a softer tone now, a reminiscing note, like the sound of a hurdy-gurdy far off on the highway.

Pistoli was as quick to note the change as an outlaw the rainbow. He rested his chin atop his ax-headed staff, and affixed a prolonged gaze at the Madame.

"Listen to me Jolán Weiss, I'm taking my hands off you," he said at last after a long pause. "I don't like your behavior. I don't like the tint in your hair. And I can't stand the way your red boots creak. And what's this new soap you wash your face with? Where are those freckles I used to love so much on your face?"

"Is that why you came here, to torment me?" said Stony Dinka, suddenly overcast, her mood shifting as rapidly as the weather on an April day. "Didn't I suffer enough since you abandoned me? First my father's illness. I thought the old furrier was on his last leg. I was rending my hair by his bedside—you know I love that man more than anyone in the world. And even then in my despair I thought of you, of the long winter nights I spent talking to you about Father. If only he could still sew, if only his blessed hands could still wield the needle... Why, he could sew you a black lambskin jacket to keep you from freezing when you stray after all those floozies... In my travels I got to see the River Sajó, where I grew up. Where I was a little girl in short skirts, listening to the foxes baying at the moon rising over the reeds. And even there I had to think of you, because I remembered how meekly you listened once when I told you about that place... Then, at a relative's cellar, I drank some vintage wine. And didn't I think of you right away... If only you could have been there, drinking this special wine... And now you've come to torment me?"

Pistoli wagged his head, twisted and turned his neck. Then slowly, solemnly, he extended one leg:

"It hurts," he said.

"I knew it!" Stony Dinka suddenly shouted. "You get wrecked elsewhere, then come here to have me treat and cure you. You want my supernatural health and vitality to restore you. Well, until now I didn't mind. But from now on I'm going to be less generous with you."

"Well, just this one last time..." Pistoli grunted like a big bear, lifting his leg repeatedly in the air. "Anyway: '*kampets dolores*'—it's all over for me. My boots will soon hang from the rafters. All I ask is: make my last days beautiful."

"Hmph, you've said that before," a teary-eyed Stony Dinka replied, and yanked the boots off Pistoli's feet. She immediately went off to soak his foot-rags. She rousted up a ruddy-cheeked serving girl from the courtyard and promised her two quick slaps for her sloth, or some pennies if she shined the frazzled boots. Pistoli just sat there like a Turk carved of wood in front of the tobacconist's. He felt most in his element when women-folk took advantage of his physical impotence and handled parts of his body as a midwife does a newborn babe.

"Is it your heel?" asked Stony Dinka.

"Right there."

"Yes, that's where all those witches went and hid. So tell me, you old rascal," murmured Stony Dinka, taking in her lap Pistoli's ailing foot, and starting to rub it with a gentle hand, "how many women's heavenly salvation have you got weighing on your conscience?"

Formerly Pistoli would have laughed at this: he would have reeled off a list of the women who went mad on his account, and spent the rest of their lives dancing or rending their hair. But now he felt as melancholy as if the end were near. His enormous intake of alcohol during the three days' bender, combined with the events recently transpired, suddenly unhinged him. He burst into such choking sobs that he could hardly catch his breath. He sobbed spasmodically, almost joyfully, copious tears easing his heart's burden, like a woman beating her forehead against the stones. Of course he could not find his handkerchief, so that, childlike, he had to reach for Stony Dinka's skirt, to wipe his tear-soaked face. There followed a few more hiccups and shooting stabs of pain, much as the rattle of a cart recedes on the highway as it carries the bride far away from her true love. At last he recovered his ability to speak:

"Stony Dinka, you're the only love I ever had in this whole wide world. Oh, if only my mother were still alive, how happy you would have made her! You've been my mother's kind of woman all your life. Your oven-baked biscuits, the leeches you applied to my side when I had pneumonia, your barbecues and your Gypsy superstitions, your smoked sausages and your downy bed, your early springtime vegetables, your life-restoring chicken soups, the unforgettable aroma of your wieners and Eastertime baked hams, your faith-healing incantations and the way you turned me over in my sleep, your nocturnal bathings, your bread-kneading, your economies, your coat-ironing, your very nature always benevolent and faithful; your desire that I should always be free of care by your side, even when business went poorly for you; the pride you took in always seeing me off rejuvenated, cleaned up, ironed out, 'fresh from the wash' when I took my leave, even when I'd come to you straight from the gutter besmirched with blood and mud...

"Everything around your white feet in this house, your friendly watchdog, the stork nesting on your chimney, the dried walnuts in the attic and your aged nanny, all, all proclaim that you are the one, the woman I ought to have married. Not to mention my heart, which was ever yours. There were times when I looked at your concerned, serious face and felt as moved as I'd been in front of the bishop the day I was con-firmed... I could always feel secure by your side—let the dogs bark outdoors, but in here, under these rafters no danger could penetrate, for your determination, your extraordinary feminine toughness would make sure that no harm came to me at your place. In my dream you were the tall chestnut mare whose neck I clasped to escape the flood. I saw your wonderful eyes looking at me through that mare's glance."

"Oh, you old scoundrel..." giggled Stony Dinka, and took off all of Mr. Pistoli's clothes. Next, she slapped and pounded the bedding into place. The quilts went flying like geese in the meadow. Pre-warmed bricks and platters lined up in a row. Vinegar water awaited its uses. Pistoli sank into the bed so deep that not even the tip of his mustache could be seen.

"Good night, sweet song of youth!" whispered Stony Dinka, and timidly caressed Mr. Pistoli's gleaming, pale forehead.

Stony Dinka was indeed a peculiar woman: she loved Mr.

Pistoli best when he, like a tusked beast, like some prehistoric creature, rooted about and wallowed in the field of dreams, snoring in three or four different tones. Had she lived in that distant era when primitive humans fought dragons in caves, Stony Dinka would surely have been the lover of the dragon that lurked about the settlement. She loved to stare at circus strongmen, lanky vagabonds, stalwart shepherds and bandit-faced tramps. But she did this unobtrusively, for she was a woman . . . Yes, she would have loved to be married to a giant, whereas fate had assigned as her lawful husband a man who was small of stature, with an apelike gait. Around the tavern the poplars, all stairways to heaven, roared in the wind, long-legged herons strutted in the wetlands, while Dinka took delight in Pistoli's enormous muscles. In the sleeping man's presence she no longer felt modesty's girdle constraining her waist.

Pistoli woke with a start, as one returning from kingdom come.

"What did you do with the amulet I hung around your neck? The one that was consecrated twice at the Pócs chapel, and I even had an old Jew bless it for me?"

"I gave it away. . ." replied an embarrassed Pistoli. "That is, it was stolen, charmed, wheedled away from its rightful place over my heart. But I'm going to get it back, because ever since then I've had the worst luck."

"Oh, those worthless hussies," lamented Stony Dinka, with the profound scorn of one who alone understood the female sex. "How many decent men's lives have they wrecked and made miserable? Why can't every cracked-heeled hussy be driven out of Hungary, so that good men can have some peace again in this country."

When Pistoli said his farewells, he realized Stony Dinka's forehead was just as clear as Eveline's. The two women did resemble each other, after all they were natives of the same region, had bathed in the flower-strewn waters of the Tisza River, shared the same long-dead ancestors, and seeds germinating in the same soil had nurtured both of them. Their eyes had followed the turning of the same windmills on the horizon, their ears had listened to the cry of the same wild birds, as girls they had danced the same dances at harvest time and at feather-plucking bees. They had the same slightly Slavic way of pronouncing certain vowels, and they had grown up hearing the same folk songs. The same April showers had washed away the springtime freckles from their faces, and lumps of earth in this corner of The Birches were equally well acquainted with the bare heels of both Stony Dinka and her ladyship Eveline Nyirjes. Ah, how alike women appear when you consider their heels! In the summer, when even young ladies went about barefoot in The Birches, the soil did not make any distinction between the soles of peasant lass and young miss. —Why shouldn't Eveline and Stony Dinka resemble each other, when the geranium happened to be the favorite flower of both! Mr. Pistoli felt a tremendous sense of relief.

"Not even Eveline's foot could be whiter," he thought, as he took his place in Quitt's cart.

He called Stony Dinka over to the cart's side, and, as if confiding a secret, whispered the following in her ear:

"I'm going now, and it's unlikely we'll ever meet again, my heart. I won't hold you to be faithful to me when I'm in the other world. Nor will I return to haunt you, for I've played the white-shrouded ghost enough times already in my life, whenever I had to frighten off superstitious women or cowardly husbands. I want you to go about your business as calmly as ever. Don't forget to take your mares to the Nyíregyháza stud; and I know you won't neglect to dilute last year's wine . . . Alas, I have too little time left to help you with that. By the way, you should dismiss your serving girl Fruzsinka, for I caught her wearing one of your shirts. Don't ever let your little daughter, who's being brought up by your Szatmár aunts, visit this region. It would be best if she found a job at the post office when she grows up. Preferably far away, somewhere in Transylvania, where no one knows her mother. And take care of yourself. Your feet still have their snowy white looks, and I can't detect any signs of those unappetizing varicose veins on your legs.

"Your hair still has its sheen, for you've always taken care to shampoo and comb it. Keep taking those baths, especially in the rainwater that you save in the pantry. You know, if you keep your eyes downcast, they sparkle more when you look up. Don't laugh too loud with open mouth, because you have a yellow tooth that shows. Try to be quiet and composed, like a lone blackbird. At your age, what men like is a dreamily murmuring voice, like a bumblebee humming in an autumn vineyard. And remember, there's only one decent man in the whole county, and his name is Andor Álmos-Dreamer. Make sure you never wear your stockings inside out! And now farewell, my love."

He kissed Stony Dinka on her forehead, whereupon Quitt started to shake the reins, like a village storekeeper driving a cart.

After many a mile of lumpy-bumpy highway, when village steeples like so many whip handles appeared on the horizon, announcing that a tavern must be nearby, the one-eyed Quitt looked back at his passenger:

"So, how was it?" he asked, in the deep, slushy voice of Jews from the Nyírség region.

"Oh, I like'em zaftig like that," replied Pistoli, who preferred to affect cultivated airs in lower-class company.

"Stop talking Yiddish, you know I don't understand that. Tell me, Pistoli, did you beat up the little woman, or did she beat up on you?"

Pistoli replied with drooping spirits:

"I'm done with fighting."

"Then you haven't got much longer to live," said Quitt, and went back to contemplating the horses' ears. When they came to the Süvöltö oaks that guarded the local sands like great shaggy komondor sheepdogs, he looked behind him once again, timid and paling, afraid that his passenger already lay dead in the back of the cart . . .

"Where to, Fanny Late's?" he asked, mumbling into his beard.

Pistoli linked his hands behind his neck, pushing his hat forward. He meditatively eyed the graying driver.

"So, you think we owe Fanny Late a visit? . . . Well, if you think so, Quitt . . . If that's what you believe . . . I guess she does deserve a kind word or two . . ."

Quitt nodded twice.

"Yes, she's been good to us . . . Even when you took a knife to her, and all the times you broke her heart . . . she was always good to us."

Of course, Fanny Late, too, was a tavern-keeper's wife, for where else could Pistoli camp out if not at some roadside inn, where of an afternoon the cat stretched out in the warm ashes, the wine jugs slumbered in the taproom, the flies hung motionless from the ceiling, and the keeper's wife sat by the window to mend her little son's pants . . . For awhile Pistoli would sit in silence like a blackbird in its cage. Noisily sipping his wine he would contemplate his hands as they lay on the tabletop. He would keep nodding pensively at his ring finger that was somehow never without a ring from one of his women. Then he would start in with his lies as the woman sat there in silence. At times he believed his own lies, and this made him supremely satisfied.

"What day is it today?" he now asked Fanny Late, entering the tavern known as the Zonett.

She kept on kneading her bread dough and answered without looking at Pistoli, as if she last saw him a day or two ago.

"It's Saint Florian Martyr's day. Fair day at Nyíregyháza. All the horse dealers will be here by nightfall."

"Well then, for one last time I'll play cards with your horse dealers."

"You could do worse," said Fanny Late in a soft voice, and went on with her kneading.

Kneading dough is a fine occupation. Women like to do it wearing a blouse, petticoats and slippers. A white kerchief goes on the head, as in some ritual. The waist jostles, the calves flex, a delicate dew sits on the forehead, as if a birth were impending, that of sacred bread itself, God's blessing on earth. But in addition to all that, Pistoli noted the white of Fanny's plump arms, the noble swan arch of her nape, and the small melons swinging free under her shirt, like little fairies at play. The scent emanating from her as she kneaded the dough was so sweet that Pistoli nearly regretted that his life must end so soon. (Again, as so often in his travels, he thought of her ladyship, Eveline. By the time she is married she would become just such a wholesome, strapping, sweet-scented female, with a light smile on her face when her man rested his head on her shoulder, as if she were also the mother of the recipient of her love. Why, a care-laden man's head weighs no more than a butterfly weighs on a flower.)

Sending up a great sigh, he took the pack of cards from the cupboard to practice for the night. Kakuk, who had arrived in the meantime, watched Pistoli's activity with eyes popping. If he could play cards with the gentleman, just once . . .

Pistoli had his favorites among the cards in the deck.

He especially loved the two kings side by side, or a pair of aces, nor did he disdain sevens in proximity whenever he dealt the cards to the assembled horse dealers. He practiced shuffling the deck at great length. His index finger with its signet ring pushed the cards in and out like old acquaintances.

Fanny Late stood behind his back, having wiped the dough from her hands. She bestowed a kiss on Mr. Pistoli's ear and placed a key in his hand.

"The money's in the drawer," she said.

Kakuk gulped so noisily that Pistoli banished him from the room.

"So, my golden man!" Fanny Late called out, and embraced Mr. Pistoli. "Tell me, am I still the one you love, or is it my youngest servant girl?"

Pistoli gave a limp, weary wave of the hand.

"I'm fed up with women. And anyway, I'm in love. Let me see, I think you look a little bit like that certain someone . . . Turn the other way! Now sideways."

Fanny Late obeyed the gentleman's requests. He gave her the once-over from top to toe.

"Your feet," announced Mr. Pistoli after lengthy deliberation, "upon my word, your feet appear to be somewhat like hers. Miss M's. Miss M—that's a capital M for you—loves to keep her feet in stirrups. You mostly go about in slippers. Still, your ankle's curve, your foot's arch, your heel's turn is as noble as a chatelaine's. It could be that in a former life you did some falconry in this land, and lived in a castle. Now you are an innkeeper's wife, and I prefer you that way."

Fanny Late shook her head in silence. Yes, there was indeed something noble about her face, her forehead, her petite hands and narrow feet, her eyebrows' arc, the hawk's curve of her nose, her mouth's straight and sensuous lines, like some Egyptian queen's. Possibly it was only some itinerant Italian who had played the hurdy-gurdy in the neighborhood when her mother was a young woman. But it could also have been aristocratic hunters stalking the egret.

"You've told me many a time that I am the rarest pipe in your collection. That I am the antique walking stick that is missing from queer old Vidlicskay's collection."

It was a May twilight, when all things appear to be full of life and purpose, and there was nothing and no one moribund or suicidal anywhere near the golden, dusty highway. Frogs had not yet struck up their evensong, although one or two concert masters in the reeds did sound a few tentative croaks, basso profundo. It was easy to see that within an hour the impromptu concert would be in full swing—and who knows why frogs sing? A bridal veil lowered over the sun's disk. A day in May is still whimsical and sentimental, like a girl who keeps a diary of her emotions. In moments of abandon, her affections gush forth upon the earth, swearing eternal faith both to weeds' upthrusting spears and to the soft laps of apple blossoms. The day plays with the ruffled pelt of the fields, like a young bride running her fingers over the wolflike backbone of a man. She distributes her kisses equally among highwaymen, hanged men, deep ditches and coldhearted old birches. She belongs to everyone and no one. Meanwhile at nightfall the clouds are ascending so that rain might start to fall round about midnight, tapping and palpating like a physician, examining roof tiles, people's dreams, and checking the resonance of windowpanes. The rain swishes over meadows, dallies with the flowering trees, speeds up and slows down, just like a skilled dancer; and plays by herself in the night, like an orphaned child. But still, this is May, and even the oldest crone would be startled to find death's ugly black spider hiding in her nightshirt.

Before it was completely dark, the cart encountered pilgrims heading for a saint's feast. Quitt pulled off the highway, rested his horses, for although as a Jew he observed only the Day of Atonement (freely consuming smoked sausages the rest of the year), nonetheless he had the greatest respect for other people's religious convictions. He believed that religiousness was a tremendous advantage in life. For this reason he took off his hat when the pilgrims, a group whom he considered fortunate individuals, approached his cart.

It was the Feast of Our Lady. Knapsack on back, the daughters of the soil marched barefoot and chanted tirelessly on their way to the chapel at Máriapócs. The Blessed Lady was already awaiting them at the church of the sandal-wearing friars, shedding her tears for her devotees, both hands laden with forgiveness and solace. So the women trudged on, like turkey hens with wings weighed down by the leaden rain of transgressions and tribulations. They had brought along one or two older men, in case men were more familiar with the way to the heavenly kingdom. These superannuated elders had regained their manhood for the occasion of the pilgrimage and marched at the head of the procession with an air of leadership, and recited their litanies as if the entire flock's salvation depended on them. ("Too bad I won't live to be a pilgrimage leader to the Pócs feast," thought Pistoli, and all sorts of mischievous prayers crossed his mind.) The women kept chanting their responses, with the same unwearying persistence with which they kneaded the bread dough: "Mary, Mother of God, have mercy on us."

The banners were held aloft by the supple arms of hefty young virgins. They would earn a special reward in heaven for this. Sunbrowned faces, white teeth, liquid eyes, lush eyebrows, these maidens of The Birches must have learned their gait from the geese, for their ancestresses had come all the way from Asia on carts drawn by buffaloes. Here came the childless ones, chanting loud enough for their voices to be heeded by the baby Moses who was no doubt floating somewhere about in the neighboring reeds. May the kindhearted Virgin Mary bless their wombs to bring joy to their husbands at last. Here came the invalids, who were losing the love of their men. They, too, were chanting, for they had placed great hopes in this pilgrimage. Those who had some clandestine goal marched with downcast eyes; those whose troubles were known by the whole village looked up to heaven. They would pass the night under God's open sky: the women would wrap their skirts around their feet, tie their kerchiefs under their chins, light small candles in the field, and under the browsing moonbeam dream about the kingdom of heaven and angels clad in crimson. Among the sleepers an old man, the lead gander, keeps the watch, nodding and dozing. If a flock of wild geese should happen to pass overhead, they would surely honk out a greeting to such kinfolk.

By the crack of dawn, when little birds stir on the branch, these women will be on the road again. As they near the village of Pócs, the ragged beggars by the roadside will become more and more pushy, penitent life crying out from their dreadful limbs; the dust is deeper, the air hotter; the bells tolling from the friars' steeple promise heavenly miracles, the whole world is steeped in a smell of gingerbread and wax candles, wandering Gypsies play their music at the barbecue stands, the organ's boom resounds from the church...where their revived and quickened steps take them, where the miracle is to be found. Year after year these faces come, wide-eyed, for a glimpse of that flame-lit heaven.

Suddenly Pistoli sat up, as if the prevailing pious atmosphere had turned even him into one of the superstitious old women. At the end of the procession, following the booted, hatted, parasoled contingent of tradeswomen in brown, officials' wives and small-town ladies, who all cast scornful glances as they passed the cart of the county's greatest reprobate, there now appeared two figures, at the sight of whom Pistoli squiggled down to lie low on the straw-lined cart bed.

Kerchiefed, clad in a flowery skirt—borrowed from a servant girl—came the petite, cherry-lipped Eveline Nyirjes, sauntering along, her waist swaying. She was carrying her shoes in her hand, her bare feet treading on sand. Her companion, the wasp-waisted Miss Maszkerádi, cast a glance of queenly cruelty over Pistoli's cart, as if her scornful eyes demanded: "How can this man still carry on, for shame..." Maszkerádi had not taken off her ankle boots of yellow leather, although Mr. Pistoli would have loved to catch sight of her feet, as well. Her peasant skirt allowed a glimpse of calf that revealed a pliant musculature, straight from the dreams of schoolboys. "After the pilgrims!" Pistoli shouted, beside himself, as soon as he regained his composure. "This is one pilgrimage that I must attend."

But before Quitt had a chance to turn the cart about, Pistoli had lost his élan. His head drooped like a very old man's.

"My time's up. Let's go home," he growled, disgruntled, as if he noticed his heart skipping a beat every now and then.

But he kept staring after the pilgrim procession, until at last he saw in the far distance Miss Maszkerádi turn around, and send a fiery glance that ran down the shadowy highway like a burning carriage, as if a mirror's shard had flashed on the horizon. Satisfied, Pistoli nodded toward the one who looked back. Just as he had thought.

All the way home he wondered whether the two ladies would confide to each other what they prayed for at the Máriapócs church..." Ah, women!" he sighed, and concluded that life was no longer worth living.

9. PISTOLI'S TWILIGHT

NOW FOLLOW those events that complete the structure of life and death, the way a clock crowns a tower.

Stonemasons belong to the most ancient craft; they know well that building is indeed a thorough science. Much labor must go into the construction of the foundations, before the roof can be raised over the bare walls—or before one can erect a tombstone over the body of a restless man.

One man's life may be paced like the tumbleweed's passage over the wasteland, all day long chased by the wind from one end of the field to the other, to arrive in unexpected places and leave without any farewells after spending the night. Blowing unnoticed past hundreds of people, until suddenly, haphazardly, catching in someone's hair: an existence that seems aimless, vanishing more rapidly than a shadow toward eveningtime. Yet such a life can cause so much trouble, howl so bitterly, crush so many hearts, create such havoc, evoke such anxieties. Yes, those with tumbleweed lives live life to the fullest, for they do not make any journeys for their own ends. Happenstance, rumors and humors, the vagaries of moods drive them hither and thither, toward good fortune or ill luck.

Yet others prepare the course of their lives as thoroughly as a fly picking its residence in amber. They build their house on a foundation of great fieldstones that will not easily be blown down by the wind. A few manage to live out their lives in a den of their own devising, to grow old, and die, all the while avoid-

ing the serpent's twisted and slippery path. Yes, there are men
and women who indeed die innocent. (I wonder if they receive
any special recognition for this in the world to come?) They
never have to howl in pain, bitter remorse, guilty misery. But
just as most of the guilty cannot help falling, the blameless ones
have no call to be haughty on account of the purity of their
body and soul. No, neither glorifying nor holding this world in
contempt is quite justified. No one is responsible for their personal fate because it is unavoidable, like the misfortunes foretold in a fairy tale. And so it is best to leave people to their
tumbleweed lives, or to their lonely isolation, as if in a humming seashell. The weather vane cannot help being placed on
the peak of the roof. And even a hedgehog in a cellar may feel
contentment. Let each live as he or she will, sad or gay. It is
equally foolish to try to avoid an hour of bitterness or a moment of joy. The picnic in May, the funeral, the wedding night
and the secret grief all have the same ending. Comes the stonemason to immure both the anxiety-ridden and the well-
behaved.

Such were Mr. Pistoli's thoughts, musing alone at home. By
now, Ossuary was gone from the garden cottage, having left behind his discarded cigarette butts and his women, who went off
on pilgrimages. In the afternoons Pistoli withdrew into a
brown study, where he caught alternating whiffs of Miss
Maszkerádi and of the precious Eveline.

"*Sic transit...*" he mumbled.

One day a ragamuffin showed up, bringing a message.

"My father couldn't come," the boy reported, pulling a letter
from his straw hat.

"And who may your father be?"

"Old Kakuk. We sacked our old lady. She yelled at us once
too often. So we sent her packing, as my Da' would put it. The
old man brought home a new woman. Now she's moved in
with us. That's why my Da' couldn't come."

"May you grow up to be as wise as your father," Pistoli said to Kakuk, Junior, and squeezed a penny into the boy's palm.

The letter was written on fine watermarked paper not commonly used in this region. Women in these parts write their correspondence on their children's notebook pages, or else they use the backs of old promissory notes. The exclusive stationery carried the following note penned in lilac ink:

"Someone implores you to hold your nasty mouth. Someone is coming to visit you, to make up. *M.*"

Pistoli peered at the note with an acerbic smile. "Young miss, you should have come yesterday or the day before," he muttered.

Face propped on his elbows, Pistoli contemplated the letter. He was not as well-versed in graphology as most provincial young ladies, but he did have some experience with mysterious anonymous letters, having written dozens in his time: to women who had not received his advances too kindly, and to men who had rudely turned their backs on him. After most country club balls, when assault or dueling was out of the question, Pistoli's hands reeked of sealing wax from all the anonymous letters he had penned; addressing women, he would fling in their faces even their mothers' dirty underwear. (Poor Pistoli was, after all, just like any other man. He liked people to greet him in advance and with respect.)

This is how Pistoli interpreted the letter:

"Mademoiselle M. happens to be in the interesting condition that makes women want to eat chalk, possibly even crave the white stucco off the wall. In other words, a condition that brings great joy to a childless household. But does Miss M. necessarily rejoice over her condition? In the present case I am to be the bit of chalk the little miss craves. But I am too old to serve as chalk for anyone."

Such were Mr. Pistoli's thoughts in his solitude and, since he was as vain as an aging actress, he resolved to avoid the meet-

ing. There are in any human life a number of such inexplicable
things, mysterious phenomena that have no apparent meaning,
and yet deep down a solution certainly exists. Perhaps the noble Pistoli was merely acting out the offended, humiliated male
rearing up to take his revenge on Miss M. for the beating she
had given him. Whereas, had he been more of an ordinary soul,
he would have elected the jolly path of reconciliation. But he
was still smarting from that whiplash...And Pistoli was accus-
tomed to women kissing his hands whenever he was kind, condescending, emotional and passionate toward them. Village
women are not spoiled by an overabundance of amorous pro-
posals. As a rule they will be astonished to hear any man's declaration of love. The most worn-out compliment is a novelty
for their ears. They cast their eyes down when they hear their
hands or feet praised. And when they are alone again, they will
stare at length into the mirror at the tresses some babbling man
had praised with such strange extravagance. In this part of the
country women are still naive, gullible, and well-meaning. The
village primadonna never drives her beaux to suicide. Take
Risoulette: she had gone out of her way to be nice to many a
man who was barely better looking than the devil himself!
(They say even the most pockmarked, puny man will find a
lover.) Therefore Pistoli's huffiness in holding out against the
society miss's summons is quite understandable. In fact, he remembered he still had to say good-bye to his deranged wives.

He had already donned his cape, and pulled the broad-
brimmed hat over his eyes, the hat that had made him unrecog-
nizable at Nagykálló (where he had perpetrated so many
pranks)—when something suddenly occurred to him.—What
if the young lady who wanted to visit him in fact had not ingested chalk? What if this visit was merely a cunning stunt on
Miss M.'s part, to oblige Mr. Pistoli never to betray her secret
to Eveline, to hold his peace forever about matters glimpsed
around the garden cottage during Kálmán Ossuary's sojourn

there? Girlfriends will grow sentimental at times, and will not shrink from the greatest sacrifice just to maintain their intimate bonds. Perhaps Miss M. had merely wanted to prevent his betraying those potentially painful and damaging escapades of hers, amorous escapades which would certainly stab Eveline to the core of her heart if she heard about them? "So, you would shove me underground, while you go on fornicating?" Pistoli muttered, gritting his teeth. "I'm going to queer this deal for you."

He worked himself into a coarse, cruel, malevolent mood, as he sat down with a sheet of Diósgyőr foolscap to write down all about Miss Maszkerádi and Ossuary: everything he knew, and things he did not know... For the moment he did not consider that his treachery would also be a fatal blow for his beloved Eveline, whose consecrated love for Ossuary he had witnessed with his own eyes. He persisted in scraping away with his goose quill, as if he were a liverish judge writing out a death sentence. When he was finished with his business, he sealed the letter and placed it in a double envelope. On the inner one he wrote: "To be opened after my death." The outer one he addressed to Her Ladyship, Miss Eveline Nyírjes. Pocketing the letter, he cheerfully set out for Kálló, to visit the madwomen.

The letter hiding in Mr. Pistoli's cape went as follows:

Pistoli Residence, May 18–

My Queen!

When for the final time I confess to you all those tender respects, my heart's wild roses, floating moods, my bygone life's aerial smoke rings, song-filled reveries, the butterflies hovering around my head; bellowing woes, deathwatch beetle–like, gnawing torments and ethereal fluttery humors that rose and fell during my days like

two lovers on a swing—I wish to report to you something that may very well be a matter of indifference to
you: that I take your memory with me to the other world
as a hunter takes the cherished edelweiss in his hatband.
You were the Fairy Queen in the apple tree of my life,
singing invisibly, seated in a blossom's calyx. You were my
sunrise—the virginal veil over my world; and you were
the sunset as well, an old man's singsong humming
prompted by memories of bygone happy loves. For your
love I would have turned comedian or gendarme, a Hail-
Mary friar or night watchman in your village, although
you, alas, never desired that I assume any role in your life.

The tiny grains of sand are inescapably tumbling in
my hourglass. A futile, blind and molelike lifetime's ashes
are heaping up on the bottom of the glass. Perhaps I
could have been master of ceremonies at your May-time
picnics, or else your estate's undertaker, sheriff, or over-
seer; but the hell with it, I had no ambition to become
anything. If you honor my memory by listening to my
glee club's songs at my graveside, I shall have accom-
plished all that I aimed for in life.

Staff in hand, I am ready to depart, and so I must not
make the otherworldy carriage wait, nor can I let my sinful eyes caress one last time your figure's lilylike lines,
your chignon, that solace of my lifetime, your heartening
visage, your precious glance. My eyes have seen much
that was never seen by other men. Love, separated from
murder by the narrowest of margins, I have always beheld
as a miracle. I was always astonished when love appeared
on my life's way. I know love backwards and forwards, as
I do my local road master; I recognize love's footfall in
the night, under my window, and do not mistake it for
anyone else, such as the watchman. Yes, I have seen love
seated up in a tree, carefree, swinging her legs. And I have

met her in the roadside ditch, in back of gardens, along the fence, where pictures cut out of old magazines decorated the planks.

I have always known more than others, for women and men told me everything, as to a father confessor. I have heard of the loves of serving girls and the passion of brother for sister, fathers' infatuation with their daughters... Secrets, voices from the cellars of the soul, in the unsteady light of the confessional's guttering oil lamp. I was a wise man, for I always listened and never told tales, no matter what women had confided to me at a weak moment, in an unguarded mood. I shall never forget seeing men in their solemn Sunday best, coming and going like earnest churchwardens, when only a little while earlier their wives had testified to me about their hidden passions, the strange histories of bedtime. In the same way, men had trusted me with everything about their wives over a cup of wine, disciplining the soul, absorbed in conversation that delved into the most labyrinthine tunnels of life. Oh, these gingerbread hussars!—But I heard them out, and only when I got home, alone with my glass of wine, did I smile to myself, for I have always despised tattletales, backstabbers, malicious gossips. Pistoli had always been a chivalrous gentleman; in fact, an honorable man. I shall have it inscribed on my tombstone: Here lies an honest man who had exposed only one woman, to another one whom he loved as he loved life itself in his youth, when life was worth living.

And so, the woman I am about to expose, my Queen, happens to be your bosom friend Miss Maszkerádi. You two still face the long vista of your young lives; mine has declined like a wilting rosebush. Why should you be bitterly, irremediably disappointed in your best friend, the one who knows all your secrets? This lady has abused your confidence by carrying on a clandestine affair with your fiancé, who was my guest. Leave it to old Pistoli, he knows what went on. There is no possibility of a mistake here, nor any uncertainty. They have had an affair, and will continue—those two were made for each other. You, my Queen, are an innocent lamb next to this pair of bloodthirsty wolves. They are audacious and ready for anything; you are not—probably not even ready to give credence to everything in this final letter of mine. But I am confident that I will rest in peace under the poplar that I have designated for this purpose.

Queen of my heart, one who secretly loved you the most sends his farewell, his greetings toward your window, and reminds you that there is only one decent man in the whole county, and his name is Andor Álmos-Dreamer.

Please accept all that a dying man can give: his blessing.

Your humble servant,
Pistoli

Pistoli, having looked around in vain to find a suitable personage to notarize his documents, went up to the county seat at Nagykálló, where he used to run loose as often as he could, back in his days as a madman.

He found his three deranged wives together in the asylum garden, for they always kept each other's company and never fought; Mishlik was digging a pit and the other two watched attentively.

For a while Pistoli observed his mad wives from the cover of the garden shrubbery, nodding repeatedly.

"Ah, so the poor things are already digging my grave. Alas, they will not be able to come to my funeral."

The poor creatures were not the least bit surprised to see

Pistoli suddenly in their midst. Since they usually talked mostly about him, the appearance of the man they so often mentioned seemed natural. The two older women merely nodded in greeting, but Mishlik, who had not yet abandoned all hope, vehemently grasped Pistoli's arm:

"Ah, good to see you here, marquis. Perhaps you could intercede on our behalf. They won't let us bury our petticoats here. But what use could we still have for a chemise, don't you agree?"

"I'll make sure to talk to the director," said Pistoli, glad to comply.

"Why, only those women need petticoats who still have a husband or lover," continued Mishlik, producing a lively variety of facial expressions. "But our lord and husband has vanished like smoke...like smoke...Is it possible to bury smoke? When it's gone, it's gone..."

Alarmed, they stared at Pistoli, but he kept his calm. He caressed their faces one after the other.

"Still, you had it pretty good, for each of you received one third of your husband's affections. Other women get only a quarter share. For a man's love is like moonlight: it has four quarters. The woman who gets the last quarter is happiest, for that's the longest lasting. But Pistoli's moon was divided into only three parts. One-two-three. There was no fourth. And there never will be one. So why should you bury your petticoats?"

After this, Pistoli soon had to make his escape from the garden, for the three women crowded about very close to him. Their careworn, grieving, cemetery-flower faces surrounded the moribund man. The first carried her worries like cobwebs from a cellar. The second one displayed images of woe seen on antique funeral monuments...The third one presented a frostbitten autumnal pallor, acrid as sumac blossoms. In the autumn of life the eyes withdraw into their orbits like a shepherd into his hut when the nights are getting cooler. Above the thinning crop of hair the moon passes on, as over a field, where once upon a time it was impossible not to linger among the lush, wild growth of young curls. The fields grow rusty red, and so does the aging woman's hair, like outdated furs.

"Alas, no matter how smart I am, I won't have the good fortune of dying in the lap of a fifteen-year-old girl," thought Pistoli, ambling in the direction of a roadside tavern to review his adventures for the final time.

It was as if he were sobering up after a twenty-year drunk. He sat high up on the ramparts of a fort, with a long-distance view over life's meandering gray and empty highways. He had danced with wild mercenaries and pink-flashing girls of easy virtue till daybreak, hitting the very rafters, trampling on top of the coffin and the cradle. But at sunrise he sobered. Now he could see how futile all that sweaty running, tramping, and hastening toward distant, beckoning towers had been. He saw only life's monotonous span, here and there a hump of land that rose for no particular reason; and valleys where only the solitary frog croaked. Along the empty highways he saw the capsized carts that would never reach their unknown destination. The wind whistled over the horizon like an invisible player's fingers over a silent piano. Yes, Mr. Pistoli was sober at last—having believed for a quarter century that drunkenness lay always in wine and women, and not in his freakish head. How much imbecility he had witnessed while loitering around life's fairgrounds, nosing about barbecue stands and white-footed females! Where were they now, those ebony and russet female pelts he had once been ready to die for? Where were they now, women thirsting for revenge, the savor of kisses, the fragrance of their bodies, soft touch of their palms, flash of their eyes, carillon of their voices, their honeyed whispers, the stupefying fume of their sighs, their high-strung legs, the thrill of their groans and precious moans, virgins' frenzied, abandoned oaths, and the wine-tasting apples of untouched maidens? The roads are empty everywhere, no matter how wide his eyes scan, shaded by his palm; all is laid to rest, like a bird fallen on dry leaves; the arrow no longer quivers in the deep wound it had struck; the inflated balloon pops under the clown's tailcoat, and life, daubed with pancake makeup, stands gaping at the source of the sound. No, it had not been all that wonderful...Nor very surprising...Not even all that interesting. It was merely like a dog panting under a hawthorn bush. At times the flag flew from life's pinnacle. Then the rain drenched the flag and the parade was over... Only the insane and the imbecilic imagine that life has not raced past them.

At this moment Mr. Pistoli had the strangest vision, as he sat in that roadside tavern by his glass of red wine, contemplating his boots, rummaging among his thoughts.

Up on one mountaintop in the far distance sat Eveline. Her benevolent face was distorted, her curls hung in grizzled knots, her dear eyes were veiled by cataracts, night had descended over her lips, like a madwoman's...And this hag had been her, once: the kind, noble, lamblike, dove-hearted one...This ancient, deranged crone had once been Eveline Nyirjes...Pistoli covered his eyes and sobbed. But even through his tears he could see the other mountaintop on the horizon, where Miss Maszkerádi bobbed like a crazed belly dancer. Her tresses undone, her voice screeching, her talons curving, her eyes spitting flames and knives, her legs like a wolf's, her neck ringed like a serpent's.

"Ah, what kind of wine is this?" cried Pistoli, and shivering, pulled the cape about himself, as he departed from the roadside inn.

It was around midnight when he got home.

The moon, like a peacock feather's eye, stood waking over the lifeless world.

Pistoli, to find some solace amidst his gloomy thoughts,

consoled himself by recalling that, after all, nothing base had ever really happened to him, and so he had no cause to complain, when a dark shadow like a bandit's glided past his porch. It had to be a man, for it wore pants. Pistoli howled out:

"Is that you, Death?"

His alien, hoarse roar gave him courage. Like a wild boar he charged the shadowy figure and his heavy fists pummeled the intruder. The shadow did not respond to the blows. It did not defend itself, nor did it strike back, but merely emitted a sound, something like a horrendous scream behind gritted teeth. At last Pistoli knocked off the nocturnal visitor's hat, and his hands felt soft, warm, fragrantly feminine hair. His arm froze as if in a spasm; the midnight fisticuffs came to a halt. He fumbled for a matchstick in his waistband, and while the uncertain bluish flame flickered up, Pistoli's whole being was pierced to the core by a tremulous thought, like a fit of ague.

When the match flared up, Pistoli's mouth gaped wide, although he could not be said to be disappointed in what he saw. On his porch he found the one he had been waiting for. At arm's length stood Miss Maszkerádi, her nose bloodied. She wore a strange getup, formal evening wear: tailcoat and trousers, and a blazing white starched shirt. It gave her the mannish and eccentric look of a circus artiste.

The match burned out, having singed Pistoli's fingertip.

"Why have you done this, gracious Miss?"

The lady still did not reply. There was something frightening in her mute immobility. Pistoli began to think he was hallucinating. The shadow was perhaps after all not Miss Maszkerádi but some assassin, who would stab him with a stiletto as soon as he turned his back. He stood, aware that he was quaking in his boots. He would have given everything to have someone light a candle in this terrifying dark. But no relief was forthcoming. Far off in the village a hound sent up a nasty howl, in premonition of an impending death.

At last Pistoli heard a peculiar noise, as if the shadow were blowing her nose. With many a soft sniffle, like all beaten and humiliated women, Miss Maszkerádi kept persistently blowing her bloodied nose. Her steps subdued and wavering, she descended the flagstones of the porch. (A far cry from her once capering, bouncy stride!) Pistoli watched her cross the yard with her head bent and could feel the drops of blood falling at each step. The shadow headed for the well, where a full bucket of water stood ready for a nocturnal fire. The water quietly plashed in the distance. Pistoli did not dare to move closer to the well. He made his way into the house and thanked God when he at last managed to light an oil lamp. He installed himself at the table and knitted his brows, drumming on the tabletop in anticipation. In the lamplight he regained his customary composure. What could possibly happen? The remorse, shame and gnawing pain he felt at first for so brutally beating up Maszkerádi had faded, and a cold, stubborn egotism now manned the gates of his soul. "At least we're even now," he thought. And Lady Maszkerádi, having scratched on the door, to timidly open it and stand abashed on the threshold, was received by the cheerful wisecrack often heard in carousing company:

"We're even-Steven, Miss."

Maszkerádi stood with downcast eyes and hands crossed in front of her lap, as if she were ashamed of her silken-trousered and -hosed legs.

"My clothes are all bloody. I can't go back like this. I need a dry set of clothes."

Thus spoke Maszkerádi, without raising her eyes. Her reddened nose quivered in mute misery. Humiliated, she stood like a schoolgirl before the severe headmaster.

Pistoli extended his arm.

"In that ancient wardrobe over there, you'll find some ratty old skirts that belonged to my former wives. If you wish, I'll turn away while you change."

Maszkerádi advanced toward the wardrobe and Pistoli sluggishly turned his chair about. Leaning on the table, he watched in the mirror as Maszkerádi, all catlike caution, rummaged among the junky clothes in the wardrobe. Then she stopped and noiselessly began to undress. The scene had all the strangeness of some fantastic story taking place at a border guardpost where a refugee, a lady of quality traveling incognito, had happened to stop for the night. Maszkerádi dared not raise her eyes while slowly taking off her jacket and the hard shirtfront. Then, pianissimo, she took off her little knickers. She took care that her blouse never hitched up during this maneuver. This blouse of hers was snow-white. It exuded feminine cleanliness, the most exquisite perfume in the world. And when the lady stood in her chemise, there by the wardrobe, she raised her long eyelashes, and her eyes flashed like a pair of green lamps. She stared so insistently at Pistoli that he was compelled to turn around and face her.

"Swear that you will never ever reveal any of my secrets!" she said, articulating each word as clearly as if she were reading a text.

Pistoli's face flamed up, as if a pistol had been fired under his nose. But the gorgeous lady in dishabille made him lose his head only for a split second. The next moment he squinted one eye like a horse trader, and began in an insidious, bartering voice:

"Before I promise anything, may I know what's the meaning of this midnight comedy?"

"I wanted to scare you," she replied calmly. "I'd wanted to raise the ghosts in your cruel heart, set the mute midnight hounds on you. I was curious to see if you would be afraid. Have you a conscience? Do you shudder with grief? Perhaps I just wanted to give you a fright..."

"So that I'd have a heart attack?" Pistoli asked, bantering.

"Yes," was her solemn reply.

Pistoli leaned forward, fascinated, as if he were trying to peer into the water under the bridge.

"Perhaps you've heard that my ticker's as weak as a junky old alarm clock? It skips, and beats unevenly, has choking fits, pants, and at times I must take enormous breaths just to keep going... Were you aware of that?"

"I know all about you, for I have loved you from the word go," came her reply, as solemn as a deposition before a judge.

"Well, you did a real good job of hiding your love..." answered Pistoli sarcastically, thrilled and fluttery, making sure to hide his shaking hands under the table.

Miss Maszkerádi crossed her bare arms over her chest, like some martyr upon the stake.

"Please recall that night at Hideaway when you with your scary stories had so upset me: what did I do then? Didn't I invite you into the silent, sleeping garden?"

"In order to strangle me."

"But I would have kissed you first."

Pistoli, red in the face, slammed his fist on the table:

"God, I've had enough of crazy women! Has everyone gone mad around here?"

Maszkerádi made a weary, melancholy gesture:

"At times I'm convinced I am not in my right mind."

"Get out of here!" bawled Pistoli.

The young woman kept her determined eyes on his:

"Not tonight. Tonight, I'm staying. You can beat me up again, if you want to. After all, I deserve it for coming here. But it's because of you. Why did you cross my path? Why couldn't you leave me alone? Why did you persecute me? Why did you show up in all my dreams? Why did you entice me? Well, here I am. You can throw my corpse out into the highway."

"Why, you rabid wildcat!" howled Pistoli. "I can sense that you want to go for my throat. But I won't let you. Go on, you devil's brood. I'm going to rouse the servants, wake the whole village, scourge you and send you packing without a stitch on! Get out before I do something we'd both regret!"

Maszkerádi remained calm.

"You have no servants, and therefore you'll do nothing unworthy of a gentleman."

"Ah, you all come up with that line," Pistoli countered, plaintive. "You expect a man to be chivalrous, generous, honorable and self-sacrificing, while you yourselves are as vile as rats. But I have paid the dues for wearing the pants. I've done my share of playing the noble man. Actually, what do you want from me?"

Maszkerádi cast down her eyes and the smile that flashed across her face was like Saul's vision of heaven. It was a smile full of secrets, lifelong playful thrills, sultry female dreams, desires stifled into the pillow.

"I would like you to dance the fox dance for me, for I've heard you are its greatest master in these parts."

Pistoli shook his head in surprise:

"The fox dance?"

He started to laugh, and Maszkerádi's laughter joined his with the tinkle of golden thalers:

"Yes, the fox dance..."

All of a sudden a madcap carnival atmosphere pervaded the gloomy manor house. As if a cheerful group of guests had pulled up unexpectedly on a sleigh in front of the house and were already on their way in.

The things that now befell Mr. Pistoli happen only in dreams. Maszkerádi draped herself over him like a swan and kissed him on the mouth so forcefully that the good squire began to choke.

"I love you," the lady said, and the shadow of a black dog ran across the room. The dog instantly disappeared in a corner and was never seen again. Weeks later, Miss Maszkerádi realized that the black canine must have been Mr. Pistoli's soul, for that noble gentleman's face was never again seen in human company after that night.

The blessed May rain kept falling in the vast night, on grasses, trees, meadows, heaven's waters descending to fertilize all things down here on earth. Each drop of rain swaddled a newborn that would grow up to man's estate by summer's end. One would become an ear of wheat, another a bunch of grapes, the third only a clunky-headed onion. A downpour, an infinite host of tiny newborns in the mysterious night. The patter of millions of little feet woke the tiller of the soil, who crossed himself gratefully lying on his cot. The fields, the shaggy trees, the sleeping and deeply respiring shrubs lay sprawled under the rain's kisses, like dreaming women. To make sure the labor of fertilization goes on underground as well, was now the task of Mr. Pistoli and his companions, the ones who died this night in Hungary. They would all stoke the furnace down below, these old men turned to coal and fuel, who sacrificed their shanks, hipbones, and enlarged livers, so that up here all sorts of beautiful new flowers may bloom, trees may unfurl their foliage, and lovers tumble in the fuzzy hair of meadows. Those pockmarked old faces give rise to tea roses that blossom on the earth's surface. Those sad old hands, weary limbs, aching backbones, knees long past their spring are the fuel that nurtures anemones in the graveyard.

The rain falls, but Pistoli's gouty foot no longer bothers him, his eyes no longer cast resentful looks at the mud, at wenches' feet treading in it; he no longer hears ghosts in the attic as the rain rattles on the roof. Motionless, at peace and forgiven, he lies sprawled on the floorboards of his house. Someone has pinned a slip of paper onto his chest:

HERE LIES

PISTOLI FALSTAFF

unhappy in life, dead at pleasure's peak

STRANGER, LEAVE HIM A LEAF

Kakuk and his wife kept the wake by the dead man's side on the following night, and the next day the talk had it that around midnight Mr. Pistoli began to hum one of his songs, on his way out: first in the coffin, then outside the window, and later on the highway. They could even hear his footsteps. That night there was a wedding somewhere in the neighborhood and the groaning contrabass could be heard from afar. Could it be that Pistoli had rushed off to the feast?

This is how the noble squire departed from The Birches.

10. PISTOLI'S FUNERAL

ANYONE who thinks that Miss Maszkerádi failed to attend Mr. Pistoli's funeral simply does not know this remarkable young lady. Yessir, off she went, having persuaded Eveline that they must not omit to pay their final respects.

"With any luck, we'll get to see every scoundrel and loose hussy in this county assembled around their gang leader's coffin. The local Falstaff, Pistoli, is dead. What hobo, tramp or callus-heeled servant girl could stay away?"

Thus spoke Maszkerádi, putting over her face a dark veil that had formerly sheltered her tender complexion on an ocean cruise. Behind that veil she was free to shed a tear or smile and turn serious. Why should these villagers get to see the private thoughts of such a fine lady at the funeral of the black sheep?

The coffin was walnut wood, and only one man was sitting next to it. It was Kakuk, who had for the occasion replenished his impoverished wardrobe by consulting Pistoli's closet. The oversize jacket and trousers hung rather loosely on the self-appointed heir. He had to stuff paper into the hat to make it fit. The bootlegs stuck out. His hands had to stay in the pockets of the pants (cut tight along traditional Hungarian lines).

Out in the courtyard the villagers stood about in solemn silence—as if Mr. Pistoli's death had not yet been quite verified. Who knows, maybe this whole thing was an elaborate prank. Any moment he might screech and thump inside his coffin.

Risoulette arrived in deep mourning.

This remarkable lady never felt ashamed in public on account of her lovers. Her only concern was that the Captain should not suspect a thing. This was perhaps the tenth time she had donned the mourning outfit she had ordered after the death of her first lover, a Calvinist clergyman. Since then, many a time did Risoulette's nose turn red from crying behind her veil, for even the most melodious lovers have a way of dying, just like any old field hand. How strange, the way a person is laid out, someone who only yesterday was still waltzing around, organizing picnics, telling subtle lies to women, roaming and fretting like a maniac. Yes, ordinary lovers die—as do exceptional ones. Those refined gentlemen, who launch midnight serenades and poems for openers, and have to be teased and encouraged until they are good and ready to do the deed, patient loving plus gorgeous words . . . Just about every man has his own peculiar manner of stringing words together, and there are many who like to regurgitate something they read the day before in some encyclopedia or book of poems. Around these parts, the poet Tompa's *Flower Myths* was a fixture of every library once upon a time. Anyway, they had all gone and died, the simple ones, the taciturn, the bored, the slow-witted, the devil-may-care. The sly ones and the play-it-safers, they too had to go and meet their Maker, and Risoulette was there to weep for them, musing about their lives, their acts, their long-expired words. The veil of mourning was earned by anyone who had ever spent a pleasant hour or two at the house where Risoulette was the reigning lady. Returning home, she laid a flower for the dead by the photo of the deceased, and recited the rogation her prayerbook designated for this purpose.—Ah, nothing remained in life now but reveries!

Yet others arrived for Pistoli's funeral, as for some event of vital importance. The deceased take away with themselves a piece of one's own life. From now on anyone who had known Mr. Pistoli would have that much less to live for.

Here came Fanny Late, keeper of the Zonett, and here came Stony Dinka, from The Rubadub. As long as Pistoli had been alive, these two women never missed a chance to revile each other. They thought of each other with envy and hatred; each held the other beneath contempt. Yet now they instinctively stood side by side, as if keeping an order of rank—well behind the sobbing Risoulette, Eveline and Maszkerádi.

Whoa, if my good lord Pistoli were to stick his head out of the coffin just now, how quickly he would pull it back in! Although the faces confronting him no longer carried the least sign of blame, still, he might recall certain threats made by this or that little woman... Why, one had threatened to tear out her rival's hair. Another had promised she would only visit his grave after all had quieted down, the feasting was over, the burial mound abandoned and awaiting a few heartfelt tears.

They were decked out as if going to a ball or wedding. Fanny Late wore two necklaces hung with gold coins; Stony Dinka sported flowery blue silk from top to toe. Even the soles of their little shoes were immaculate. The two stood with arms linked, proud, not one whit ashamed of having been the eminent man's affairs of the heart. From time to time they measured the assembled company with a scornful glance. Strictly speaking they were the only ones who had a right to cry, for they were the ones who had been nicest to Pistoli while he lived. They had not wanted anything from him, except to love him. They had not taken up his time, robbed him of his good mood or health. Maybe they stood guilty of a thing or two, for who on earth is not guilty of one thing or another—but with regard to Pistoli, they could maintain their snow-white innocence in front of the highest heavenly tribunal. Therefore they were the preeminent ones here, and condolences should be addressed to them... They put their heads together and decided to hold Pistoli's wake that very night at The Rubadub. After the funeral they would notify a few older women who had been

Pistoli's lovers so many years ago that they themselves had forgotten about the affair by now.

"Let me cook dinner, I know our dear departed's favorite dishes," offered Stony Dinka.

"And Kakuk should bring the Gypsies," added Fanny Late. "Let'em play once more my good man's favorite songs."

The two women warmed up to the idea of their bereavement, achieving a kind of Christmastime mood. All of life should be a feast. Even a death may have its beneficial as well as its harmful aspects. Many a wake has turned into a dance.

Back in a corner of the yard stood the village poor, who had claimed only an hour or two in Pistoli's crowded life. Old peasant women dabbed kerchiefs at the corner of their eyes, and tradeswomen clad in black gossiped about the gentlefolk. The usual audience of village funerals was awaiting the performance.

At last the members of the glee club Pistoli had presided over made their entrance. Men in threadbare black suits, walrus mustaches, some lanky, some stout, and all of them flustered. There were six songsters in all, and all of them wore over their shoulders the national colors muffled with black. Their entrance was somewhat timid and uncertain, for they lacked Mr. Pistoli's self-confident figure at the head of their company, leading them into battle. So they stumbled and stepped on each other's heel, and it took a considerable effort on the part of Gerzsábek, the director of funerary affairs and the sender of death notices, to settle them down on the left of the coffin. It was rather miraculous that Pistoli had lain motionless in the box all this time. When the glee club was at last installed in place, the members' necks started craning toward the open gate. For they were still without their famous basso profundo, who, in order to fortify his singing voice, had dropped in somewhere on the way for a pint. And Mayer, it appeared, was still fortifying his voice.

Meanwhile other problems had arisen.

The Catholic priest sent the sexton with a message that he would not undertake Mr. Pistoli's funeral service, for the good gentleman had been an atheist from way back, having lapsed from the faith decades ago.

So what had been Pistoli's religion?

Nobody knew. Only the deceased could have told now whether he had believed in God, and if so, according to what rite he had praised the Lord. No one seemed to recall ever seeing him in church.

So the funeral would have to be held without the priest.

Eveline's sensibilities were excessively offended by the abstention of the Church.

"I'm leaving," she told Maszkerádi, and could hardly hold back her sobs.

"Stay," her friend whispered. "Gerzsábek's already sent for the vicar. A Calvinist clergyman won't refuse to bury the old reprobate."

"I am a Catholic," Eveline insisted. "I respect my religion. I cannot participate in the funeral of a heretic."

"Then go," snapped Maszkerádi. "But I'm staying to the end, even if the dogcatcher comes to bury him. Go on, I can walk home."

Eveline, shamefaced, slipped out of the yard. Her example was followed by others. Some of the old women sidled away from the coffin, as if it carried contagion. Once outside the gate, they hung around to keep an eye on the proceedings from the safe distance of the far side of the street.

But the general mood turned agitated after Gerzsábek returned empty-handed. Apparently the Calvinist preacher had gone to the next village for a funeral, and would not be back before nightfall. There was no other man of the cloth in the area.

Maszkerádi had to adjust the veil over her face so that no one would notice her smile.

Now Fanny Late stepped up. Timid at first, she gathered her pluck and surveyed the scene.

"Ladies and gentlemen, why don't we say the Lord's Prayer. That should be enough for a soul's salvation."

"And what about the glee club?" Kakuk argued.

"Ah, the hell with'em," replied Fanny Late. "So who can recite the Lord's Prayer here without a mistake?"

Again it was Kakuk who stepped forth, determined to save some of the dignity of the occasion, as if he had been specifically instructed to do so by Mr. Pistoli.

He crossed himself and began to recite the Lord's Prayer in a loud voice.

But in vain did Kakuk pilfer Pistoli's pants and jacket. The assembled company was well aware that the man leading the prayer was nothing but a common tramp. In ones and twos, women and men began to slip away. Maszkerádi and the two tavern keepers were the last to remain. At last Fanny Late venomously hissed at the young lady:

"And what about you, pretty mask?! Why don't you, too, beat it?"

Maszkerádi shuddered. She gave the flushed woman a withering glance, then hurried out of the courtyard.

Quitt drove up the hearse, and now the coffin had to be hoisted. They tried levering the black wooden box with poles, but it was as heavy as lead. The two hefty females and the two older men had a sweaty time of hoisting Mr. Pistoli up for his last carriage ride. Stony Dinka quite forgot herself and let out a couple of oaths, sotto voce.

"Oh, I always knew my darling carried his weight well. But I had no idea he was this heavy. He must have drunk a lot of water."

It was now around three in the afternoon.

The cloudless sky was as clear as a conscience with nothing to hide. The May sun stood high up above the earth, indifferent to the fact that a funeral was about to take place down here. But just as Quitt's cart pulled out of Pistoli's gate, a tiny little cloud appeared on the western edge of the sky. In shape it resembled a black dog cavorting on the horizon.

The cemetery was quite far from the manor. People who live in these parts prefer not to keep the dead in everyday sight. They are enough trouble showing up in your dreams, when you are defenseless. They enter the atrium, sit around at length in front of the cold fireplace, drink up the leftover wine on the dinner table, rest their head on their arm and their expression contains such pain that the dreamer wakes next day to ponder: what sort of mortal sin could weigh upon the dearly beloved departed one? And all the useless lottery numbers they give! Plus they spout tales about one's jealously guarded women! They divulge one's most painful secrets... Yes, better keep the dead far apart from the living. No one can thrive on the friendship of the dead.

So the cemetery was quite far, tucked away in a valley from where no evil waters from the malicious dead could descend upon the village, no seepage from old crones to affect the new wine. Let their tears flow into each other's graves. Most of the people lying here were related, anyway. One lived ninety years, another only thirty; no matter, they were all the same flesh and blood. Former lovers must surely get together here, regardless of what obstacles life had raised between them. Grandmothers can sneak off at night to join their quondam beaux, no one would notice that their beds are empty. Even if the lawful husband does occupy the neighboring grave (for old people like that sort of thing), the aged husband would never think of asking his better half what she did in the adjacent pit all night long until cock's crow. Yes, it is a fine world, underground.

Everyone can live it up with their mate.—Why, many was the time Mr. Pistoli had passed the cemetery in the course of his journeys. The trees of quietude: cypresses, willows, locusts full of crows' nests, bushes humming with bees all knew him well, since the old cemetery was a most suitable place for conducting amorous trysts. The neglected grave mounds had been long ago abandoned by the old women who visit graveyards for no reason at all. Atop Darabos (lived 80 years) or over the widow Fitkonidesz (lived 76 years, and in the meantime helped bring Mr. Pistoli into the world, being a midwife) it felt oh so good to stretch out in the company of some sweet young thing, on those grave mounds where the knobby toes and skinny arms had long ago turned into larkspur. No wonder Mr. P. loved to sing the song that went: "In the graveyard, that's where I first saw your face..." On his way back from a wake (having said goodbye to the dead man), from Phtrügy (where he'd gone to taste the fresh horseradish), from a wedding (where he kept hugging the bride), or hearing Gyula Benczi play old Hungarian songs—Pistoli never failed to tip his hat and raise the wineskin in front of the cemetery's old inhabitants. "Here's to you, old buddy!" he shouted at the ancient headstones and crosses. At other times, usually in his cups, wrapped in his cloak he crossed the entire cemetery at midnight, curious to see if the dead would snag his coat, as they did the proverbial shoemaker's. Yes, Pistoli was quite well known here. Maybe one or two old drinking companions and a few bored women were already lying in wait for him.

And so they trudged onward, carting Mr. Pistoli to the cemetery, to a remote corner where the solitary poplar stood, designated by the deceased as his final resting place. That's where he wanted to repose, where the wind blows the hardest, out at the far edge, all alone, as if he required something out of the ordinary even six feet under. Only crows and peregrine falcons ever perched on the swaying branches of that lonesome poplar. Though in the nighttime witches riding brooms might have landed there.

By the time the funeral procession reached the highway, that black dog had leaped up from the horizon into the middle of the sky. And it shed its coat. First it turned into a bear, then into a lion, and finally into a monster with hindquarters somewhere south of Debrecen, and its head way up near Miskolc in the north. Thunder rolled all along the vast upstairs, a rumbling giant was approaching; the wind, like some bandit, blew a sharp whistle in the fields, and hunched-over assassins rushed behind bushes and fences. The atmosphere was ominous and oppressive; the last few stragglers were hurtled like dust balls back toward the village.

The carter Quitt had not taken his pipe out of his mouth all this time. His two little horses ambled along, heads hung low.

By the time they reached the grave in the cemetery's corner, the grave diggers were gone. They had run off seeking shelter from the storm. But there rose the eternal mound by the open grave, the last stop for all of us under the sun. Last stop for rich and poor, where the loud wails ring out one last time, and the priest prays while the grave diggers solemnly hold the ropes. The sandy loam was yellow here and the pit profound. Kakuk, on peering into it, gave a terrified yelp. They say he saw Mr. Pistoli standing down there, shrouded in white head to toe, exactly as he had been when laid into his coffin. Still, there he stood, his face chalk white, his hair in his eyes, his hand groping for help.

After that, no one dared approach the grave pit. The sky crashed like kingdom come. The clouds howled. Kind heaven now screamed raving mad. The last escort of the dead man at last turned tail: abandoning the coffin by the open grave, they flew headlong toward the shelter of distant trees. Only the thief Kakuk could still hear behind his back Mr. Pistoli's thunderous, clattering voice . . . Even Quitt drove off in a hurry, as if he had suddenly lost his mind.

There was a tremendous crash.

The two women looked back from the distance. The poplar

in the cemetery's corner was one flaming torch. The fire flew and blew sparks, as if souls from hell were hopping around in the flames. It was blue and yellow and ghostly, that flame.

Run, run, from this place of horror...

Soon after the storm broke and raged until next morning.

The next day not a trace remained of poplar, coffin, grave. Just black cinders, mixed in with the wasteland clods. Pistoli was nowhere to be seen. Only the spider spun its web in the cemetery's corner, accompanied by an occasional song blowing in the wind.

11. AUTUMN ARRIVES

EVELINE had suffered plenty, until autumn arrived at the Bujdos manor, like a mailman on foot who at long last brings in his pouch the sheet music, the books and magazines, the news that promote forgetting and help pass the time away. At last the landscape reddened, the wind limped around in the copses, rattly noises arose in the evening garden (dry leaves rehearsing the concert soon to come), midnight drummed in the chimney and attic, and the roadside sunflowers could now pass for emaciated scarecrows.

Eveline spent the summer at the salt lake spa of Sóstó, as had her mother, grandmother, and every other female relative before her. She may even have occupied the very same ramshackle Swiss cabin where her mother had once upon a time waited for the arrival of the stork. She had sought refuge in the provincial, village ways of her ancestors, once the cosmopolitan Maszkerádi, after a brief scene, had stormed out of Bujdos. (Kakuk had faithfully delivered Pistoli's posthumous letter.) Eveline calmly announced that Maszkerádi now held all rights to a certain young man who had for a few years muddled Eveline's life, whose initials were entered both in her heart and in her account book, who occasionally dropped by clad in a dream mantle, and spurred on the girl's fantasies. And so Maszkerádi packed and departed, following him to the capital. Her last words to Eveline were: "Silly goose, go fly a kite!" Eveline waited, composed, without saying a word, until her friend cleared out of her house. Afterward, it felt so good to be a little village miss again!

To sit on a lonely bench under the Sóstó oaks, watching the summer play of sunlight and shade; listen to Mr. Aladár Virágh, registrar of mortgages from Kistata, playing the flute on the lakeshore in the evenings; soak in the alkaline lake water until one's fingertips were all wrinkled; eat savory dinners; in the afternoons, wait for the Nyíregyháza dogcarts bringing amusement-hungry gentlemen through the woods; hear the tall and distinguished-looking Gypsy violin virtuoso Gyula Benczi, who towered in front of his band like some morganatic prince —and above all, to be bored; for the women of the Nyírség came here to be bored and to relax. These ladies now stepped softly, their plump white legs tipped with sensible shoes, the corsets laid to rest for the season, their light, loose summer dresses an occasion to air out their wintery selves, once the May and June picnics were over, and the Sóstó spa resumed its usual blissful summertime tranquility. It did not take much effort on Eveline's part to renew childhood acquaintances with local matrons. The Budapest winters, the capital's hauteur, had temporarily taken her away from here, from the company of her kinsfolk and well-wishers, but lo, the local genteel ladies readily accepted her, the returned prodigal, back into their bosoms as soon as Eveline showed the least sign of interest. The gentlewomen of the Nyírség really know how to love, caress, befriend and be loyal...As if they were all sisters indeed, regardless of differences in wealth or rank. The husband might be a mighty subprefect or merely a lowly scribe at the county courthouse, but the women among themselves are the best of friends who unite their busy hearts in all their trials and tribulations, childbirth and illness. The savings association's loans are often voted by women members, and the eligible bachelor is frequently railroaded by a united front of females toward a marriageable young lady. And cares are shared, as for instance when a maiden cannot find a husband. Therefore much of the summer talk at Sóstó revolved around the question of why someone like Eveline was still unmarried, such a decent and noble soul, and a native of these parts, too; the gift of her heart and hand would make any man happy.

It was a fine summer. Sweet, like cream kept in a cool cellar. Tranquil, like the breeze swaying over the flat fields. Bright, as the little birds' songs at dawn. This was the threshold to a clear, calm and unpretentious way of life. The plump ladies of Sóstó on their woodsy benches knitted their words together like stitches in a stocking, recommending this or that one among the county's unmarried gentlemen for Eveline's attention. She quietly smiled to herself whenever Andor Álmos-Dreamer's name cropped up on the list. (That sentimental bachelor never showed his face at Sóstó—as if he intended to give Eveline ample time for undisturbed convalescence.)

This was one of those summers when the diary's pages would surely remain blank. Aimless and passionless days followed in succession like the weather vane swinging to and fro. The only things worth noting down were the old-time tales of the region told by the good ladies in the afternoons while shadows lengthened. But one as a rule does not scribble down such stories, for they are kept in people's memories, anyway. The tall trees know each one well; the layer of fallen leaves remembers; the still, pearly lake encloses it within, the bird of passage carries it away, the crow will caw it out on the silent white fields of winter, the hunters with greyhounds will gallop away with the news in the russet fall: just who had been unhappy in these parts? Whose life had turned sunflowerlike toward the sun of happiness, and whose melancholy head hung low, before its time, during the springtime storms? The stories of these yellow-booted, cat-whiskered, weather-beaten Nyírség gallants and their kind, modest, reverentially smiling womenfolk with their mignonette-scented hair, these stories quietly live on in this land, like gossamer floating over the autumn stubble.

One fall day Andor Álmos-Dreamer at long last stopped in at Bujdos.

"I've been waiting for you so long," said Eveline, offering her hand.

"And I've been meaning to come for a long time," replied Andor. His voice and gestures were solemn, tranquil and deliberate. He seemed as dreamy as if he had stepped out of an old photograph.

The wind rattled the empty poppy heads, red-brown shadows played in the garden, the shingles topping the stonewall fence creaked, crumbling under the damp moss.

"There is much that needs to be repaired here before winter," Álmos-Dreamer said. "Wouldn't you like me to take care of one or two things around the house?"

"I would be most grateful."

"I think your stoves could use a cleaning. The old men are predicting a long winter, and you haven't had a supply of firewood put in. And what about your storehouse?'

"That, Andor, is taken care of. I'm a pretty good housekeeper."

"All right, I'll make arrangements with the carpenter and stonemason, I'm better at that," continued Álmos-Dreamer. "Make sure your rose bushes are covered with straw. We'll have to set traps, this year there are a lot of foxes around. And I better look over your watchdogs. I think I'll send you a couple of my wolfhounds. They'll guard your backyard."

"And perhaps you could check on me too, from time to time."

"As for your beehives, toolshed and stables, I'll have to see what condition they're in. Your granaries, wine cellar, pigsties . . . I'll see to everything before winter's on us."

"Already the afternoons are shorter, and the evenings are getting long."

"I want you to have everything, as long as you've decided to stay the year in the village, like all your ancestors and kinsfolk. I'll see to the walnuts, filberts and apples spread out to dry in the attic, the hams smoking in the chimney. I'll make sure the ice cream and soda contraptions are put in good repair. And order the latest sheet music and games. If you have a visit from those two Budapest journalists sporting hunting hats and outlandish jackets, the ones who sell books published by Aufrecht and Goldschmidt, go ahead and sign the subscription sheets. Books are indispensable company in the countryside. I find myself consulting the encyclopedia and dictionary every day."

"Still, I'll be lonely."

"If you feel like it, you can come hunt with me later in the fall when it gets drearier. You'll find the afternoons pass more quickly outdoors, in the yawning meadows and sleepy woods, among meditative, wild marshes. Of course you'll have to write letters, and all those dogcarts, *britskas* and antique carriages will gladly set out from all over the neighborhood to bring visiting ladies, young and old, to your house. The Nyírség roads never get too muddy for family visits. You know even the fireplace snaps brighter sparks when there's a guest in the house, the hours pass more quickly, the servants are sprightlier, the days friendlier. In the evenings you play dominoes or a game of hearts, as in old Russia. At times the young folks feel like dancing, so you just take up the carpets. For the old gentlemen, you must have plenty of Tokay wine, you can serve your Szerednyei to the curate, and for the more distant kin, there's the local wine. The hunters will get homemade brandy, the ladies cherry *pálinka*, there'll be rum for the cartomancers, soda water for the young ones, and Parád bitters for myself, thank you. You'll see how quickly the time will pass."

"But I won't always have guests, and then I'll be rather sad."

"When you find yourself alone, and feel endless sorrow nearing your soul's gates, melancholy rearing up near the keyhole...well, I'll visit you then, and sit down quietly in a corner. You'll play the piano for me, something new or one of the classics. And I'll read you passages from the books I love. Or else we'll have a calm chat about life, like two people who meet in a cemetery, by a graveside. I would recommend that we raise a memorial in the garden, in memory of our friend Pistoli. A regular funeral mound, complete with a cross and his name on it, so we can meditate about our noble friend's life. No one else thinks of him. If we too were to forget him, his whole life would have been in vain."

"Pistoli thought very highly of you..."

"He was a man who understood me."

"And what about me, couldn't I understand you?"

"Let's wait for winter. The first, the second, the third winter...Let's wait for the monotonous evenings of this place, the courses of the moon, the howling-wolf nights. We'll just have to make sure to wind the clocks each day, bury our memories, sit in tranquility by the warm fireside, play enough tric-trac, and never, ever write letters without each other's knowledge, no matter how overcast the twilight."

"I'll be waiting for you."

"Let crazy life rush headlong on the highway for others; we shall contemplate the sunflowers, watch them sprout, blossom, fade away. Yesterday they were still giants, but now, in autumn, they are thatch on the roof."

(Margaret Island, 1918)

NOTES

p. 5 *when Jacobins lurked in old Pest:* the Hungarian Jacobins were led by I. J. Martinovics, who was executed, along with several co-conspirators, in 1795.

p. 9 *Berzsenyi:* Dániel Berzsenyi (1776–1836), poet, often called "the Hungarian Horace."

the poet Kisfaludy: Sándor Kisfaludy (1772–1844) was an early figure of Hungarian Romanticism, famous, among others, for a sequence called *The Sorrows of Love.*

p. 34 *Fanny's Posthumous Papers:* novel in the form of letters, written by József Kármán (1769–1795).

p. 44 *Mrs. Baradlay in Jókai's novel:* Mór Jókai (1825–1904) was the leading Hungarian novelist of the nineteenth century; Mrs. Baradlay is a character in his most famous work, *The Sons of the Stone-Hearted Man* (1859).

p. 75 *kuruc:* late-seventeenth-, early-eighteenth-century freebooter, partisan of Prince Rákóczi's insurrection against Austrian imperial rule.

p. 93 *cimbalom:* hammer dulcimer.

p. 106 *Louis the Great:* Louis I (1326–1382), called "the great," of the House of Anjou, king of Hungary and Poland.

p. 112 *Prince Rákóczi:* Francis II. Rákóczi, prince of Transylvania (1676–1735), who led an insurrection for Hungarian independence from the Austrian empire, 1703–1711.

p. 123 *Jósika:* Baron Miklós Jósika (1794–1865), father of the Hungarian historical novel.

p. 159 *aszú:* fine sweet wine of Tokay made by adding choice grapes dried on the vine to ordinary must, producing a surface scum dubbed "noble rot."

p. 179 *Mrs. Blaha:* Lujza Blaha (1850–1910), popular actress and singer.

Queen Elisabeth: Elisabeth of Wittelsbach, wife of Francis Joseph: assassinated in 1897.

p. 180 *Kossuth-style:* à la Lajos Kossuth (1802–1894), leader of the 1848–49 Hungarian revolution, after which he lived in exile in Italy.

p. 183 *kampets dolores:* (Hungarian Yiddish) no more sorrows; it's all over.

p. 215 *the poet Tompa:* Mihály Tompa (1817–1868), a popular poet of lyrical subjects.

TITLES IN SERIES

J.R. ACKERLEY Hindoo Holiday
J.R. ACKERLEY My Dog Tulip
J.R. ACKERLEY My Father and Myself
HENRY ADAMS The Jeffersonian Transformation
CÉLESTE ALBARET Monsieur Proust
DANTE ALIGHIERI The Inferno
DANTE ALIGHIERI The New Life
WILLIAM ATTAWAY Blood on the Forge
W.H. AUDEN (EDITOR) The Living Thoughts of Kierkegaard
W.H. AUDEN W. H. Auden's Book of Light Verse
ERICH AUERBACH Dante: Poet of the Secular World
DOROTHY BAKER Cassandra at the Wedding
J.A. BAKER The Peregrine
HONORÉ DE BALZAC The Unknown Masterpiece *and* Gambara
MAX BEERBOHM Seven Men
ALEXANDER BERKMAN Prison Memoirs of an Anarchist
GEORGES BERNANOS Mouchette
ADOLFO BIOY CASARES Asleep in the Sun
ADOLFO BIOY CASARES The Invention of Morel
CAROLINE BLACKWOOD Corrigan
CAROLINE BLACKWOOD Great Granny Webster
MALCOLM BRALY On the Yard
JOHN HORNE BURNS The Gallery
ROBERT BURTON The Anatomy of Melancholy
CAMARA LAYE The Radiance of the King
GIROLAMO CARDANO The Book of My Life
J.L. CARR A Month in the Country
JOYCE CARY Herself Surprised (First Trilogy, Vol. 1)
JOYCE CARY To Be a Pilgrim (First Trilogy, Vol. 2)
JOYCE CARY The Horse's Mouth (First Trilogy, Vol. 3)
BLAISE CENDRARS Moravagine
EILEEN CHANG Love in a Fallen City
UPAMANYU CHATTERJEE English, August: An Indian Story
NIRAD C. CHAUDHURI The Autobiography of an Unknown Indian
ANTON CHEKHOV Peasants and Other Stories
RICHARD COBB Paris and Elsewhere
COLETTE The Pure and the Impure
JOHN COLLIER Fancies and Goodnights
IVY COMPTON-BURNETT A House and Its Head
IVY COMPTON-BURNETT Manservant and Maidservant
BARBARA COMYNS The Vet's Daughter
EVAN S. CONNELL The Diary of a Rapist
JULIO CORTÁZAR The Winners
HAROLD CRUSE The Crisis of the Negro Intellectual
ASTOLPHE DE CUSTINE Letters from Russia
LORENZO DA PONTE Memoirs

ELIZABETH DAVID A Book of Mediterranean Food
ELIZABETH DAVID Summer Cooking
MARIA DERMOÛT The Ten Thousand Things
ARTHUR CONAN DOYLE The Exploits and Adventures of Brigadier Gerard
CHARLES DUFF A Handbook on Hanging
ELAINE DUNDY The Dud Avocado
G.B. EDWARDS The Book of Ebenezer Le Page
EURIPIDES Grief Lessons: Four Plays; translated by Anne Carson
J.G. FARRELL Troubles
J.G. FARRELL The Siege of Krishnapur
J.G. FARRELL The Singapore Grip
KENNETH FEARING The Big Clock
KENNETH FEARING Clark Gifford's Body
M.I. FINLEY The World of Odysseus
EDWIN FRANK (EDITOR) Unknown Masterpieces
CARLO EMILIO GADDA That Awful Mess on the Via Merulana
MAVIS GALLANT Paris Stories
MAVIS GALLANT Varieties of Exile
JEAN GENET Prisoner of Love
JOHN GLASSCO Memoirs of Montparnasse
P. V. GLOB The Bog People: Iron-Age Man Preserved
EDMOND AND JULES DE GONCOURT Pages from the Goncourt Journals
EDWARD GOREY (EDITOR) The Haunted Looking Glass
VASILY GROSSMAN Life and Fate
OAKLEY HALL Warlock
PATRICK HAMILTON The Slaves of Solitude
PETER HANDKE A Sorrow Beyond Dreams
ELIZABETH HARDWICK Seduction and Betrayal
ELIZABETH HARDWICK Sleepless Nights
L.P. HARTLEY Eustace and Hilda: A Trilogy
L.P. HARTLEY The Go-Between
NATHANIEL HAWTHORNE Twenty Days with Julian & Little Bunny by Papa
JANET HOBHOUSE The Furies
HUGO VON HOFMANNSTHAL The Lord Chandos Letter
JAMES HOGG The Private Memoirs and Confessions of a Justified Sinner
RICHARD HOLMES Shelley: The Pursuit
ALISTAIR HORNE A Savage War of Peace: Algeria 1954–1962
WILLIAM DEAN HOWELLS Indian Summer
RICHARD HUGHES A High Wind in Jamaica
RICHARD HUGHES The Fox in the Attic (The Human Predicament, Vol. 1)
RICHARD HUGHES The Wooden Shepherdess (The Human Predicament, Vol. 2)
HENRY JAMES The Ivory Tower
HENRY JAMES The New York Stories of Henry James
HENRY JAMES The Other House
HENRY JAMES The Outcry
RANDALL JARRELL (EDITOR) Randall Jarrell's Book of Stories
DAVID JONES In Parenthesis
ERNST JÜNGER The Glass Bees

HELEN KELLER The World I Live In

YASHAR KEMAL Memed, My Hawk

YASHAR KEMAL They Burn the Thistles

MURRAY KEMPTON Part of Our Time: Some Ruins and Monuments of the Thirties

DAVID KIDD Peking Story

ROBERT KIRK The Secret Commonwealth of Elves, Fauns, and Fairies

ARUN KOLATKAR Jejuri

TÉTÉ-MICHEL KPOMASSIE An African in Greenland

GYULA KRÚDY Sunflower

PATRICK LEIGH FERMOR Between the Woods and the Water

PATRICK LEIGH FERMOR Mani: Travels in the Southern Peloponnese

PATRICK LEIGH FERMOR Roumeli: Travels in Northern Greece

PATRICK LEIGH FERMOR A Time of Gifts

D.B. WYNDHAM LEWIS AND CHARLES LEE (EDITORS) The Stuffed Owl: An Anthology of Bad Verse

GEORG CHRISTOPH LICHTENBERG The Waste Books

H.P. LOVECRAFT AND OTHERS The Colour Out of Space

GEORG LUKÁCS Soul and Form

ROSE MACAULAY The Towers of Trebizond

JANET MALCOLM In the Freud Archives

OSIP MANDELSTAM The Selected Poems of Osip Mandelstam

JAMES McCOURT Mawrdew Czgowchwz

HENRI MICHAUX Miserable Miracle

JESSICA MITFORD Hons and Rebels

NANCY MITFORD Madame de Pompadour

ALBERTO MORAVIA Boredom

ALBERTO MORAVIA Contempt

JAN MORRIS Conundrum

ÁLVARO MUTIS The Adventures and Misadventures of Maqroll

L.H. MYERS The Root and the Flower

DARCY O'BRIEN A Way of Life, Like Any Other

YURI OLESHA Envy

IONA AND PETER OPIE The Lore and Language of Schoolchildren

RUSSELL PAGE The Education of a Gardener

BORIS PASTERNAK, MARINA TSVETAYEVA, AND RAINER MARIA RILKE Letters: Summer 1926

CESARE PAVESE The Moon and the Bonfires

CESARE PAVESE The Selected Works of Cesare Pavese

LUIGI PIRANDELLO The Late Mattia Pascal

ANDREI PLATONOV The Fierce and Beautiful World

J.F. POWERS Morte d'Urban

J.F. POWERS The Stories of J. F. Powers

J.F. POWERS Wheat That Springeth Green

RAYMOND QUENEAU We Always Treat Women Too Well

RAYMOND QUENEAU Witch Grass

RAYMOND RADIGUET Count d'Orgel's Ball

JEAN RENOIR Renoir, My Father

FR. ROLFE Hadrian the Seventh

WILLIAM ROUGHEAD Classic Crimes

CONSTANCE ROURKE American Humor: A Study of the National Character

GERSHOM SCHOLEM Walter Benjamin: The Story of a Friendship

DANIEL PAUL SCHREBER Memoirs of My Nervous Illness

JAMES SCHUYLER Alfred and Guinevere

JAMES SCHUYLER What's for Dinner?

LEONARDO SCIASCIA The Day of the Owl

LEONARDO SCIASCIA Equal Danger

LEONARDO SCIASCIA The Moro Affair

LEONARDO SCIASCIA To Each His Own

LEONARDO SCIASCIA The Wine-Dark Sea

VICTOR SEGALEN René Leys

VICTOR SERGE The Case of Comrade Tulayev

SHCHEDRIN The Golovlyov Family

GEORGES SIMENON Dirty Snow

GEORGES SIMENON The Man Who Watched Trains Go By

GEORGES SIMENON Monsieur Monde Vanishes

GEORGES SIMENON Red Lights

GEORGES SIMENON The Strangers in the House

GEORGES SIMENON Three Bedrooms in Manhattan

GEORGES SIMENON Tropic Moon

CHARLES SIMIC Dime-Store Alchemy: The Art of Joseph Cornell

MAY SINCLAIR Mary Olivier: A Life

TESS SLESINGER The Unpossessed: A Novel of the Thirties

CHRISTINA STEAD Letty Fox: Her Luck

STENDHAL The Life of Henry Brulard

ITALO SVEVO As a Man Grows Older

HARVEY SWADOS Nights in the Gardens of Brooklyn

A.J.A. SYMONS The Quest for Corvo

TATYANA TOLSTAYA The Slynx

TATYANA TOLSTAYA White Walls: Collected Stories

EDWARD JOHN TRELAWNY Records of Shelley, Byron, and the Author

LIONEL TRILLING The Middle of the Journey

IVAN TURGENEV Virgin Soil

JULES VALLÈS The Child

MARK VAN DOREN Shakespeare

KARL VAN VECHTEN The Tiger in the House

ELIZABETH VON ARNIM The Enchanted April

EDWARD LEWIS WALLANT The Tenants of Moonbloom

ROBERT WALSER Jakob von Gunten

ROBERT WALSER Selected Stories

SYLVIA TOWNSEND WARNER Lolly Willowes

SYLVIA TOWNSEND WARNER Mr. Fortune's Maggot *and* The Salutation

ALEKSANDER WAT My Century

C.V. WEDGWOOD The Thirty Years War

SIMONE WEIL AND RACHEL BESPALOFF War and the Iliad

GLENWAY WESCOTT Apartment in Athens

GLENWAY WESCOTT The Pilgrim Hawk

REBECCA WEST The Fountain Overflows

PATRICK WHITE Riders in the Chariot

JOHN WILLIAMS Butcher's Crossing

JOHN WILLIAMS Stoner

ANGUS WILSON Anglo-Saxon Attitudes

EDMUND WILSON Memoirs of Hecate County

EDMUND WILSON To the Finland Station

RUDOLF AND MARGARET WITKOWER Born Under Saturn

GEOFFREY WOLFF Black Sun

STEFAN ZWEIG Beware of Pity

STEFAN ZWEIG Chess Story